LOCH
AND
KEY

LOCH
AND
KEY

A Church Street Kirk Mystery

Daniel K. Miller

First published by Level Best Books 2022

This novel is entirely a work of fiction. The names, characters and incidents portrayed in it are the work of the author's imagination. Any resemblance to actual persons, living or dead, events or localities is entirely coincidental.

Author Photo Credit: Chera Hammons

First edition

ISBN: 978-1-68512-194-5

Cover art by Michael Tompsett

This book was professionally typeset on Reedsy.
Find out more at reedsy.com

To Chera

Praise for Loch and Key

"A smartly written, fun read, *Loch and Key* will transport readers to the outwardly tranquil Scottish Highlands at Christmastime. What could possibly go wrong in this idyllic setting? Author Daniel K. Miller puts his hero, the charming, slightly bumbling Rev. Darrow, through his paces by having him chase after a murderer, romance a bonny lass, and uncover a nefarious scheme. There's no shortage of lies, secrets, and didn't-see-it-coming twists in this fast-paced tale. But at its heart, it's also about something deeper: the power of friendships and the realization that people aren't always what they seem. I simply couldn't put it down."—Karin Fitz Sanford, author of *The Last Thing Claire Wanted*

"*Loch and Key* by Daniel K. Miller will keep you reading into the late night. It's a story that pits the honest instincts of a good heart against the garish ploys of an evil hand, the imitation of the natural against the intricacies of nature. It shows hidden strength rising from one who questions himself, and a gentle love. An easy and quick read that will coax you to turn the page one more time."—DonnaRae Menard, author of the Katelyn Took, It's Never Too Late series.

"*Loch and Key* is a mystery that will keep you hooked . . . as you wait to see the pieces of the puzzle come together."—Jordan Reed, author of *The Wizard's Brew*.

Chapter One

A vigilant hand grasped young Finn's arm before he could drop a new branch on the fire.

"What are you doing?" the hand's owner asked, alarmed.

"I'm keeping us from freezing to death out here," Finn said.

"You're going to get us caught, is what you're doing," the other boy said. "It's like you've never had a Bonfire Night. That branch is too green. It'll just smoke, and someone will see. Do you want Reverend Darrow to accuse us of burning down the whole forest too?"

Finn and the other teenaged boys laughed, recalling the night one year ago when their reverend, fresh off the plane from the States, had chased them through the streets of Inverness. They had always suspected adults of having a misguided grasp on reality, and that moment had confirmed it. How could they have started the fire that had brought Broonburn House, that centuries old castle, to its charred knees? Still, the fact that they could be so easily suspected made them extra cautious tonight.

"No. I'm just so cold."

"I can fix that!" another boy said. The boy patted his belly with pride, making a metallic thud sound.

"What've you got there, Brodie?" one of the boys asked.

Brodie unzipped his coat and lifted his sweater to reveal a giant, novelty-size flask. He held it up with both hands and sang the opening refrain from *The Lion King*. This caused another round of laughter followed by an anxious "Shhh."

"You're a regular free trader, aren't you," one boy said, laughing.

"Free trader?" Finn asked.

"Liberator," Brodie said. Finn shrugged, not understanding. "A smuggler," Brodie said, exasperated. He unscrewed the cap and coughed down a too-big swallow of the whiskey he had "liberated" from his father's cupboard earlier that day. "Smuggling is a proud tradition along the Ness," Brodie said. The other boys laughed. Brodie took another drink and passed the flask to the boy nearest him.

* * *

Flett pulled his cloak tight over his shoulders and head. His body had hoped for better weather, but his mind told him this misty cold was the best kind for tonight's business. He walked with purpose up the streets of Inverness town. No one would think twice over his hurry or reluctance to meet their eye. The wind was such that passersby also kept their heads down and faces shielded. Flett nearly passed the tobacconist shop on Petty Street. He opened the door and quickly shut it, taking in the shop's warmth and sweet tobacco aroma with pleasure.

The shop was more crowded than he liked. But on a night like this, he wasn't surprised. No one wanted to be out in the weather. He loosened his cloak and browsed a shelf of pipes and dried leaves. He recognized a few of the men in the shop, but most were foreign to him. Where was his contact, the shop's clerk? Flett's shipmates wouldn't wait all night. When the clerk finally appeared behind the counter, Flett handed him an empty snuff box.

"Dreadful night for a ride, no?" Flett said. He gave the clerk a knowing look and tapped on the box's lid.

"Aye. Though men have been known to brave worse," the clerk said. He took the tin to a storeroom in the back.

Flett waited impatiently. He scanned the room, but no one seemed to be paying him any special attention. Or if someone was, they did so discretely. That was what worried Flett. What was keeping the clerk? This should not take so long. The clerk returned, and Flett took back the snuff box, perhaps too eagerly. He opened it. Only half full. Flett gave a questioning eye to the clerk. The clerk just nodded. Half full then. Flett paid the man and left the shop. His mates would not be happy about this news.

When he reached the shore, Flett retrieved a small lantern and flint and steel from under his cloak. He knelt and shielded the newborn flame from the wind blowing in off the North Sea, much stronger away from town. He stood, holding the lantern above his head, flashed its light three times with his hand, and then blew it out. Within a few minutes, two men appeared from behind a boulder. Flett hurried to meet them.

"What's the story?" one man asked.

"Not good," Flett said.

"Riding officers out on a night like this?" the man asked.

Flett nodded. He didn't want to believe it either. Excisemen patrolling the beaches tonight of all nights. And in this dreadful weather! Flett helped the men push their rowboat to the water and then jumped in. They had planned for this possibility. It was a riskier plan than he preferred, but circumstances had forced his hand. They would have to travel through Inverness rather than along the shore. Though, perhaps the weather would still work to their advantage. With most people inside and those outside fully covered from the elements, the chances of their faces being seen were greatly diminished. He simply had to hope that a group of pregnant women strolling through town this late at night wouldn't raise too many eyebrows.

The ship's captain wasn't pleased with Flett's news either. He had already waited longer than he'd liked to unload his elicit cargo. "If you don't return by dawn, we sail without you. I can blame contrary winds for delay only so many times before the customs agents become suspicious. They already believe me to be the unluckiest captain in all of Scotland," the captain said. Flett promised they would be as swift as possible in their mission.

Below deck, Flett was relieved to see that the other men had already removed the ship's load of herring to reveal several barrels of illegal French brandy. With Napoleon showing no sign of tiring from the war, such a rare commodity should fetch a high price. Certainly enough to compensate for their risk. Flett helped unload the barrels' contents into two-gallon iron canteens that his captain had commissioned specially for this shadow business. Each man selected for the mission then strapped a canteen to his belly and had a mate help him into a large dress.

Flett's dress was tan in color with cheap lacing around the cuffs. He refused to wear the light women's shoes. He could bear much discomfort, but he drew the line at cold, wet feet. His crewmate added a tartan sash over his shoulder and a horsehair wig. The helper looked him over and frowned. "You couldn't have shaved cleaner, could you?" the helper asked.

Flett rubbed his chin and shrugged. "Let's get on with it." He supported his belly canteen with both hands as he walked. The thing was terribly heavy. Once on shore, he and the other newly pregnant men waddled their way into town. It took longer than expected, and by the time they had made it midway through Inverness, they were all exhausted. How on earth did women do this for nine whole months? Several of the men begged Flett for a five-minute rest, but Flett knew they could not afford it. Every minute they were in town was a minute a customs or other officer might spot them and grow suspicious.

They plodded on, slowing making their way up the muddy and cobblestone streets. Their large-bellied troop turned many heads, but none stopped to question them. When they reached a path that paralleled the River Ness out of town, Flett breathed a sigh of relief. Nearly there. He wondered what time it was. If they could make it to the riverboat drop-off and then back to shore before dawn, they might just pull this off. It would be easier going back. With no contraband weighing them down, they could ditch their disguises and cut through the wood without fear of being caught.

"Halt!" A man in a long, dark cloak hurried toward them. He held up a badge. "'Tis an odd hour for a stroll, ladies."

Flett offered a falsetto "Aye" and continued walking. He pulled on his wig, trying to cover his face.

"There's word of smugglers about. Have you seen—" The officer paused. He squinted at Flett and took a step closer. His eyes widened. He looked at the other poorly disguised men, sweaty from their long walk and several in need of a closer shave.

Before the officer could react, Flett punched him in the gut. A second blow to the face sent him splashing to the ground. The officer cried out, and two other men began kicking him mercilessly. Flett noticed a light come on in the window of a nearby house. "Make haste!" Flett shouted.

"But—" one of his men said.

"Leave him," Flett said. He ran as quick as he could, carrying the iron canteen over his belly. The others followed. They ran along the river for another half hour before reaching the boatman, who impatiently relieved them of their illegal burdens. Lighter and out of his stuffy costume, Flett peered up through the tall Scots Pine trees. The sky was noticeably lighter than when they had begun their journey. If they hurried, they might just make it.

∗ ∗ ∗

"Hold this," Brodie said after taking another large gulp from the much lighter flask. Despite the weak light from their small campfire, the other boys could see he did not feel well. Brodie put his hand to his mouth to stop the coming flood.

"Ew, not here!" one of the boys said. "Go down by the loch."

Brodie stood up weakly, then hurried away. When he reached the shore of Loch Ness, he unloaded much of the Scotch he had so carefully smuggled out of his father's cupboard. He wiped his mouth with his sleeve. His stomach no longer burned, but his head was still spinning. Because of this, he did not trust his eyes when he spied the body. It lay half submerged, caught between two large rocks several feet from shore. Brodie approached it to assure himself he wasn't hallucinating. He couldn't see much in the cloudy moonlight. He dared not approach too close. What he could see reminded him of one of his younger sister's ragdolls, with its arms waving in motion with the tide. Brodie's stomach turned again, but it was already empty.

He stumbled back to camp. The other boys cracked jokes when they saw him, but quickly fell silent at the sight of his wild eyes. They questioned him, but Brodie could not speak. He only pointed toward the loch.

Chapter Two

D aniel Darrow stood at the main doors of Church Street Kirk greeting parishioners as they exited. He pulled at the too-tight collar of his clerical robe. Though he had served for just over a year as the assistant reverend at Church Street, he still felt out of place in the costume. It reminded him too much of a high school graduation ceremony. At this time of year, though, he was thankful for the extra layer of warmth it provided. Having grown up in the Carolinas, where even the whisper of a snow flurry could shut down schools, he feared he would never grow accustomed to these bitter Scottish winters.

He took note of two elderly parishioners, fully bundled up in matching coats. Hugh and Marjory Macpherson, who also happened to be his landlords, were all smiles as they shuffled toward him. Daniel smiled to himself. They were likely coming over to congratulate him on his sermon. He had worked hard on it and was glad to see it had resonated.

"Reverend Darrow, have you heard the good news?" Hugh said.

"How could he? We only just received it, didn't we," Marjory said. "Sorry for texting during the service. I'm afraid we quite missed your sermon."

"Nonsense, the Reverend doesn't mind. He can't expect people to pay attention through the whole thing. Besides, my mobile was on silent," Hugh said, fiddling with his phone.

In fact, Daniel had heard a series of melodic dings during his sermon. He had assumed they came from social media-addicted teens, though he had not spotted them at their usual back corner of the sanctuary. He would have never suspected the Macphersons, who were now eagerly awaiting his reaction.

"Good news?" Daniel asked.

"Why Young Hugh is to arrive today," Marjory Macpherson said.

"We haven't seen nor heard from the boy in ages. Not since, well… Then out of the blue, a message pops up on my mobile saying his ship arrives this eve," Hugh Macpherson said.

"Oh, I do hope he can stay for a bit. You must try to get on with him, Hugh. He's our only son, and it's been so long since we've all been together for Christmas and Hogmanay," Marjory said.

"Why wouldn't he stay at our home?" Hugh asked.

"HOGMANAY, Hugh. I said I hope he stays for Hogmanay," Marjory said.

"Eh? Hogmanay? That's at least a month away. Young Hugh is arriving today, Marjory," Hugh said. He tapped on his ear and, turning to Daniel, said, "Her hearing's going."

"That is good news, Mr. and Mrs. Macpherson. I've heard so much about your son. I look forward to meeting him," Daniel said.

"You won't have to wait long. He'll be sharing the flat with you. You won't mind, will you?" Marjory said.

"Oh, um, no?" Daniel said, trying to mask his surprise. "He's certainly welcome."

"Of course, the Reverend won't mind. That is a stipulation of his tenancy," Hugh said.

Daniel didn't need Mr. Macpherson's oh-so-subtle reminder. He knew that the cheap rent he paid for the two-bedroom house attached to their own in Belfield Park came with certain strings attached. But after a year, he had grown accustomed to living alone. And with everything he'd heard of their son's itinerant lifestyle, Daniel did not think that particular string would be pulled quite so soon.

"Look at the time. We must be off. So much to prepare before Young Hugh arrives," Marjory Macpherson said.

Daniel pulled out his own phone to see the time. "I'm leaving soon, too," he said.

"A hot date?" Marjory joked.

"Well, I wouldn't call it that," Daniel said. Though, if he were honest, he wished he could call it that. "I'm meeting Ellie for lunch."

"Ah, the Gray lass. I'm happy you two could work things out after that *unpleasantness* with her mother last year," Hugh said. That's not quite how Daniel would describe it. But, then, the Macphersons were of a generation and upbringing for whom understatement was a virtue and keeping polite society meant never mentioning scandal out loud. Ellie's mother was, in fact, the most notorious arsonist in Inverness, having burned down the centuries-old Broonburn House. The only reason she had been caught was because of Daniel's snooping. Ellie had initially blamed him for her mother's incarceration.

"I thought wee Ellie was in Edinburgh?"

"The University is on winter break," Daniel said.

"It's so wonderful when all the chicks return to the nest, isn't it. But we truly must be off. Ta," Marjory said. She squeezed her husband's hand and led him out the door.

Daniel hugged and shook hands with other parishioners robotically, his mind trying to process the Macphersons' revelation. He hadn't had a roommate since his undergraduate days some four years ago. As soon as he could, he snuck away, changed out of his robe, and headed to the nearest bus stop.

The Inverness city bus took Daniel across the Ness River and then the Caledonian Canal to a coffee shop near the Kinmylies Veterinary Clinic where Ellie Gray had just finished her morning shift. She was waiting for him when he arrived. He had expected to see her in scrubs, but she wore slacks and a light blue sweater, or *jumper* as she called it. Her cinnamon-colored hair was pulled back in its usual ponytail.

"How's your mother?" Daniel asked after he sat down. He passed her one of the two steaming cups of coffee he had just carried back from the counter.

"She's as good as can be expected. She seems to be eating more. Gave me several letters to post. One is to the Shaws. I still can't get over them striking up a correspondence," Ellie said.

Daniel was surprised, too, when he'd first heard Elspeth Gray and the

8

Shaws had become pen pals. The last time he'd seen them, they nearly threw him out of their house at the mere mention of her name. He didn't blame them. They'd thought she'd murdered their son when she'd set fire to Broonburn House over a year ago. If it were not for Ellie's unwavering belief in her mother's innocence, they would have never discovered the true murderer. How could he tell her how much he admired her?

"Tragedy has a way of bringing people together," Daniel said.

"I know. I guess I just wouldn't want to be reminded of it all the time. But Mum doesn't have much of a choice, does she. Everywhere she looks is a reminder. This will be such a weird Christmas."

"I suppose the prison doesn't have much of a Christmas celebration," Daniel said.

"No. And I've never been one to make a big deal of the holiday, but I'm finding myself strangely nostalgic this year. All I want is to be a wee lass again, with both my parents back home, a fire in the hearth, the smell of mince pie from the oven, a sea breeze frosting the windows." Ellie sighed and sipped her coffee. "I'm sorry. I'm sure listening to me feel sorry for myself isn't how you wanted to spend your Sunday afternoon."

"No, I get it," Daniel said. Ellie raised an eyebrow at him. "Well, I don't get it exactly, but I will be away from my family too. A video call just isn't the same. Maybe we can smuggle some mince pie in for your mom. I have some influence in the community."

Ellie laughed.

"Okay, not me, but maybe Reverend Calder," Daniel said.

Ellie nodded and chuckled. They sat in silence for several minutes, sipping their coffees.

"How is the auld kirk? Mr. MacCrivag manage to talk you into any more treks out to the Hebrides?" Ellie asked.

"He thinks he can get his friend Philly down here, if you can believe it. Some fishing trip along the Ness, I think. But I do have news. Do you know the Macpherson's son?"

"Hugh?"

"Yes, Young Hugh, they call him. Very confusing naming your kid after

9

yourself. Why would anyone do that?" Daniel asked with a pointed smirk, for he knew that, like Young Hugh, Ellie was truly named Elspeth after her mother.

"Why indeed," Ellie said.

"Anyway, he's arriving in town tonight. On a ship, I think? So, it looks like I have a housemate now."

"Young Hugh Macpherson is going to live with you?" Ellie said, shaking her head.

"Is he that bad? His parents are so nice."

"Growing up, he had a reputation for trouble. Nothing too serious, mind you, a few scrapes with older boys, mostly partying. I lost track of him after secondary school, high school. But you hear stories don't you."

"Like?"

"Like how he pretended to go to Uni but spent the first year's tuition on a romp through North Africa," Ellie said.

"Really? His parents have told me he has an adventurous spirit, an insatiable curiosity that never allows him to stay in one place, or career, for too long. Mrs. Macpherson makes it sound romantic."

"Mothers have a tendency of looking at their children through rose-tinted glasses. I should've guessed Hugh was in town, with all the police sirens waking me up last night."

"Now I'm getting worried," Daniel said. Ellie just smiled and sipped her coffee.

"You might be alright. It sounded like the police were headed away from the dock, west in the direction of Loch Ness," Ellie said.

Chapter Three

Inverness's fickle weather had teased bright, clear skies that morning. Yet by the time Daniel and Ellie's lunch date was finished, a dark troop of clouds had rolled in off the North Sea. Daniel hadn't dressed for rain. As he rounded the corner of Bellfield Park, he pulled his coat snugly around his torso. The familiar whiff and ping of tennis balls in flight assured him he was nearly home. He admired these stubborn residents, determined to eke out every last ray of sunshine from this winter's day. Daniel could not see them, of course, hidden as they were behind the ivy and tree-lined fence that separated Bellfield Park's lawn and tennis courts from its rectangular perimeter of houses.

He paused in front of a gray stone house that, like many houses along this road, gave the appearance of two smaller, twin structures conjoined in the middle. Yet, something was amiss. The red front door of the elder Macphersons' side stood secure, but the matching blue door of his side was ajar. Daniel was sure he had closed and locked it that morning. Marjory Macpherson would never stand for him leaving either door open for anyone, most likely children who had strayed from the park, to just walk in uninvited. Daniel crossed the small front garden and knocked on the open door. "Hello?" he called. No answer. He took a step inside. Daniel heard a shuffling from one of the two bedrooms in the back. "Hello? Is anyone there?" he called out again. A bedroom door opened and out popped, or more accurately staggered, a young, shirtless man.

"Shut the door. You're letting the weather in," the young man said. In his state of surprise, Daniel stepped inside and shut the front door without question. The young man turned to return to the bedroom.

"Wait, who are you? What are you doing in my house?" Daniel asked.

"Your house? This is my house, mate," the young man said.

"Young Hugh Macpherson?" Daniel asked. The man's black hair was short and disheveled, matching his beard. It was of such a striking contrast to the snow-white heads of the elder Macphersons that Daniel struggled to see the family resemblance.

"Just Hugh. You must be the Reverend. Mum told me I'd be sharing with a man of the cloth. I didn't take your room, did I? I was so tired when I arrived, I simply crashed on the nearest bed I saw," Young Hugh Macpherson said, pointing down the hall.

"No, I'm in the other room. I'm sorry. I thought you were arriving later tonight?"

"Got in early. Thought I'd have a wee nap and shower before I met up with the parents. Couldn't sleep much, though. Mobile over there's been ringing like crazy. Thought it was mine at first, but mine's here," he said, holding up the same older model phone as Daniel's. "I assume that one's yours?"

Daniel was wondering where he'd left his phone. He was terrible about forgetting the thing. Ellie complained that she had to type three phone numbers into her address book for him because she never knew which he would pick up: his cell, the kirk, or his flat. But he had just come from seeing her. Who else would be calling him on a Sunday afternoon?

Daniel retrieved his phone and scrolled through the recent calls list. Rev. Calder's name appeared three times. "I'm sorry, I've got to go," Daniel said.

"Take that blasted thing with you, will you? We'll have a proper meet tomorrow night, after I've slept off my sea legs," Young Hugh said. He shut the door to his room. The old mattress springs groaned as they received the sailor's tired body.

Daniel returned his boss's call.

"Daniel, where have you been? I've been ringing you the past hour," Rev. Calder said.

"I'm sorry, I forgot my phone again. What's going on?" Daniel said.

"Some lads from the kirk, they…. Well, perhaps you should come hear for yourself. I'm at the MacGill's. Do you know where that is?"

"Um,"

"I'll text you the address."

Daniel switched out his coat for a waterproof and headed out the door, mindful that it shut and locked as he left.

* * *

Three bus stops later, with only one being on the wrong line, Daniel arrived at the MacGill's house. When he entered, he found the MacGill family, Rev. Calder, and three teenaged boys from the kirk sitting in the living room. The room had a serious, gloomy tone about it, as if he had just entered a wake. Rev. Calder stood to greet him. "Let me catch Reverend Darrow up on what has happened. No sense in the lads reliving last night more. Shall I put on the kettle?"

Mrs. MacGill nodded and motioned toward their kitchen. Rev. Calder took Daniel's arm and led him out of the room. She found an electric kettle and filled it with water. "Now, where would we find the tea?" she asked. She reached above the counter for the cupboard door, stretching on the tip of her toes to open it.

"What's going on out there? It feels like someone died," Daniel said.

"Well…"

"Oh no, did someone die?"

"It's a bit more complicated than that. See, the lads snuck out to Loch Ness last night to have a wee bonfire and drink, as lads sometimes do. Young Brodie MacGill nicked a bottle of his father's best Scotch for the evening. Naturally, they were reluctant to come forward with what they saw. Wiser angels prevailed, however, and one of them rang the police. Finn, I ken," Rev. Calder said as she rummaged through the MacGill's cupboard in search of tea.

"What did they see?"

"A body, half submerged in the loch. Put them all in quite a fright."

"Do they know who?"

"Aye, I just received word this afternoon. It was poor Archie Caird," Rev. Calder said. "Grab that for me," she said, pointing to a tin of black tea at the back of the cupboard.

Daniel handed it to her, then took a step back, scratched his head. "You don't mean Archibald Caird, do you?"

"Aye, the very same. His mates called him Archie," Rev. Calder said.

"And his wife is…." Daniel thought for a moment, "Edna?"

Rev. Calder nodded.

"I'm sorry to say I don't know them well," Daniel said.

"Kept to themselves mostly. Archie was fonder of spending his Sundays out of doors than in the kirk hall. Poor Edna, though. I'm headed there next. She'll need a comforting shoulder after hearing the news. They've no other family close. Her children moved south many years ago, London, I ken."

"Do the police know what happened?"

"Ongoing investigation is all I've heard. Though how Archie Caird could end up drowned in the loch, I can't imagine. He's been a wilderness guide for as long as I've known him. Was more at home in the water and wood than in the city."

The tea kettle was near boiling now. It emitted a whisp of steam and the slightest of high-pitched whines. "Och, forgot to bring in their cups. We'll just have to top them off with this," she said. She took the kettle off its electric heating plate. "Bring the tin, will you?" she said to Daniel. Daniel picked up the tea tin and followed her back into the living room.

* * *

Rev. Calder dropped Daniel off near the kirk on her way to visit Edna Caird. This visit, she explained, required a woman's touch. Daniel thanked her for the ride and promised to check in with the MacGill boy and his friends again later in the week. The boys seemed to be handling the tragedy well, though Daniel figured it was more likely that the initial shock of having seen a dead body had not yet worn off. He decided to stop by the kirk before heading home. Rev. Calder kept a file in her office with the contact information for professional counselors in Inverness and their specialties. He wanted to have options in case he got in over his head when talking with the boys.

As he walked along Church Street, about a block from the kirk, Daniel saw a familiar face walking toward him. Two familiar faces, on second glance—Eliza MacGillivray and her pet rabbit. The elderly woman was bundled up in a black and white checked coat that flowed down past her knees, revealing a black dress and old-fashioned black shoes. She carried a large, black umbrella, though only a light drizzle remained of the day's rain. The ensemble belonged to a previous era. Daniel imagined that if she could hold on another couple decades, she might be in fashion again. Today Eliza MacGillivray appeared more than simply out of place in time. She appeared entirely lost. She walked in an unpredictable path, zigzagging down the sidewalk, following the whims of the rabbit as it pulled her along on its leash.

Daniel quickened his pace to meet her. When the rabbit led her toward the street, Daniel caught her just before she stepped out into oncoming traffic. He pulled her and the rabbit back onto the sidewalk.

"Ms. MacGillivray, you must be more careful. You'll get run over," Daniel said. He leaned down to pet the rabbit, who seemed more irritated than thankful. "And you, I expect you to take better care of your owner," Daniel said.

"Take care, my hare, my dear," Eliza MacGillivray said.

"What?"

"Oh, Reverend, it's you. We were just, what were we?" she asked, looking down at the rabbit. The rabbit looked up at her and then hopped over to munch on a small patch of lawn. "No, that's not it," Eliza said.

"Eliza, you nearly walked right into the street," Daniel said. "Are you alright? Do you need help getting home?"

"Home? I can't go home now. I'm looking for someone."

"Who are you looking for?"

"Reverend, it's you. We were just on our way to see you. I've a message for you."

"A message?" Daniel winced. Everyone at Church Street Kirk knew that a message from Eliza MacGillivray was more than a casual exchange. Her messages were often prophetic, always enigmatic, and never expected. She fancied herself the spiritual descendent of Coinneach Odhar, the Brahan Seer, Scotland's very own seventeenth-century Nostradamus. "Are you sure this message is for me?" Daniel asked.

"Quite. I haven't slept in days. This vision, it haunts me. I cannot see it clearly, even through my seeing stone. It is looking for its owner."

"And you think that's me?"

"Most certainly. Perhaps now it will leave me in peace. I don't summon these prophecies, you know. They find me on their way to where they belong. Hold this, will you," Eliza said as she handed Daniel the rabbit's leash. She took off one glove and unzipped the collar of her coat. In her bare hand, she held the smooth, donut-shaped stone that hung from her necklace. The stone had once belonged to the famous Seer himself, or so Eliza claimed. She held the stone to her eye, then rubbed it between her finger and thumb. Her eyes glazed over, and she appeared more absent than usual.

"Listen," she said, "strange as it may seem, the time will come, and it is not far off, when full-rigged ships shall sail eastward and westward by the back of Tomnahurich, near Inverness."

"Tomnahurich? That's the hill down by Bught Park, right? By where the Caledonian Canal meets the Ness River? The one with the old graveyard on it?" Daniel asked.

"Shh!" Eliza hissed. She held the stone to her eye. "I see the time has come, tis already past when, through a fog on the silt muddled burn, a pearl from white to blood red shall turn."

She dropped the stone and held her head. She blinked several times then looked up at Daniel as if she had just awoken from a hard sleep. "The message is yours now," she said. She took the rabbit's leash from his hand and continued walking down the sidewalk. The rabbit followed obediently behind her.

Daniel shivered. This was the second time he had received a message from Eliza MacGillivray. The first had occurred just over a year ago. She had foreseen his arrival at Church Street as well as the destruction of Broonburn House. Despite the tragedy that ensued, Eliza insisted that her vision had

16

also precipitated his budding relationship with Ellie Gray. Now, try as he may, he could not see a silver lining in this latest vision.

Chapter Four

After his unnerving meeting with Eliza MacGillivray, Daniel Darrow headed to the kirk garden. He wanted to sit for a moment in a peaceful place before tending to his clerical duties or returning to his upturned home at Bellfield Park. Sheltered from the noise and busyness of after work traffic, Church Street Kirk's small garden was a favorite spot for quiet reflection. It was beautiful in summer with patches of colorful, fragrant flowers: marigolds, bluebells, and roses against a small backdrop of heather. Now, along with the summer, all the color had faded from the garden. Still, its tranquility remained.

Daniel sat on a stone bench near a tree long emptied of its leaves. He rested his head in his hands and recalled the somber scene at the MacGill house. Those poor boys must be traumatized after what they'd seen. And Mrs. Caird, now a widow with no other family close to comfort her. As difficult as the boys could be, Daniel was thankful Rev. Calder had not tasked him with seeing to Mrs. Caird today.

An inhuman yowl followed by a very human string of curses interrupted the garden's peace. Daniel lifted his head with a start, just in time to see a flash of orange fly across the ground and onto his lap. The cat stayed there for only half a second, long enough to dig in its claws and propel itself onto the nearby tree trunk. Daniel cried out in pain and swatted with his arms, but he was too late. The cat had already scurried up to the closest branch and hunkered down out of reach. Daniel stood, rubbing his punctured thigh, and glared at the cat. Sir Walter Scott, the kirk's adopted cat, ignored him, as he often did. Or was it the cat that had adopted the kirk? Daniel wasn't sure. But he was certain that his duty as the cat's yearly veterinary checkup chauffeur had not put him in good graces with the illustriously named feline.

"Sir Walter, ow. What did I do to deserve that?" Daniel asked the cat. Sir Walter Scott paid him no mind and instead curved his back and hissed toward the direction from which he had come. "Now, what's got you so riled up?"

Daniel walked to the far end where the garden met the kirk's stone outer wall. A door Daniel had never noticed before was opened. Inside, someone was hunched over, rummaging around. The weak light from a single bulb on the ceiling kept the figure in shadow.

"Hello?" Daniel called.

The figure stood and faced him. He was tall, male, and holding something that was both unsettling and eerily familiar. What was it? It resembled a small melon in size and shape. The shadowy figure took a step forward. Daniel took a step back. The thing he held was now partially revealed—an eye, a nose, rose-colored lips. A female head, unattached from its body. Daniel stumbled back.

"Oh, Reverend Darrow, I didn't know anyone else was about today," the man said.

"Fisher? Who? What are you doing?"

Mr. Fisher, the kirk choir director, noticed Daniel's wide eyes and became suddenly aware of the object in his hands. "Ha, I must've given you quite a fright with this." He stepped fully into the light and held up the ceramic head. "That blasted cat knocked the head clean off my Mary."

Daniel caught his breath and laughed. "The nativity scene! Of course. I've seen them popping up around town."

"Aye, I wanted to get ours up by week's end."

"Why the rush?"

"I got word the Old High Church, up the road, is revealing theirs Sunday. Their choir director and I have a wee rivalry with these displays. You may remember last year, they expanded their manger, added fresh hay and two lambs, didn't they," Fisher said.

Daniel didn't remember, but he nodded anyway. The Old High Church was the oldest church, the oldest structure in Inverness. Parts of the building dated back to the fourteenth century. It sat on a mound at the north end of Church Street, complete with its own cemetery. Their own Church Street Kirk was a lovely building, but quite humble in comparison. Fisher could not possibly hope to outdo such a setting.

"Well, I've a mate who can get us a second camel and a fourth wise man this year. I'd like to see the Old High top that! But now I don't know what to do," Fisher said, looking dolefully at the severed ceramic head.

"But aren't there normally just three—" Daniel stopped himself before finishing his thought. He didn't want to add further injury to the man's spirit.

"She's always been a bit wobbly, but now," Fisher held the head up, reminding Daniel of a scene from Hamlet.

"I suppose putting her out there like that would send the wrong message to your rivals, huh?" Daniel said with a laugh.

"A rather strong message indeed. I might as well pack it all back up."

"Maybe we could find some glue? Wrap a nice scarf around her neck to hide the break?"

Fisher ignored Daniel's suggestions. "Reverend Calder usually helps me with this, but with Archie Caird's murder, she's been so busy."

"Word travels fast," Daniel said. He'd only found out about Archie Caird a few hours earlier. "Wait, did you say murder?"

"Oh aye, just my own musing, of course. Archie's an outdoorsman, a practical gillie, or he was. He would never let himself die out in the wood alone. I've seen the man finish a twenty-mile hill walk on two twisted ankles."

Daniel wasn't sure whether two twisted ankles was a statement for or against Archie Caird's wilderness prowess. He was curious, though, to hear a second voice questioning the circumstances of the outdoorsman's death. Daniel looked at the sky and saw dark clouds gathering again. In truth, they had never left, simply stalled for a time.

"It'll be dark soon and looks like rain again. I have some free time tomorrow afternoon. I'm sure we can come up with something to do about the nativity scene," Daniel said.

Fisher looked at the sky and grumbled. He hesitated between Daniel and the open door before finally conceding. "Ta," he said and returned the Virgin Mother's head to the storage room with care. "A few of us, George Fraser, William MacCrivag, old mates of Archie's, we're planning a wee vigil out by where his body was found Saturday. You should join us."

"I didn't know him that well, but—"

"But you know us," Fisher said.

Daniel nodded. "Count me in."

* * *

When Daniel arrived home, he noted that the front door was closed. Music blared from inside. Young Hugh must be awake, he thought. Though the sun had set, it was too early for dinner. He had wanted to read or watch TV to unwind, but with the flat sounding like a nightclub, he couldn't focus on either. Instead, he went to his room and retrieved his laptop computer. His bedroom shared a wall with Young Hugh's room, the music's epicenter. So, Daniel went to the kitchen, which had at least two walls between it and Hugh's stereo. Still, the thumping bass made the coffee mugs in the cupboard rattle.

Daniel googled Archie Caird. Several images appeared on his screen. A few resembled the man Daniel had seen in the pews on high holidays like Christmas and Easter. He clicked on the link for *Caird Highlands Adventures*. The website's homepage showed Archie Caird in weatherproof slacks and jacket, posed with a group of smiling tourists in front of a breathtaking view of Loch Ness and Urquhart Castle. "A family-run business for over twenty years. Offering guided tours of the Highlands' most iconic and wild places," the site read. As Daniel clicked through images of the various tours offered, he began to understand Rev. Calder and Fisher's suspicion regarding Archie Caird's death. How could a man who had spent the better part of his adult life trekking across the wilderness wind up drowned at the shore of one of Scotland's most famous lochs?

Chapter Five

Daniel was so engrossed in the *Caird Highlands Adventures* website, that he did not notice the sudden silence in the house.

"Planning a hill walk, are you?" Young Hugh Macpherson said, peeking over Daniel's shoulder at the screen. Daniel jumped and shut the laptop screen. "It's okay, mate, I won't tell." Young Hugh laughed.

Daniel didn't know why he'd shut the screen. He was surprised and acted instinctively. *Was* he trying to hide something? Perhaps that he, too, was beginning to question the circumstances of the wilderness guide's death? "I was just looking up a member of the kirk, Archie Caird. Did you know him?"

"No, but I've been gone a long time. My folks might. I can ask them for you. I'm going to dinner with them just now," Young Hugh said.

Daniel noticed that his new flatmate did appear dressed for dinner. His hair was gelled into a mess of short spikes, and his chin was shaved smooth. He wore an almost iridescent button-down shirt that shined in the kitchen's florescent light like blue-tinted sheet metal. Young Hugh pulled at his collar and winked. "Might hit a club after. You should join. Bound to be a cracking time."

"Maybe another time. I've got a lot to do here. There's the unfortunate case of Mr. Caird and then the kirk's nativity display. Mr. Fisher is in a tizzy over it. Evidently, his Virgin Mary has lost her head," Daniel said.

"Well, I wouldn't know about your Mr. Caird, but I can help you with your nativity problem. That's actually the reason I'm in town for the season. In the morning, I'll take you to a mate who'll get you all sorted. Not too early, though!" Young Hugh said. He then grabbed his coat, took a last look at his hair in a mirror beside the door, and left.

Daniel opened his laptop and continued scrolling through Archie Caird's website. He clicked the "book a tour" tab. A calendar popped up displaying open days and trips already planned. Caird was supposed to take a group on a walking tour of Loch Ness this weekend. "I wonder if he was scouting out the trip when he died," Daniel said to himself. His stomach growled. He hadn't realized how hungry Young Hugh's talk of food had made him. "I suppose I should cook something up for myself," Daniel said. He closed the laptop again. Maybe it'll be good to have a roommate, after all, he thought. It would give him someone to talk to besides himself.

* * *

Daniel woke at his usual time in the morning. He got dressed and made breakfast, put on a pot of coffee. He often grabbed a cup to go at the little café on Church Street on his way to the kirk. But this morning he had company. He'd heard Young Hugh Macpherson come in sometime late last night or very early that morning, long after Daniel had gone to bed. Young Hugh had promised to help him solve his nativity problem, and Daniel figured his new flatmate might appreciate, or more likely need, a caffeine boost this morning.

When Young Hugh did not appear after half an hour, Daniel walked to his room and listened at the door. No signs of movement. Young Hugh *had* warned he couldn't help too early in the morning. Daniel returned to the kitchen and topped off his coffee mug. He flipped through the morning paper. No news about Archie Caird's death. Half an hour later, he opened his laptop to see what work he could get done from home while he waited. At noon, Daniel made lunch—for one this time. With Young Hugh still asleep, Daniel left a note with his mobile number on the refrigerator and headed for the kirk where Fisher was likely waiting, growing more flustered by the hour at the state of the nativity display and the delayed arrival of promised help.

Daniel tried his best to calm Fisher with vague assurances of a fix that Daniel himself was growing less confident in. Young Hugh and whatever solution he promised remained yet unseen. Daniel spent the remainder of the afternoon catching up on a week's worth of minor errands and calling in vain around town for a life-size Virgin Mary figure. Just as he was beginning to lose hope and wondering why he had ever agreed to help such a headless cause, his mobile rang. The number was that of his own flat.

"Hello, Hugh?" Daniel said.

"Oi, Rev, where are you? I thought we were meeting today?" Young Hugh said.

"Yes, this morning, I was," Daniel paused. "Never mind, what did you have in mind?"

"Come pick me up, and I'll get you a new Santa, a whole Santa's village, no problem."

"Well, it's a Mary that I need, life-size, and—"

"Sure, whatever you need. I'm at the flat now. You'll have to swing by and pick up my mate, Carmen too. She'll arrange everything."

"That sounds great, but I don't have a car. And I'm actually supposed to meet someone for drinks in a bit," Daniel said. That someone was Ellie, and however much he didn't want to disappoint Fisher, he was not about to miss a date with Ellie. She was set to return for her final semester of veterinary school in Edinburgh after the Christmas break, so any chance to see her was precious.

"Drinks? Even better. Where should we meet you?"

"MacCallums, but-"

"I'll tell Carmen," Young Hugh said and hung up. Daniel rang back, but no one answered. He hadn't really wanted a business double date, but there didn't seem to be anything he could do about it now. He only hoped Ellie wouldn't mind the extra company.

MacCallum's Bar was a short walk down Church Street and around the corner of Union Street. It was a small, friendly pub. Tinsel hung from the perimeter of the bar, and a three-piece band - guitar, fiddle, and accordion—was setting up in the corner. Daniel ordered two pints for himself and Ellie and secured a table with space for four. Ellie arrived next.

"This is just what I needed today!" she said and sat down.

"Long day?"

"The holidays are always extra busy for some reason. And they don't often bring out the best in people—or their pets." She took a drink and leaned back in her seat. "I just want to sit back and enjoy a relaxing pint and some pleasant company," she said with a wink to Daniel.

Daniel sunk into his seat. "Well, speaking of company."

"What?"

Before Daniel could answer her, Young Hugh Macpherson walked through the door with a woman wrapped around his arm. "Rev!" he shouted and headed to their table. "Wait, is that? Little Ellie Gray? It can't be, can it?"

"Young Hugh Macpherson?" Ellie said.

"Our folks weren't too creative when it came to naming us, were they?" Hugh said. He gave her a peck on the cheek and sat down.

"I'd heard you were back. Inverness is such a small city," Ellie said.

"Oh, the Rev invited us out."

Ellie shot Daniel a look that he knew was coming and had been dreading ever since Hugh had invited himself along. He smiled an *I'm sorry*, then turned to the woman who'd entered with Hugh and was still standing.

"Sorry, this is Carmen Oteiza. I told you about her," Hugh said. "Carmen, sit down. Seems we're two pints shy. You two can talk business while I remedy the situation." Hugh left them for the bar. Carmen combed her hand through her long black hair and sat down. She wore a short, lowcut black dress and coat lined around the hood and seams with what appeared to be fur.

"You are the Rev who needs a Christmas display?" Carmen said.

"Yes, you can call me Daniel. How do you know Hugh?"

"Since we were young. His family rented a house near mine in Costa Calida for holiday. We work together now."

"Costa Calida? Spain?" Daniel asked. Carmen nodded. "That explains your lovely accent."

"And the outfit," Ellie said under her breath. Carmen raised an eyebrow at her.

"Well, thank you for meeting me. I didn't mean for you to have to come all the way down here on such short notice," Daniel said. He gave Ellie another apologetic smile.

"Is no problem. I am sure I have what you need," Carmen said.

"Hugh never told me what exactly you do," Daniel said.

"We're in shipping," Hugh said, returning to the table with a pint in each hand. "Right now, it's holiday stuff, outdoor décor. Many of the displays around town are ours. The big Santa's village at the Eastgate Mall, manger scenes at loads of churches, even a big Hanukkah display. Rentals mostly. I'm part of the loading and setup crew. Carmen here's the brains of the operation."

"Wonderful! You don't know how many places I've called trying to get a replacement Mary for the kirk's nativity display. Ours had an unfortunate encounter with Sir Walter," Daniel said.

Ellie laughed. "That sounds like him. How's he doing? I haven't seen him since you brought him in for his yearly checkup."

"Well, he's keeping clear of Mr. Fisher, that's for sure," Daniel said.

"Sir Walter? I thought my folks said you were a vet?" Hugh asked.

"I am," Ellie said. Hugh gave her a quizzical look but offered no further explanation. Daniel laughed. She was enjoying this.

"So, you think you have a Virgin Mary for me?" Daniel asked Carmen.

"I don't know about the virgin part, but Carmen can hook you up!" Hugh laughed. Carmen simply smiled.

"I have what you need. Satisfaction guaranteed," she said. Then to Hugh, "Bring him tomorrow."

"Actually, tomorrow, I'm busy. Fisher won't be happy about the delay, but can we pick it up Monday?" Daniel asked.

"Don't make me wait too long," Carmen said with a wink.

Ellie rolled her eyes. "I didn't know you had plans. That's a shame. I'm off tomorrow."

"I didn't know either until yesterday. Fisher asked me to join him out at Loch Ness for a vigil for Archie Caird. I think it's just some men that knew him, or I'd ask you to join," Daniel said.

"A bunch of old men stumbling around in the wood talking about old times? I'm sure I'll manage on my own somehow," Ellie said.

"Caird? Is that the bloke you were talking about last night? You didn't tell me he died," Hugh said. "Is ol' Mr. MacCrivag going to be there?"

"I believe so," Daniel said.

"Ol' MacCrivy, what a funny old man. That's what we used to call him. Remember Ellie? He'd lose his head if it weren't attached to his body. No offense to your Mary statue! He was always so nice to me growing up, though. I'd love to see him again before I leave town. What time are we going?"

"Um, I, Fisher said to meet him in the morning around nine. But-"

"That's early, but I'll be there," Hugh said. "We can't stay out so late again tonight," he said to Carmen.

"Then we should leave now. This place is quaint, but I want to dance," Carmen said.

"You heard the lady. Cheers," Hugh said. He finished off the last of his beer and put on his coat.

After Hugh and Carmen left, Ellie asked Daniel, "What just happened?"

"I don't know. Hugh is, I don't know."

"Hugh is Hugh. I warned you."

"You did."

"Well, be careful out there with him tomorrow. Hugh's quick to make friends, but just as quick to lose them. He doesn't have a great track record for making great decisions. Plus, I don't trust that woman."

"Carmen? She seemed nice enough, I thought," Daniel said.

"You would. You and every other man in here. You didn't notice how she made sure every eye was on her when she came in?"

"I guess not. Anyway, she's helping with the broken nativity display. It's just business."

Ellie gave him a skeptical look and took a drink.

"It is," Daniel insisted.

"Okay, just don't say I didn't warn you." Ellie leaned in closer to him and rested her head on his shoulder as the band warmed up.

Chapter Six

Daniel and Young Hugh took the bus to meet Fisher and the others for Archie Caird's vigil. Daniel usually walked the mile distance from their flat at Bellfield Park to Church Street Kirk. He enjoyed the calming walk along the Ness River, past the shops and Inverness Castle, the tree-lined pedestrian path of Bank Street. This morning, though, Young Hugh had slept late and insisted on taking the bus. When a cold breeze swept in from the North Sea, prompting Daniel to quickly retreat back inside to add a scarf to his coat, he did not begrudge the bus ride. They arrived to find a small group of men huddled under the shelter of the kirk's entryway.

"The ol' kirk. She looks just as I remember," Young Hugh said as they departed the bus. "Can you believe I actually missed this place while I was away?"

They paused for a moment to admire the building. Its centuries-old gray stone walls, the square tower that reached up to the heavens. Church Street Kirk did not have the grand, ornate design of older, medieval churches in the Catholic or Episcopal traditions. Its modest simplicity reflected the austere, sometimes rigid inclinations of its own Reformed tradition. Though the building preserved some touches of gothic flair and, like its congregants, its share of quirks. The roof was a splash of dark gray hues from the repair campaign that had been ongoing for as long as many members could remember, with no foreseeable completion date. The tall, pointed, wooden doors where the men huddled were encased in decorative stonework. The back garden, now in its winter slumber, would bloom with such abandon in the summer that John Knox, himself, would surely have blushed at the sight of it.

Daniel felt a sadness, a loss, that he had already grown accustomed to the building's beauty. He recalled the day he first arrived in Inverness, and Rev. Calder had driven him past the kirk and the heart of the city. She had a nostalgic look in her eye then, too, when she'd watched Daniel take in the place for the first time. He understood that look now as he watched Young Hugh reminisce about the place that had been such a large part of Hugh's childhood.

Fisher, the choir and crèche director, waved them over. The huddled group consisted of six men, with Daniel and Young Hugh making eight. Fisher, bundled up in a thick wool coat stood a head above the rest, second in height only to George Fraser. Fraser, or Mr. Tweed as Daniel fondly referred to him with no one else but Ellie, did not disappoint in his brown tweed pants and jacket with matching overcoat and hat. He was one of the more well-to-do members of the kirk and had a hand or at least an eye on most of the goings on in the city. Daniel was not surprised he was also a friend of Archie Caird. William MacCrivag, whom Young Hugh was so eager to see, appeared exceedingly short next to Fisher and Mr. Tweed. He resembled a puffin bird in his black and white coat. He kept rubbing his bald head with his gloved hand, having clearly forgotten his hat. Two of the other men, Daniel recognized, but did not know well. The sixth was a true surprise.

"Philip Morrison? Is that you? I didn't think you ever left the island?" Daniel said.

"Aye, I try not to if I can help it. But when Willie told me of poor Archie's passing, I had to come show my respects, didn't I? Archie was a good man. Often took tours up to Lewis," Philip Morrison said. He hailed from the Island of Lewis and Harris, one of the Hebridean islands that crowded the northwest coast of Scotland. His short beard and mane poked out from under his wool hat and reminded Daniel of a lion. "Gave me a chance to enjoy this balmy southern weather too, didn't it," Philip Morrison said.

William MacCrivag huffed. "If you're so warm, you won't mind loaning me your hat." He reached up to Philip Morrison's head, but Philip swatted his hand away. He huffed again, then noticed Young Hugh. "And who's this you've brought with you, Reverend?"

"Don't you recognize me, MacCrivy?" Young Hugh said.

"No one's called me MacCrivy since....is that Young Hugh Macpherson?"

"It's me! I'm back. You really don't recognize me?" Young Hugh said, disheartened.

"Of course, I recognize you, lad! I'm simply giving you a hard time. Payback for years of abuse. Now come here." William MacCrivag pulled Hugh in for an embrace.

"Seems we're all here. I suggest we carry on before the weather has a chance to grow worse," Mr. Tweed said, the unofficial leader of the group. He tapped his cane twice on the stone walkway and headed toward his car. Fisher and the other two men got in Mr. Tweed's spacious sedan, while Philip Morrison, Daniel, and Young Hugh crammed into William MacCrivag's little green compact. They drove southwest out of town. Daniel was surprised at how suddenly the city seemed to simply end, and the road opened up into trees and farm fields.

Just as suddenly, about twenty minutes later, the fields gave way to the deep, blue waters of Loch Ness. They drove along the northern shore farther than Daniel had ever been on the loch, past the ancient, crumbling castle of Urquhart, nearly to the small village of Invermoriston. Just past a cottage with white walls and a dark gray roof, Mr. Tweed's sedan slowed and then pulled off to the side of the road. William MacCravig parked behind him. "Well, lads, looks like we're on foot from here," he said. Further from Inverness and the coast, the weather was less dreary, or *dreich*, as Young Hugh had called it earlier that morning. The air was still chilly and damp, but the drizzle had faded. Daniel buttoned the top button of his coat and stepped out of the car.

The group followed Mr. Tweed across through a line of trees and down a hill. He walked, as he always did, with the confidence of a man who seemed to know exactly where he was going and was determined not to be late arriving. Daniel admired this trait in Mr. Tweed and was equally astonished by it. When Fisher had first mentioned the impromptu vigil, Daniel had wondered how they were going to get to the place where Archie Caird's body was found. He should have known that Mr. Tweed would lead the way.

They did not have long to walk before they could hear the rush of a river emptying into the great loch. The tree line receded, and they walked along the open shore for several minutes. The length of the loch stretched out in either direction, seemingly without end. Daniel didn't see how a person could become lost here and fall in, especially a renowned nature guide like Archie Caird. Mr. Tweed passed the blackened and partially buried remains of a campfire before stopping near the mouth of the Moriston River. Three large, oblong stones stood in a line at the edge of the water like a rough stair leading straight into the heart of Loch Ness. The two nearest stones were closer together than the third, separated only by a sharp, narrow crevasse. The men huddled together in a tight circle. No one spoke. They simply looked around at their hands or feet or the water.

"Should someone say something?" William MacCrivag asked.

"Reverend, a kind word or a prayer?" Fisher suggested.

"Unfortunately, I didn't know Mr. Caird well. I can start us out with a prayer. Then perhaps those of you who knew him better can share a favorite memory?" Daniel said. After the prayer, each man, in turn, offered his own story of the deceased. Most involved some hill walk or fishing trip. Philip Morrison observed, rather grimly, that Archie died as he lived—outdoors. No one knew exactly how to end the impromptu ceremony. Someone suggested lighting a candle in Archie's honor, but no one had thought to bring one. Philip Morrison retrieved a lighter and carton of cigarettes from his coat pocket. He shrugged, pulled one out, and lit it. "To Archie," he said.

William MacCrivag shook his head and rummaged through his own coat. He pulled out a flask and held it up triumphantly. "A proper farewell," he said. He poured a small portion out on the ground and then took a drink before passing the flask around the circle. When it returned to him empty, he crossed himself with his free hand and said, "Amen."

As they prepared to leave, Daniel turned to Young Hugh only to find he was missing. "Where's Hugh?" he asked.

"I saw the lad walk off up the shore. Must have needed some time alone," Fisher said.

Daniel saw Young Hugh several yards away, crouching at the shoreline. "We're about to leave," Daniel said when he reached him. Hugh ignored him. Daniel leaned down to get a better look at where Hugh was staring. Daniel didn't see anything unusual, just a small, calm eddy and the lakebed beneath. Steam and mist rose where the cold water met the sandy, rocky shore.

"Just there," Hugh said, pointing. Daniel still didn't see anything. By now, the rest of the group was standing behind them.

"What've you found?" Philip Morrison asked. Hugh pointed again. Philip knelt and peered into the water. He stuck his arm in and pulled out a stone. It had a familiar saucer shape that Daniel could not quite place. Philip then retrieved a knife from his pocket, flipped out the blade, and put it to the edge of the stone. He pierced the blade slightly into an opening in the stone and pried it open further.

"Found a pearl in there, did you?" William MacCrivag asked.

"Aye, have a wee look," Philip said.

"What? I can't believe it. Let me see," William said, moving in for a closer look.

"A pearl? I didn't know oysters lived in Scotland?" Daniel said.

"Not an oyster. A freshwater mussel," Philip said. "They like the cold waters of the loch. Quite rare to see 'em nowadays, though."

Fisher stepped in front of Mr. MacCrivag for a look. Then Daniel took a turn peeking into the partially opened shell. It was hard to see inside. Philip didn't open it very wide, claiming he did not want to harm it. But there, in the center of its slick flesh, was a tiny white pearl. When everyone has seen it, Philip placed it gently back in the river. Daniel saw them now, a whole mussel colony, dozens of them, sitting nicely camouflaged along the riverbed.

"Good eye, lad," Philip Morrison said to Young Hugh. Hugh smiled and shrugged.

"That's enough nature for today. Let's be off," Mr. Tweed said. He led them out of the woods and back across the road to their cars.

On the drive home, Daniel could not stop thinking about the pearl and what Eliza MacGillivray had said to him the other day on the street. Something about a fog and mud and a blood pearl. How did it go? Daniel pulled a small notebook from his coat pocket. He liked to keep it close to jot down stray thoughts or sermon ideas. You never knew when inspiration could strike. He flipped to the page where he'd written down Eliza's unsettling messages. There was the one about Tomnahurich, the old cemetery hill south of town. No. He turned the page. Here.

The time has come, tis already past when, through a fog on the silt muddled burn, a pearl from white to blood red shall turn.

Had she actually prophesied Archie Caird's death? They had found a pearl near where Caird's body was found. Daniel chuckled at himself for even venturing the thought. Eliza had a way of making her cryptic prophesies align generally with current events or the personal lives of those she gave them to. But surely, this was too much of a stretch even for her. It was simply the power of suggestion, Daniel assured himself, the way the human mind seeks out patterns, even when there are none.

Chapter Seven

"Reverend?"

Daniel felt an elbow jab in the side. He looked up from his pocket notebook to see Young Hugh and Philip Morrison staring at him. "Where'd you go there, Reverend?" Philip Morrison asked.

"Sorry, I was thinking. What did you say?"

"I said, it was a nice wee service, wasn't it? For Archie," William MacCrivag said. Daniel saw eyes in the rearview mirror looking back at him.

"Oh, yes, it was. I wish I'd have known him better. From the stories, he sounds like he was a quite a man," Daniel said.

"Must be quite a book you have," Young Hugh said.

"This?" Daniel said, closing his notebook. "It's just a little journal for random thoughts, sermon notes, appointments, boring stuff." Young Hugh and Philip Morrison continued to stare at him. "Well, I was just thinking of something someone said to me a few days ago. Seeing that pearl reminded me."

Philip Morrison raised his eyebrow expectantly. "Go on, lad," William MacCrivag said. Such a nosy couple. Daniel knew he shouldn't have taken the bait and told them that much. But he knew they wouldn't let up until he gave them a few crumbs of gossip.

"I ran into Eliza MacGillivray, quite literally, actually. But it's really nothing," Daniel said. He regretted immediately having let slip her name. Anything regarding Eliza was like catnip to these two. Even Young Hugh perked up when he heard her name. Daniel couldn't really blame them. Ms. MacGillivray's Victorian-esque clothing and cryptic way of talking caused everyone at the kirk to view her with an eye of curiosity. Daniel believed she enjoyed the notoriety as being Church Street's very own self-proclaimed prophetess, though she would never admit to it.

"Old Ms. MacGillivray's still around? She must be a hundred years old by now," Young Hugh said.

"Older I've heard," Philip Morrison said with a laugh.

"Always scared me growing up," Young Hugh said.

"I wouldn't speak ill of her if I were you. She prophesied you would leave home for a life at sea, didn't she?" William MacCrivag said.

"Did she?" Young Hugh said. He thought for a moment, mumbled something to himself, then said, "Oh my God, she did! Rev, you can't tell her I made fun of her age."

"Don't be daft. Eliza MacGillivray's a seer. She doesn't cause the future. She only sees it," Philip Morrison said.

Young Hugh still looked suspicious. "Don't worry, my lips are sealed," Daniel said.

"You said the pearl reminded you of something. Did she give you a prophesy?" Philip Morrison asked.

"If she did, you must tell. They can be quite mysterious, they can. We'll help you decipher it," William MacCrivag said.

"Okay," Daniel relented. "There were two, actually." Daniel recited the prophecy of the pearl turned blood red. After he finished, he could feel a chill run through the car, though its windows were all up and its little heater was churning out as much heat as it was able.

"I told you, she's scary," Young Hugh finally spoke up.

"That was rather grim," Philip Morrison said. "Perhaps the second one will be cheerier."

Daniel flipped the page in his notebook. "I don't know, but it's certainly as enigmatic. Here goes: *Listen, strange as it may seem, the time will come, and it is not far off, when full-rigged ships shall sail eastward and westward by the back of Tomnahurich, near Inverness,*" Daniel recited. "At least there's no mention of bloody clams."

Young Hugh giggled like a child. "That's not what I meant," Daniel stammered. Now Philip Morrison chuckled. "Never mind," Daniel said.

"See, that was cheerier. Though it's not much of a prophecy," Philip said.

"No?" Daniel asked.

"No, well it was at one time, though that was long ago. Are you sure you wrote it down right?" Philip asked. Daniel nodded. "Hmm, she must be losing her touch. Or that seeing stone she has truly did belong to the auld Brahan Seer. That prophecy isn't from Eliza MacGillivray, at least not originally. It's one of the Seer's. But it must've been fulfilled over two centuries ago."

"Aye, Philly's right. That's a prophecy about the building of the Caledonian Canal, though that doesn't make it any cheerier," William MacCrivag said.

Everyone now turned to Mr. MacCrivag.

"What could be cheerier than a trip up the canal?" Young Hugh asked. "Why that prophecy could be for me, not the Rev. We're planning a trip after we're done in Inverness, my company, I mean. Setting up holiday displays as we go."

"It's not the canal that's troubling. It's Tomnahurich," William MacCrivag said. Philip Morrison shook his head. "You doubt, but it's a faerie hill, and it's trouble."

"I thought it was a graveyard?" Daniel said.

"And the faeries are none too keen on us digging up their hill to bury our dead in," MacCrivag said. "It's just up the road if you want to see." He turned at a roundabout onto a road that led to a bridge across the Ness River. They traveled for a short distance along the Caledonian Canal before hitting the A82 into Inverness. "There on the left," he said.

Daniel and Young Hugh both leaned to the small left side window to see the wooded hill that rose unexpectantly at the edge of the city. Daniel had seen it before, but never so close. It was larger than he'd realized. They passed rows of gravestones circling the foot of the hill.

"The oldest graves are at the very top. But it's not open today. Likely for the best. Faeries are attuned to the mystical world you know. Gave the Brahan Seer his gift of second sight, didn't they? With Eliza possessing his seeing stone and her own prophesy hanging over you, Reverend, it's best you stay clear of faerie folk for the time being," William MacCrivag said.

Philip Morrison shushed him. "I was just telling—" William said.

"Shhh, Willie, the radio," Philip Morrison said as he turned up the volume on the car's stereo.

"Thank you, Terry. For those of you just joining us, that was Terry Adair with the latest press release from the Inverness police who now believe that local Inverness wilderness guide, Archibald Caird, found deceased on the shore of Loch Ness last week, was murdered."

Philip Morrison turned the radio back down. "Murdered? Archie?" he said.

"Faeries," William MacCrivag mumbled. The little green car's speed increased noticeably as they drove away from Tomnahurich Hill.

* * *

Sunday morning, Church Street Kirk was abuzz with talk of the recent police report. Everyone seemed to have a theory about how Archie Caird had died. A drug deal gone bad, a mugging gone too far, poachers, eco-terrorists. Some refused to believe he could have been murdered, preferring instead a hiking accident or suicide. Mr. Tweed claimed to have already known that the police suspected foul play. Mr. Fisher had a more difficult than usual time herding his choir into formation. No one wanted to practice hymns when the gossip was so rich. A few minutes before the service was set to begin, Edna Caird, Archie's widow, walked through the front doors. The whole sanctuary fell silent while all eyes watched her take her seat. Only a few hushed voices could be heard: *Poor Mrs. Carid. And so close to Christmas. I heard she has no other family. How brave she is to show this morning.*

Edna Caird sat, stiff-backed, in her usual pew, ignoring the looks and whispers. She looked straight ahead. She removed her gloves one finger at a time, the picture of composure. Rev. Calder whispered to Daniel, "Edna's a strong woman, but no one could take much of this. Let's go ahead and get started." Daniel agreed and nodded to Fisher. Fisher pulled at his hair and looked back at Daniel with wild eyes that screamed, *We're not ready!* Daniel shrugged. Fisher shook his head in defeat and raised his hands to get the choir's attention. Only half of them noticed and began on the first verse together. By the second verse, the rest of the choir had caught on, and most of the people in the pews had joined in too.

After the closing prayer and blessing, most of the congregation headed to the kirk hall to socialize over coffee and biscuits and to resume their gossip, having been only momentarily interrupted by hymns and homilies. Daniel looked for Edna Caird. He didn't know what he would say to her, but he felt he should say something. A reassuring smile or hug at least. But she must have left early. He and Rev. Calder greeted the last of those who left at the front doors and were about to join the rest in the kirk hall, when Rev. Calder tapped Daniel's arm. She motioned toward a corner of the nave. Edna Caird had not left early after all.

"Edna, we're so happy to see you this morning. How are you?" Rev. Calder said. Daniel was glad she was there to take the lead.

Edna Caird sighed. "I'm simply ready for this all to be over. I can't even bury my Archie, give him some peace. The police won't release his body now that they suspect—" she couldn't say the word. She pulled a tissue out of her purse, and for the first time that morning, Daniel saw her cry.

"There, there," Rev. Calder said. She embraced Edna and patted her back. Rev. Calder was shorter than Edna so that Edna's head rested on Calder's. Daniel envied the ease with which his mentor was able to comfort parishioners. He always felt so awkward around people in mourning.

Edna reached for another tissue. "Thank you, Sarah. You've been more help than you can know during this time. Would you mind if I spoke to Reverend Darrow alone for a moment?"

Rev. Calder raised an eyebrow to Daniel. She was as surprised as he was. "You give me a ring if you need anything, anything at all," she said to Edna and then left for the kirk hall.

Daniel was now alone with the crying widow. "Mrs. Caird, I'm so sorry for your loss. I can't imagine how hard this must be for you."

Edna Caird nodded. "I heard about the wee vigil you had for Archie out on the loch."

39

"Yes, I'm sorry for not inviting you, but it was just a few men that wanted to pay their respects and remember your husband. I—"

"No, it was just as Archie would have liked it. No fuss or big ceremony. Thank you."

"I'm glad to hear that. Though Mr. Fisher deserves the credit. It was his idea."

"I'll have to thank him later."

"I think I saw him head to the kirk hall," Daniel said.

"Later," Edna said. "I must ask a favor of you, Reverend."

"Anything," Daniel said.

"The police are saying that my Archie was..." She paused.

"I know," Daniel said.

Edna retrieved another tissue. "When he didn't come home that night, I didn't think anything of it. He often does that. He'll go off scouting a tour or fishing trip and get caught up in nature. Forget to phone. He loved being outdoors. But he always came back." She closed her eyes to fight back more tears. "He always came back."

"I'm so sorry. What can I do?" Daniel asked.

"It simply doesn't make any sense. Archie didn't have enemies. He was a quiet man, but he got on with everyone." She wiped her eyes. She took a breath, then stared straight into Daniel's eyes. "You must discover who killed him."

Daniel took a step back. "Mrs. Caird, I'm not –" He didn't know what to say. "I'm sure the police have got it covered. It's what they do. You need to have patience and let them do their job. I can pray for you and for them, help you make funeral arrangements, but –"

"Last year, you uncovered the truth about that poor boy in the Broonburn House arson. The police had already closed the case. But you didn't give up. You cleared Elspeth Gray's name. She was one of our own, and you helped her. Now I'm asking you to do the same for me."

Edna Caird reached for his hand and squeezed it. Daniel tried to take another step back, but she would not let go. Did she know what she was asking of him? He was no detective. The last time he had inserted himself into such matters, he had nearly gotten fired, deported, and lost Ellie. But here was Edna Caird, tears in her eyes, pleading with him. And she was right. When Ellie's mother Elspeth had asked for his help, he had given it to her. How could he say no to Edna now?

He placed his hand over hers. "I don't know what I can do, but I'll help in any way I can."

Chapter Eight

Late Monday morning, the last small cloud faded from the skies over Inverness. For the first time in over a week, the sun was able to shine brightly over the city without any impediment. Daniel stepped outside into the Church Street Kirk garden, eyes closed, face to the sky. His vitamin D-starved skin soaking in the sun's rays. He felt warmed and satisfied, such a welcome contrast from the past two days' dreary weather and ever drearier news.

He still found it hard to believe that a member of his own kirk had been murdered. "Archie didn't have any enemies. He got on with everyone," Daniel heard Edna Caird say in his head. Why had she come to him? What did she think he could possibly do that the police couldn't? But the most pressing question on Daniel's mind that morning: Why had he agreed to help?

Daniel stood facing the sky for another minute. He tried to clear his mind, focus only on the warmth. He breathed in deeply, opened his eyes, and exhaled. He saw the stream of heat from his breath float away and dissolve into the outside air. He sighed. This winter seemed to drag on more than most. He pulled his coat tight and left the garden.

Church Street was busier than usual for a Monday in December. It seemed he and Ellie Gray were not the only ones set on making the most of this sunny weather. Daniel checked his phone to make sure he took the correct bus. When the clouds had cleared, Ellie suggested changing their lunch plans and meeting in Clachnaharry, a former fishing village, now incorporated into the northwesternmost part of Inverness at the mouth of the Caledonian

Canal. It was farther from the café they were going to meet at in the center of the city, but, as Ellie said, it had a lovely walking path. And no one would begrudge them for taking a long lunch on such a beautiful day. Half the city was already out of doors, enjoying this impromptu public holiday.

Daniel nearly didn't recognize her when he arrived. She was bundled up in a thick coat and hood. Once he'd stepped off the bus and made his way to the walking path, he understood why. The sunny skies did nothing to help the chilly wind blowing in from the North Sea. When they kissed, Ellie's glasses immediately fogged up. They both laughed and started down the narrow strip of land that jutted out into the Beauly Firth like a knife, just wide enough for a gravel footpath. They passed a few other walkers, families with small children, dogs running off their leashes and chasing each other up and down the shore.

They talked of their mornings, the weather, the city's upcoming Christmas festivities, avoiding for as long as possible the glaring subject at the head of city gossip—the death, turned murder investigation, of Archie Caird.

"My mum is friends with Edna," Ellie said. "Well, they knew one another at least. Through the kirk. When I was a girl, we all went on one of Archie's hill walking tours to Glen Affric. Such a beautiful place. Have you been?"

Daniel shook his head.

"We should go sometime. That's one of my favorite memories."

"I talked to Edna yesterday."

"How is she? This must be so hard for her. When Dad died, Mum and I were devastated. I don't think she's ever gotten over it. I don't know that you can, really," Ellie said. She stopped walking and looked out across the waters of the Beauly Firth to the Black Isle peninsula. The cold sea wind made Daniel's eyes water.

"She asked me to look into Archie's murder. I don't think she trusts the police to do it," Daniel said.

"Really? What could you do?"

"That's what I tried to tell her, but she was so insistent, and she was crying. What was I supposed to say?"

"So, you're an inspector now?" she asked. Daniel shrugged. "Just don't go accusing anyone in my family again."

"I'm sorry, I…." Daniel turned from her. Ellie grabbed his arm.

"I'm joking. You're so uptight today. Look, if you want my advice, well, you're going to get it anyway, so listen up. Obviously, be careful. Whoever killed Archie clearly isn't afraid to hurt people. Don't go trying to be a hero, for my sake, if not for your own," Ellie said. Daniel nodded. "As far as investigating, did you know Archie well?"

"No. That's what made Mrs. Caird's request so baffling. I don't even know where to start."

"I can ask Mum, next time I visit."

"Do you think she would know anything?"

"Perhaps she can trade intel for a pack of ciggies or put pressure on one of the other gangs," Ellie said.

"What? Elspeth joined a prison gang?"

"Oh my god, you're so gullible! You truly think my dear ol' mum would join a gang? Burn a house down, sure, but join a gang? She's much too shy for that. You've really got to learn to know when people are joking if you're going to be a proper inspector."

"I think all this sun is getting to your head." Daniel laughed. "But you did get me thinking. Even if I didn't know Archie very well, I do know some folks who did. I suppose it couldn't hurt to ask a few questions."

"That's the spirit! Now, let's go get some food. I'm starving, and it's getting a touch chilly out here."

Daniel shook his head and laughed again. "Hey, this was your idea. I could've eaten an hour ago."

* * *

After lunch, Ellie went back to work at the veterinary clinic, and Daniel traveled the short distance over to the Port of Inverness, where he was due to meet with Young Hugh. When he arrived, he looked around the warehouses and storage units. Completely lost, he phoned Hugh.

"The port can be a bit confusing for a newbie," Young Hugh said. He brought Daniel to a large building with a small front office. "Here's Carmen, eh, Ms. Oteiza, sorry, luv. She'll get you sorted." Hugh took one of the two chairs on the other side of Carmen Oteiza's desk.

Carmen gave Hugh a look that seemed, to Daniel, irritated, though Hugh did not appear to notice. She motioned for Daniel to sit in the other chair. "Reverend Darrow. It is nice to meet you again. You do not have your young friend with you? Elene?"

"Ellie. Um, no, she's…. Well, Hugh said you're who I need to talk to about arranging a nativity display for my church?" Daniel said.

"Ah, Americans. You are always business, business. Okay, you want a Christmas display. Let me show you what I have," Carmen said. She pulled a binder out of a desk drawer and flipped through a few pages. "Ah," she said and handed it to Daniel, opened to a page of Christmas displays. Daniel looked through the images of snowy villages, Santa's workshops, and finally to nativity scenes. "You will want it set up and taken down, no? Do not worry, it is all included. Do you see something you like?"

The book had three nativity options. One of them looked similar to Fisher's. "How much for this one?"

"You have a good eye. This is a very popular model," Carmen said. They discussed the price and how soon the display could be set up. Young Hugh, in charge of setting up and dismantling the displays, assured Daniel he could have it delivered and up by the end of day tomorrow.

"This all sounds great. Mr. Fisher should be relieved he won't have to deal with it. I know I will," Daniel said. "Oh, he might want to add a few of his own figures. I know he was excited about a camel or an extra wiseman? Would that be alright? They wouldn't get too mixed up?"

"Yes, yes. All our set pieces are coded for sorting and storage," Carmen said.

"Great. I suppose all that's left is for me to write you a check."

"One more thing," Carmen said.

"Oh?"

"Yes, we must celebrate. Tonight!" Carmen said.

"Tonight?" Daniel said.

"Tonight," Carmen insisted.

"That's how we do business here. Come on, Rev, show us you Americans are more than just business, business." Young Hugh laughed.

"Looks like it's two against one. Okay, but I have an early morning tomorrow," Daniel conceded.

"Don't worry, we'll get you home before then," Young Hugh said.

"That's what I'm worried about," Daniel laughed. He filled out the form Carmen had put in front of him and then paid her. "Hugh, I think you'll have to point me towards the bus stop. I got all turned around getting here." He said goodbye to Carmen and followed Young Hugh out.

"Do you want a wee peak at your purchase? They keep all the displays in that warehouse there," Young Hugh said.

"Sure," Daniel said. He didn't have anything else pressing to do at the kirk that afternoon. He doubted anyone would even be there with the nice weather today. Besides, he could tell Young Hugh enjoyed showing off. Why not indulge him?

Young Hugh showed Daniel through the large doors of the warehouse. "This is usually for employees only," Young Hugh said proudly. The lighting was not great inside. One wall was covered with stacks of wooden crates. The corner beside it held a series of opened crates, some with life-sized figures standing beside them. Santas, elves, reindeer, camels, Marys, and Josephs. Two men seemed to be repairing broken figures in another partially walled-off corner of the building.

"Let's see, yours would be over here," Young Hugh said, looking at the numbers stamped onto the crates. "I don't see an open one. Sorry, Rev, you'll have to wait until tomorrow to see it in person."

"That's fine. I'm sure it'll look great. The pictures were nice."

"Oi, who's that?" a man shouted from behind the repair wall.

"It's just me, Hugh," Young Hugh shouted back.

"Who's that with you? I don't recognize him?"

"A friend, eh, new client. I was showing him around."

The man said something to his partner, then walked toward Young Hugh and Daniel. "Sorry, mate, but this area's restricted. You can't be here. Health and safety, you understand. Get him out."

"He's with me. It's not—"

By now, the man was only a few paces away. For such a large man, he could move quickly. "You deaf, Macpherson. Restricted. Now."

"I should be going anyway," Daniel said, taking a step back toward the entrance.

"Fine, we're leaving," Young Hugh said to the man as they left. Once they got outside, Hugh said, "Forget about him. He's always in a bad mood. What's so dangerous about some crates and broken ceramic figures?"

"Don't worry about it," Daniel said.

"No, he shouldn't have been so rude. You're a client. This job pays decent, but some of the guys...." Young Hugh's voice trailed off. He kicked a rock as they walked. "We'll have a cracking time tonight, though," he said, cheerier.

Chapter Nine

After dinner, Daniel turned up the flat's thermostat and settled in with an Agatha Christie novel. He had a growing collection of her novels, especially those featuring the brilliant Hercule Poirot, on the small bookshelf beside his bed. He had read this one before. It was like getting together with an old friend. Daniel had completely forgotten that he was supposed to go out that night with his actual new friend until Young Hugh burst through the front door like a blizzard.

"What are you up to, Rev? You can't go out like that," Young Hugh said.

Daniel jolted up from the couch he had been lounging on and sat his book down. He looked at what he was wearing. "Out?"

"Aye, with Carmen and me. To celebrate our partnership."

"I just rented a Christmas display. I don't know if that warrants a whole celebration," Daniel said. The cloudless sky had given Inverness a warmer than usual afternoon, but now, with the sun set, all the heat had faded. Daniel did not relish the idea of going out again into the cold.

"Come on, mate. What are you, an old man? The night is young. Drinks are waiting. Let's go!"

Daniel looked at his book and then back to Young Hugh. His flatmate reminded him of a puppy eager for a game of fetch. The book would have to wait. "Okay, give me a minute to change." Daniel didn't own anything as flashy as what Young Hugh wore, but he found a pair of jeans and a shirt that Ellie had picked out for him. She said it brought out his eyes. If it was good enough for Ellie, Daniel figured, it was good enough for a night out with Young Hugh and Carmen Oteiza.

They met at a club just north of the city center. Carmen was already at the bar. She called Daniel and Young Hugh over. "Ah, my men are here. What do you want? For my new client, I buy the first round!"

"Wow, can't beat that deal. Do I get one as a finder's fee?" Hugh asked.

"Two more," Carmen signaled the bartender.

"I love this job!" Hugh said to Daniel.

Young Hugh bought the next round, and Daniel, not to be rude, bought the next. Then Carmen wanted to dance. Daniel declined, but she and Hugh dragged him out on the dance floor anyway. Scottish dancing was so much faster and energized than he was used to, whether it was the traditional ceilidh dances or the modern bass-thumping club dancing. It was fun, though. By the second song, he was cheery, exhausted, and no longer cold. He went to the front to remove his jacket and take a breather. When he returned, he found Young Hugh and Carmen back at the bar with more drinks in hand.

"I don't know. I'm still feeling the first ones," Daniel said as Carmen passed him a pint.

"Come on, don't embarrass me, Rev," Young Hugh said, gulping down his own beer.

"How about another dance," Daniel said. He handed his glass to Hugh and took Carmen's hand.

"Yes, more dancing. Hugh, finish mine as well," she said to Hugh, passing him her half-full glass.

Hugh smiled and raised his glasses. "Cheers." After a while, he joined them on the dance floor and a while later, they all returned to the bar in need of more refreshment.

"Excuse me, boys," Carmen said, tapping her cell phone. She went to the entrance, where the music wasn't quite as loud. Daniel looked at his own phone.

"Wow, how'd it get to be so late? I should head home after this one," he said. Hugh nodded. When Carmen returned, Daniel thanked her for the drinks and dancing and suggested they call it a night.

"It is still early. We have more dancing to do," Carmen said.

"I have an early morning tomorrow, or today I guess it is now," Daniel said.

"Let me buy more shots, and then we dance," Carmen said.

"She is the boss," Hugh said, already signaling over the bartender.

"Y'all have fun, but I'm spent. I'm going to call a cab," Daniel said. He stood from his stool, a little wobbly. Carmen grabbed his arm.

"You cannot leave me alone with this one. He is not the dancer you are," Carmen said.

"Now I know you've had too much to drink," Daniel said with a laugh. He had seen Young Hugh on the dance floor and of the two of them, Hugh clearly had more rhythm. Young Hugh looked at him with his eager puppy dog eyes. Daniel sighed. "I'm going to regret this in the morning."

* * *

Daniel woke up with a dry throat and full bladder. He staggered to the toilet and realized he was fully dressed, wearing the same jeans and shirt from last night. What time did he get in? He vaguely recalled riding in a cab with Young Hugh and Carmen. He passed Hugh's room on his way back from the restroom. The door was open, and Daniel peaked in. Hugh was asleep on top of the bed. Daniel returned to his own room and collapsed on his bed. He closed his eyes, but the light coming in from the window seemed extra bright. He rolled away from it on his side. Then he shot up. What time was it?

Daniel reached for his phone, but it was not in its usual place on his nightstand. He went to the kitchen to view the clock on the microwave oven. He was late. Or nearly so. If he hurried, skipped a shower and breakfast, he might make it. But he needed a shower and was very hungry. He could kill for a cup of hot coffee right now. But he would have to make do with an extra layer of deodorant, a quick change of clothes, and a handful of whatever dry cereal he could swipe from the cupboard on his way out the door.

He couldn't find his jacket. Had he forgotten it at the club? No time to look for it now. At least his phone was there on the kitchen table. He flew out the door and to the nearest bus stop. When he arrived at the prison, he saw Ellie already waiting.

"I was beginning to wonder if you would ever show," Ellie said.

"Sorry, I'm late. It's a long story."

"Looks like it," Ellie said. Daniel self-consciously patted his hair down and tried to smooth out one of the multiple wrinkles in his shirt. "Doesn't matter. They're running late. I don't know how that's possible this early in the morning. I hope Mum doesn't think we forgot her," Ellie said with a sigh.

Daniel's phone rang. The ringtone seemed extra loud. The guard behind the front desk scowled at him. Daniel looked at the screen. *Carmen O.* Why was she calling him? He quickly pushed the button to end the call.

"Uh, do you think I have time to stop by the restroom?" Daniel said. Ellie shrugged.

"I'll be right back."

Daniel left his phone and gloves on the seat beside her. When he returned, he found an even more irritated-looking Ellie. "Still waiting?" he asked.

"No, they just called us in."

"That's good," Daniel said. He grabbed his gloves.

"Why did you say you were late?" Ellie asked.

"Hugh took me out last night. We got back later than expected. I must've slept right through my alarm."

"So just you and Hugh, eh?"

"Well, he invited his boss, Carmen. You met her the other day."

"I remember her," Ellie said. "Oh, you forgot this." Ellie held up his phone. "It kept ringing. I had to put it on silent."

Daniel took the phone. Carmen's name appeared twice more on the lock screen. "Wait, Ellie," Daniel said. But she was already at the guard's desk. Daniel followed her.

"Perhaps it's best if you stayed here," she said. The guard led her out of the room.

Daniel returned to his seat. He looked at his phone again. Why was

Carmen Oteiza calling him? He didn't even remember putting her contact info in there. In a few minutes the guard returned. "You've got to be more careful, mate. That modern technology will get you every time," the guard said to Daniel.

Daniel put his phone in his pocket. "It's not what you think."

"I've been there, believe me. No judgment. But that Miss Gray seems a good lass. Just be more careful is all I'm saying."

Daniel closed his eyes and shook his head. "I need coffee. Is there any place close?"

"Just round the corner. I'll take a vanilla latte with almond milk," the guard said with a wink. Daniel glowered at him. "Cheers," the guard called as Daniel walked out the door.

Daniel returned with three cups. Two for Ellie and himself and one, reluctantly, for the guard. "I've been thinking on your problem, mate," the guard said. "You want my advice—" Daniel didn't want his advice, but the man was clearly going to give it anyway. "You want my advice, you just give your lady some space. Let her cool off, then give her a present. The coffee's a nice start, but it's not near sufficient. You'll want something more expensive, like a necklace or something. Depends on how attractive this, eh, Carman was it? The more attractive the side bird, the more expensive the make-up present. That's my experience anyway."

"Thanks, but it's really not like that. I only went out with her and a friend once and...I don't know why I'm telling you this," Daniel said. The guard gave him a knowing look and sipped his coffee.

When Ellie returned from the visitation room, she didn't seem to be in a mood to have Daniel try to clarify the Carmen situation. So, whether he wanted to or not, Daniel ended up taking the guard's advice and gave her space. She left for an afternoon shift at the veterinary clinic, and Daniel headed to Church Street to check on the display set up. He was halfway there when he realized he'd forgotten to ask Ellie if she'd mentioned Edna Caird or her late husband to her mother. Ellie had said that Elspeth and Edna had known one another. He decided he would use that as an excuse to see her again soon and hopefully smooth things over. Hopefully, without having to resort to shiny, expensive gifts.

Daniel arrived at the kirk to find a very flustered Mr. Fisher. "Where is this company that's supposed to set up my nativity?" Fisher asked Daniel. "I'm already two days behind the Old High! This display you ordered better be truly something, or I'll never live this down."

"Hugh told me he would set it up today. Let me see where he's at," Daniel said. He pulled his phone out of his pocket. He frowned at the lock screen. *Carmen O* had appeared twice more since he'd left the prison. He tapped in his passcode, but the phone just buzzed. *Incorrect passcode*. He tapped it in again. Same result. "That's odd."

"Eh?" Fisher said.

"My phone, I can't unlock it," Daniel said.

"I can't wait for young Mr. Macpherson all day. If he doesn't show before too long, I will have to set up whatever I can salvage from the storeroom, headless Mary or no," Fisher said. He rubbed his head. "We'll be the laughingstock of Inverness."

"I'm sure it's not that bad," Daniel tried to reassure him. Fisher shot him a look that said otherwise. "I'll run home and check on Hugh."

Daniel arrived at Bellfield Park to a scene of flashing lights. But it was too early in the day for Christmas decorations. No, these red and blue lights were from two police cars parked in front of his flat. He saw the elder Mr. and Mrs. Macpherson standing outside their door, holding one another. The door to his own flat was open. Daniel walked cautiously to the short gate separating the street from the front garden. "What's going on?" he shouted to his landlords.

Before they could answer, he saw a man and a woman in blue police windcheater jackets exit his flat. Behind them came Young Hugh Macpherson with his hands cuffed behind his back, followed closely by another officer. "Hugh, what's happened?" Daniel asked when they passed by him.

"Rev, you've got to help me! I didn't do it. You have to believe me," Young Hugh said.

"Do what?"

One of the officers opened the back door of the police car and ushered

Young Hugh in. "You have to help me! I didn't murder Archie Caird!"

Chapter Ten

Daniel sat with Marjory Macpherson in her sitting room. Neither had spoken for a while. What was there to say? They needed company more than words. Daniel drew lines with his finger on the velvety red-purple fabric of his chair. Marjory held a framed photograph.

"He was such a happy lad," she said.

"Huh?"

Marjory showed Daniel the photograph. In it he saw a younger version of Mr. and Mrs. Macpherson, their hair with more color, their faces less wrinkled. They stood with their son between them. In the background was the broken tower of Urquhart Castle on Loch Ness. Daniel recognized the place and also had fond memories of it. It was there, over a year ago, that he and Ellie had shared their first kiss.

"He couldn't have been more than eight here," Marjory said. A long hiss, then a whine came from the kitchen. She stood and returned the photograph to its former place on an end table.

Daniel stood too. "Do you need help?"

"No, no. It's no bother. Gives me something to do," she said.

And something to think about besides Young Hugh, if only for a few minutes, thought Daniel. Marjory returned with two cups of tea. She handed one to Daniel and returned to her seat by the photograph. The tea was too hot yet to drink. She put her cup down and stood. "Do you think I should put on another? They're sure to be home soon. Young Hugh will want a hot cuppa after spending all night in that awful jail," she said.

"I'm sure he will." Daniel wished he could do more for her. Eventually, she would run out of people to make tea for. But sometimes, simply being there in the same room was the most another person could do. She returned to the kitchen. Daniel heard her filling the kettle with water.

"I simply don't understand it," she said when she returned. "Young Hugh hadn't even arrived in Inverness. How can they arrest a person for something that happened when they weren't even in the country?"

"The police haven't told you anything?" Daniel asked.

"Just that they found evidence in the house. But they won't say what. You live there. Did you see anything?"

"No, nothing unusual. I haven't bothered Hugh's room, but he's hardly there anyway, other than to sleep."

"Why would they even suspect him? He was at sea when Mr. Caird was killed. He was…" Marjory said. Her voice trailed off. She winced when she sipped her tea. Still too hot. The sound of a car door shutting came from outside. She and Daniel looked up at the front door expectantly, like eager dogs waiting for their owner to arrive at the end of a long day's work.

Mr. Macpherson entered the house, followed by Young Hugh. Marjory flew straight past her husband to embrace her son. After they had settled on the couch, she busied herself in the kitchen, preparing two more cups of tea. Young Hugh had an oppressive, worn-down look about him. Daniel had seen him on several mornings after all-night parties, but he'd never looked as tired as he did now.

"Do you know anything more about why they suspect you?" Daniel asked.

"He needs to rest," Mr. Macpherson said.

"Yes, but…." Daniel said. He stopped when Mrs. Macpherson returned with their tea. She sat down next to Young Hugh, scooting her husband aside.

"I was just telling Reverend Darrow how I can't understand why they think you're involved in Mr. Caird's death. You hadn't even arrived," she said. Young Hugh smiled and blew on his tea to cool it, but remained silent.

"Surely the ship or dock or someone keeps logs that could prove you weren't here," Daniel said.

"Aye, the Reverend's on to something. I'll ring the Port immediately. We'll get this sorted. I can't believe I didn't think of it sooner," Mr. Macpherson said.

"Don't bother. It won't help," Young Hugh said.

"What? Yes, your father is helping. Of course, I'm helping," Mr. Macpherson said. He had a look of dejection on his face, as if Young Hugh had slighted him.

"No, I said don't BOTHER. Calling the Port won't help," Young Hugh said.

"No?"

"When I first called to tell you I was arriving in Inverness, I didn't tell the whole truth. We'd actually docked a few days earlier," Young Hugh said. He stared at his cup as he spoke.

"But that doesn't make sense," Marjory said.

"I just wanted a couple days to myself first. I wanted to blow off some steam after being away so long. It's hard to settle back in. I wasn't sure if you even wanted to see me," Young Hugh said.

"We always want to see you! How can you say that?" Marjory asked.

"Well, you know, after last time," Young Hugh said. He looked up at his father. "The argument."

The elder Hugh Macpherson sighed. "I may not agree with some of your decisions, but you're my son. Like your mother said, we always want to see you."

Young Hugh nodded and sipped his tea. "I'm sorry, I should've said something sooner." He took another sip. "But I swear I had nothing to do with Mr. Caird."

"You have an alibi?" Daniel asked.

"I was playing poker with some mates from work. It was Saturday night, right? We always played poker on Saturday night," Young Hugh said.

"Good, that's good. And you told the police that?" Daniel asked. Young Hugh nodded.

"It's settled then," Marjory said.

"But…." Daniel said. Everyone looked at him. He thought for a moment. "But the time of death. Police aren't certain it was Saturday night. That's just when the body was found. I saw a story in the paper the other day. It could've happened Friday or Saturday. Coroners can't nail down a more specific time because of how Caird was found, half frozen in the water."

Mr. and Mrs. Macpherson looked at Daniel like he was the enemy. Young Hugh simply returned his gaze to his cup.

"Friday? I had the day off that Friday. I went to the Innes Bar. Planned on spending some time with Carmen. Show her around town. This is her first time in Scotland. But she had a meeting. An inventory issue or something," Young Hugh said.

"Have they talked to the police? They can confirm your story," Daniel suggested.

"They fired me."

"What?" Mr. Macpherson said.

"Said it looked bad for the company. Said they don't employ criminals," Young Hugh said. He took another sip of tea. "I didn't do it. I couldn't do it. I... I didn't even know Mr. Caird."

Daniel stood. He couldn't bear to see Young Hugh, once so full of life and high spirits, now so dejected. And his parents, who had been nothing but welcoming since he'd moved to Inverness, now so seemingly lost and desperate. "I'll go speak to them, the guys at your work and Carmen. I'm still a client, remember. They have to talk to me. Just stay here."

"Don't worry about me. I can't leave the city until there's a trial," Young Hugh said.

* * *

Daniel decided to walk to Church Street first. He wanted to check on the nativity display and, if he was lucky, he hoped to catch the workers before they finished setting it up. After his curt dismissal from the warehouse the other day with Young Hugh, Daniel preferred to talk with the men on his own home territory. He also needed to process what had happened overnight. His flatmate arrested for murder and lying about when he had arrived in town. With the reputation he brought with him for getting into trouble, things did not look good for Young Hugh Macpherson. But Daniel knew Hugh, didn't he? Hugh wasn't a murderer. He said he'd never even met Archie Caird. But could he have been lying about that too? Daniel had only met him a week ago. What did he truly know about Young Hugh or what he was capable of?

"Time to find out," Daniel said to himself as he approached Church Street Kirk. He headed immediately to the small lawn in the front where the display was to be set up. A narrow barnlike structure with a thatched roof stood in the center of the space. Inside were a few square bales of hay and a wooden manger. No figures populated the scene yet. A white truck was parked along the curb in front of the kirk. Blue lettering across the side of the truck read: Highland Removals.

Daniel inspected the barn and manger. They looked just like the ones he'd picked out of the catalogue in Carmen Oteiza's office. "Reverend Darrow!" Daniel jumped. He turned around to see Fisher walking toward him, carrying a plastic sheep. "You're finally here. I'm not at all sure about these men you hired," Fisher said.

"What's the problem?"

"They haven't done a blasted thing, have they? Three days now, Old High has had their display up. And look at this. It took less time for Peter to betray our Lord," Fisher said.

"It looks like they've got a good start," Daniel said. He didn't have time for Fisher's ecclesial rivalries.

"And where is the young Mr. Macpherson? You told me he was to set it all up yesterday?"

"You don't know?" Daniel asked. Fisher looked at him incredulously. "Never mind. Where are the workers? I need to speak with them." Fisher could find out about Young Hugh's arrest on his own. Nothing remained secret for very long on Church Street.

"They've been at lunch for over an hour now. That's their truck there," Fisher said, pointing to the white Highland Removals truck. "I wish you would speak to them. They are refusing to help me set up my animals. They said, 'Not our figures, not our problem,' they said."

"Do you need to use your old animals? The rental includes everything."

Fisher gave Daniel another exasperated look. He rubbed his head. Daniel did not know how the man had any hair left. "Have you seen Old High's?" he asked, as if that answered Daniel's question. Fisher placed the plastic sheep he had been holding inside the barn near the manger. "They better not make off with my animals or wisemen when they take all this down."

"The rental figures all have barcodes or serial numbers or something. I'm sure you don't have to worry."

"I'll make a mark on mine just in case," Fisher said. He pulled a black marker out of his pocket, turned the sheep upside down, and wrote an *F* on the sole of the back-left foot. He nodded, satisfied, and looked at Daniel.

But Daniel was watching the moving truck. Two men approached it. They rolled open its back door with a bang. "Wait here," Daniel said.

"Ask about my animals," Fisher called after him.

The two movers climbed inside and began taking the protective sheet off a ceramic camel. Daniel approached them and introduced himself. He asked them if they knew Hugh Macpherson.

"Yes. But he does not work here any longer," one of the men said. He was a hulk of a man, a born mover, and he had an unusual accent. He certainly wasn't from Scotland or England. *Eastern European?* Daniel wondered. And he knew about Young Hugh's firing. Did he know why?

"Can I ask you a few questions about him?" Daniel asked.

The two men exchanged glances before the first one answered. "Be quick. We must finish this job."

"Thank you. I was wondering if he was with you last Saturday?"

They carried the camel off the truck and set it on the sidewalk. "Da," the first man said. He thought for a moment. "We played poker."

The second man laughed. "*We* played poker. *He* just lost money."

Daniel had heard that voice before, but he couldn't remember from where. The first man laughed. "Hugh and your friend there. Both big losers!"

"Who?" Daniel asked. "Fisher?" Daniel glanced back at Fisher, who was busy rearranging the sheep in the display.

"Da," the first man said.

"So, they were both with you all night?" Daniel asked. Why hadn't Hugh mentioned Fisher earlier? Why hadn't Fisher mentioned knowing these two men?

"No, Hugh's a terrible poker player. They both are. Hugh only played a few hands before he was out. Don't know what happened to him after that," the second man said.

Daniel recognized the voice now. This was the man that had shooed him out of the warehouse. The warehouse hadn't had good lighting then, but the voice was definitely the same. "So, Hugh left early?" Daniel asked.

"The sun had barely set. Look, mate, if that's it, we really must finish up. We've got other jobs to get to today."

"Of course, thank you," Daniel said. They had confirmed Young Hugh's story, but only partly. If Hugh had left the card game early, he still had a lot of time unaccounted for. Daniel needed to find Carmen next. He began to walk to the nearest bus stop.

"Reverend," Fisher called after him.

"Mr. Fisher, I'm sorry, I don't have time for.... Wait. You played poker with Young Hugh and those men last Saturday night?"

"Only for an hour or so. Hugh rang me when he arrived in town. I enjoy a good game ever so often. Those boys cleaned out poor Hugh right quick. I held my own for a while longer but had to bow out. I wanted to keep enough in my pocket for dinner, didn't I," Fisher said.

Daniel now understood Fisher's disdain for the two movers. "Do you know when Hugh left that night?"

Fisher thought for a moment. "Don't recall. Oh, you've got a message. Someone rang the kirk earlier. I was the only one here. She said she had your coat and mobile."

"Huh?" Daniel patted his pocket. He had his phone with him.

"From a club or bar, what was the name?" Fisher said. He scratched his head, thinking.

"Oh, of course! Thank you. You're a life saver!" Daniel said. As he hurried away, Daniel pulled out his phone. He saw Carmen's calls on the lock screen. That was why it wouldn't accept his unlock code. This was not his phone. He had left his in his jacket at the club the other night and grabbed Hugh's by mistake the next morning. *What a relief*, he thought. Now, if only Ellie would believe it.

Chapter Eleven

Daniel thanked the woman at the bar. "You don't know how glad I am to get these back. I can't believe I left them here."

"You'd be surprised the things people forget," the woman said. "We try to return as much as we can, but as you can see...." She stepped out from behind the bar and opened a nearby door. Inside were several coats, some hung on hangers, some in a pile on the floor. Beside the coat pile sat a large cardboard box with the words Caledonian Brewery inscribed decoratively across the front. It was filled nearly to overflowing with bags, purses, phones, scarves, a few umbrellas, and canes, among other abandoned items. She thumbed through the coats on the hanging rack.

"That one there," Daniel said, pointing. She handed him his jacket. Zipped up safely in the front pocket was his phone. Daniel took it out. The battery was nearly dead. But it had enough power to light up the home screen showing two missed calls. One from Rev. Calder and one from Fisher. He could guess why Fisher had called, but why had Rev. Calder? Well, she had waited this long; she could wait another hour or so until after he had finished his mission.

"How did you know these were mine?" Daniel asked.

"There's a receipt in the pocket."

Daniel looked in the other pocket and found the receipt for the kirk's nativity display. His contact information was printed at the bottom: Rev. Daniel Darrow, Church Street Kirk, Church St., Inverness, along with the kirk's phone number. Below that, he saw Carmen Oteiza's name and number, no address. That didn't matter. He knew where to find her.

* * *

All the warehouse buildings at the Port looked confusingly similar to Daniel. He took a minute to get his bearings, trying to remember which direction Young Hugh had taken him just two days earlier. It felt like so much longer than that. After a couple of wrong turns, he found Carmen's office. She was inside.

"Darrow, yes?" she said, glancing up from her laptop computer screen for only a second.

"Yes. I'm glad I caught you. I was wondering if you could answer a few questions for me."

"Is there a problem with your display? Allen said he would set it up this morning," Carmen said. She typed as she talked.

"No, I just came from there. It looks fine. I actually wanted to ask you about Hugh," Daniel said. He sat down in one of the two chairs in front of her desk. At the mention of Hugh's name, Carmen stopped typing and looked at him.

"Hugh? He does not work here anymore."

"I know. He told me. He came home this morning."

"So, he is not still in jail?" she said. "I have heard what he has done. It is hard to believe. My Hugh, a murderer."

"That's why I'm here. I don't believe it, either. He said he was with you that weekend, the weekend Archie Caird was killed. I was wondering if you could confirm that?"

"When was this?" she asked.

"Nearly two weeks ago."

Carmen shook her head. "I do not think so."

"He said he saw you that Friday evening? Please try to remember. If Hugh has an alibi, we may be able to prove he's innocent."

Carmen thought for a moment. She pulled up a calendar app on her laptop. "Ah, yes. I was to meet Hugh that day. We had plans to go away for the weekend. This is my first time in Scotland. Inverness is pleasant, but it is so small. I told Hugh I desired to truly see this land. He wanted to take me out to the country, eh, the country, not how do you say? Not the nation."

Daniel nodded. "The countryside, out in nature. So, you two went hiking or camping for the weekend?" *Did you go to the north shore of Loch Ness, to the mouth of the Moriston River?* This was going to be Daniel's next question.

"No. Hugh wanted to walk up some hill or take me fishing, but that is not what I meant when I told him I want to see the country. I want to go to a big city with big shops and nightlife. I thought Hugh would understand. He likes to party. But he must have gotten angry. He canceled our trip. I did not see him the whole weekend. Perhaps he went hiking, as you say, on his own."

Daniel left Carmen Oteiza's office with more questions than answers. For starters, how did Carmen and the movers already know about Young Hugh's arrest? Fisher seemed still under the impression that Young Hugh was going to set up the display at the kirk earlier. With the kirk gossip lines traveling faster than the latest high-speed internet, he should have been one of the first to know. Just last month, when the MacNally boy had gotten suspended from Millburn Academy for starting a fight and stealing another student's lunch money, Fisher had warned Daniel to keep an eye on the boy when passing the tithe around the next Sunday. And that was before school had even let out. Daniel was informed by William MacCrivag the next day that it was not, in fact, a student's lunch money, but actual cash from the cafeteria's till that the boy had nicked. Young Hugh Macpherson's arrest was a much bigger story than stolen lunch money, but Daniel was seemingly the only other member of Church Street to know about it. And he had only found out because he was there when it happened. As far as he could tell, the news hadn't even made it online yet.

Further, how had Carmen known that Young Hugh was arrested under a charge of suspected murder? Daniel didn't imagine that's information the police would readily share with a curious employer. Unless Young Hugh had told Carmen himself. But how – he'd had Hugh's phone. And what about Hugh's claims to have been with her Friday evening and at a poker game Saturday night? Something wasn't adding up.

From the Port, Daniel went straight back to Bellfield Park. Fisher could handle the movers himself. He saw a light on in the window of Young Hugh's and his side of the flat. Hugh was sitting on the couch watching TV. Daniel returned Hugh's phone, checking first to make sure that it was, in fact, Hugh's phone, and recounted his conversations with Hugh's former workmates.

"Carmen said she didn't see me at all that weekend?" Hugh asked. Daniel nodded. Hugh turned off the TV. "Why would she say that?"

"You never told me you two had plans to go away for the weekend," Daniel said.

"I didn't want to in front of my parents. They're old-fashioned. Would've frowned on it. And I didn't want to add another ember to the fire with everything else. Yes, we were planning a wee holiday, but I didn't cancel on her. She canceled on me."

"Because you had differing views of what seeing the country meant?"

"I had suggested a hill walk or a trip up to Loch Ness at first, but I was fine with a trip down to Edinburgh or Glasgow if she wanted a bigger city."

"So, you weren't upset about not going hiking?"

"Of course not. Glasgow has some cracking clubs. I just wanted to spend the weekend with her, away from here and the boys from the ship. You don't get a lot of alone time on a boat, if you know what I mean. I was all set to go, packed a bag and all. Then she said something had come up, and we'd have to wait. I ended up drinking at the Innes Bar alone, like I told you, then poker with the boys the next night."

"About that. They told me you left the game early. You ran out of money?"

"I never said I was any good at poker," Hugh said.

Daniel's phone rang. It was Rev. Calder. "Can we talk about this more later?" Daniel asked. Young Hugh shrugged and turned the TV back on. Daniel took his phone to his room and shut the door.

"You're a hard one to get a hold of," Rev. Calder said.

"I know, I'm sorry. I misplaced my phone," Daniel answered.

"For two days?"

"It's a long story."

"Well, I'm glad I've got you now. I was just at Edna Caird's when I heard about Young Hugh Macpherson's arrest. I was shocked."

"Me too. I was actually here when it happened. Thankfully Young Hugh is back home now," Daniel said.

"How is the family? Should I come over?"

"They're holding up as best they can. Mr. and Mrs. Macpherson are putting on brave faces, but I know they're afraid for their son. Young Hugh seems like he's still in shock. I don't know if the full weight of what happened has hit him yet. I'm sure they would appreciate a visit. You're much better at comforting people than me. I'll suggest it to Mrs. Macpherson tomorrow," Daniel said. "You said you came from Edna Caird's. How did she take the news? I'm afraid I haven't done much of a job at helping her with the case."

"I didn't tell her. I don't know how close she is with Hugh and Marjory. She's in such a delicate state, I simply don't know how she might react to a member of the kirk being suspected. Though I fear she will find out on her own before long."

"With the way news travels on Church Street, you're probably right," Daniel said. "Speaking of which, how did you hear about Young Hugh's arrest? Did Mr. Fisher tell you?"

"No, but if I found out, you can be sure Fisher has known for ages," Rev. Calder joked.

"That's the thing, Fisher didn't know," Daniel said. He proceeded to tell Rev. Calder about his day's investigation. "What do you make of it? Three different people, three different stories, and not a one from the usual Church Street gossip lines."

Rev. Calder did not respond for several minutes. So long that Daniel wondered if they had gotten disconnected. Finally, she answered with a question, "You've heard the story of the trial of Susanna?"

Daniel wasn't in the habit of keeping up with local crimes or trials, unless they involved members of his own parish. She had said, *story*, though. Could she mean the biblical story? It had been a while since he'd read that one.

"I should think you would know it, it being from your namesake book after all," Rev. Calder said.

"Refresh my memory," Daniel said.

"Susanna was the lovely young wife of a rich man. What was his name? Eh, he's not important. Susanna was bathing one afternoon in her garden, when she unwittingly attracted the attention of two elders. It wasn't her fault, of course; these were cheeky old men. Though as many times as this type of scene seems to play out in the bible, one wonders why indoor plumbing wasn't invented sooner. Well, these cheeky elders approached Susanna and insisted that she sleep with them or they would tell her husband they caught her cheating on him. At the time, this was a crime that carried the death penalty. A rather strict bunch back then.

"Susanna refused them, as you might expect, so there was a trial and the elders testified against her. As you might also expect, her husband took the side of the men. Susanna was convicted. But just as she was being taken away, young Daniel, sitting in the audience, was stirred to action. He demanded that the elders be cross-examined. A reasonable request I kin. The husband agreed, such a magnanimous bloke, and Daniel separated the two elders. He asked each where the illicit action supposedly occurred. One said under a mastic tree, the other said beneath an evergreen oak. Thus, proving the elders had lied, Susanna was declared innocent. Happy ending. Though, if you ask me, Susanna's husband had better have had a fine apology gift in mind if he ever wanted to see her in a, eh, *compromising* state again!"

"What does all that have to do with Young Hugh?" Daniel asked.

"Seems to me one or more of them is not telling the truth. Between Young Hugh, those movers, and Ms. Oteitza, you've got your own modern-day trial of Susanna."

"So, which one is Hugh? Susanna or one of the two lying accusers?"

"That's what you've got to find out."

Chapter Twelve

Daniel Darrow awoke early Thursday morning. He laid in bed, chasing sleep, for eternal minutes or hours; who could tell in that dark timelessness before the sun rose? But his mind wouldn't grant him rest. Every time he felt himself drifting off toward sleep, some stray thought would inevitably needle him back to waking. Young Hugh Macpherson's arrest and dubious alibi. Susanna's trial. Ellie and Carmen. Would Ellie believe the phone mix-up? The boys who'd found poor Archie Caird's body in the woods. He must make a point this Sunday to check in on them.

Finally, he gave up on sleep. He got out of bed, dressed, and made a quick breakfast of oatmeal and frozen strawberries. He would grab a coffee on his walk. An early morning walk was just what he needed to think clearly, objectively. He headed south along the small two-lane road that paralleled the Ness River. It was never very busy, and as the sun was just now rising, it was all but empty. Despite the nonexistent traffic, he veered off onto the tree-lined footpath to be closer to the water. He enjoyed the steady sound of the river and its fresh, earthy scent, so cold now that it made his head ache if he breathed in too deeply.

As he walked, Daniel let his mind wander through yesterday's interviews. First, Young Hugh, his new flatmate, prodigal son of the Macpherson clan. Hugh's reputation preceded him. Ellie had known him growing up and had warned Daniel of Hugh's propensity for getting into trouble. Young Hugh was a storied partier and certainly lived up to the hype. But was he a liar and murderer as well? To Daniel, Hugh seemed generally good-natured and carefree, if a bit reckless. He seemed the type whose antics were more likely to injure himself than anyone else. But then, first impressions could be deceiving. Reputations were often earned for a reason, and Daniel had only known Hugh for less than a fortnight.

Daniel reached a narrow suspension bridge with white painted metal railing that looked like it belonged more naturally around a garden than a bridge. He crossed the bridge onto one of two small islands that rose from the middle of the Ness. The rush of the river was louder here. Wind whistled through the mostly bare tree branches. He wondered if Archie Caird had heard the river before he died.

The night Caird's body was found, Young Hugh had said he was playing poker with a few of his shipmates. But the two men Daniel had talked to said Hugh ran out of money and left the game early. Where did he go after that? Would he have had enough time to make it to the far end of Loch Ness? Hugh said he had never met Archie before. But surely that wasn't true. Hugh's parents seemed to know the Cairds, and they did all attend Church Street Kirk. But why would he be all the way out there with Archie? Unless the two movers were lying. Daniel got the impression that Young Hugh felt a greater affinity for them than they felt for Hugh. But did they dislike him so much that they would lie about his whereabouts? And for what reason?

The path through the first island came to an end at another short bridge. Daniel crossed it. The path now split, each leg winding around the perimeter of the second island rather than through its middle. Daniel took the path to the right. This route through the islands was a favorite walk for him, particularly in the early mornings or during the fall and spring when tourism was lighter. His legs, well used to this routine, took over while he thought about Carmen Oteiza.

Young Hugh had said he'd been with Carmen the weekend Archie Caird had died. But Carmen had told Daniel otherwise. They had planned to go away for the weekend, but Hugh had suddenly canceled because he was angry at her? Because she had wanted to hit up some clubs in Glasgow, and he had wanted to go for a hike in nature. On the loch? Maybe Hugh had arranged for Archie Caird to take him and Carmen on a guided wilderness tour? Maybe the trip was nonrefundable? The two movers had indicated Hugh had money problems. But would that be enough to kill someone over?

The whole puzzle reminded him of an ice-breaker game he'd played at a conference years ago: *Two Truths and a Lie*. Each participant wrote down three statements about themselves—two were true, and one was a lie. The object of the game was to read your three statements to the group and see if anyone could guess the lie. Daniel had not been very good at this game. He couldn't come up with a believable lie. Now he was faced with a game of much higher stakes. A game more aptly called *Two Lies and a Truth*, or possibly, simply, *Three Lies*.

Before he could get close to sorting out the truth from the lies, or the Susanna from the cheeky elders, as Rev. Calder had put it, Daniel found himself at another white suspension bridge. This bridge was identical to the one he'd taken onto the first island. Without any specific destination in mind, he crossed to the opposite shore and walked the short distance to Whin Park. There he saw signs of Inverness's annual Winter Wonderland coming to life. Workers in thick coats and gloves strung lights through the trees. Others put the finishing touches on a snowy candy cane platform for Santa's chair. Children's fair rides lay in a semiconstructed state to the side. The sight reminded Daniel of the nativity display at Church Street Kirk. He'd been so distracted by Young Hugh's plight, he'd forgotten to check on it.

Daniel looked at his watch. 8:30 on a Thursday morning. Fisher would be at the Millburn Academy, where he worked part-time. If he headed over now, Daniel could inspect the display without the choir director's watchful eye. He turned around in search of a bus stop. His early morning walk had helped clarify the problem, but it had done nothing to illuminate a solution.

* * *

When the bus let Daniel off at Church Street, he grabbed a much-needed coffee to-go from the café on the corner. No white removals truck was parked in front of the kirk this morning. In its place stood a nativity display complete with a small thatch-roofed barn, pastoral animals, and baby Jesus in a wooden manger laced with hay. A shepherd boy and Joseph and Mary, all with their ceramic heads fully attached, watched over the infant. It was a scene straight out of the catalogue, except for a few additions that could have only come from Mr. Fisher. Daniel counted two sun-faded sheep that were clearly not part of the fresh catalogue display, an impressive three camels, and a total of four, no five, wisemen crowded into the barn. Old High, eat your heart out!

Daniel entered the kirk. He knocked on Rev. Calder's office door, but no one answered. She was likely out on a house call or helping at the senior home. Daniel went to his own small office by the kirk hall. It was a windowless room that he suspected had once been a pantry. Even after a year, he would occasionally find a tin of biscuits or boxes of tea or canned goods stacked on top of his desk. The gifts of some kind-hearted parishioner who had clearly forgotten that he had moved into the space.

Today his desk was bare, except for a laptop computer, a notebook, and a stack of books he had been studying in preparation for Sunday's homily. The stuffy room was not his favorite place, especially after such a pleasant morning's stroll, but he could not spend all day walking along the river, contemplating murder. So, leaving the door open to let in a little light and heat from the adjoining room, he settled in behind the desk.

Before he turned on the computer, he pulled out his phone and clicked on Ellie Gray's contact info. He texted: *Do u want to have dinner 2night? Auld Lang Naan?* It was a little pricey, but it was her favorite restaurant. And some spicy Indian food might be just the thing for this cold winter's day. He checked that the phone wasn't on silent and set it on the desk with its screen easily visible in case she responded.

A couple hours later, it was easy to lose track of time in that cramped pantry office, Daniel was lulled out of his study by the phone's buzz. *Just the 2 of us?* Ellie responded with a sarcastic-looking emoji.

Ha ha. Yes, Daniel responded, adding his own smiley.

I'm off at 6, Ellie texted back.

Daniel smiled. "And with that, it's time for a break," he said out loud to himself. He closed the laptop, stretched, and left the room, not bothering to shut the door. Perhaps a visit to the kirk garden? His stomach growled, telling him he had worked through lunch. Scratch the garden, he would go for a stroll down the street to the café. He chuckled as he passed the overcrowded nativity barn.

He stopped. One of the extra wisemen was leaning precariously close to its twin. Daniel imagined a domino effect that would send the whole menagerie crashing down. He stepped carefully over a sheep. "Pardon me," he said as he squeezed past the Virgin Mary to reach the unstable wiseman. He heard a sound from the hay behind one of the camel's feet. A mouse? Daniel leaned down for a closer look. Nothing. He shrugged and squeezed back past Mary.

Now the sound came from under the manger. He knelt down, taking a position much like that of the little shepherd boy figure. What must some passerby think upon seeing this absurd scene? Daniel shook his head and was about to stand back up, but there it was again. A distinct rustling of hay. He got on hands and knees now to peer under the manger. He caught sight of a furry orange tail. But before his brain could comprehend what he saw, Sir Walter Scott burst from beneath the manger. The cat leaped onto Mary's outstretched arms, using them as a springboard to fly over Daniel's head to the lawn behind him. Daniel leaped up in surprise, knocking his head hard against the side of the manger.

"Mother...Mary!" he shouted, catching his tongue as he spotted an actual mother with two small children watching from across the street. One of the children laughed while the mother instinctively covered the other's ears. Daniel rubbed his head and offered a sheepish smile.

"Your cat went thata way," the mother said with a laugh.

Daniel waved and looked where she pointed, but Sir Walter was already long gone. The manger was on its side. He righted the manger and stuffed it back full of hay. He gasped when he went to retrieve the baby Jesus which lay a couple feet away against the side of a sheep. Fisher was going to kill him! Well, maybe Sir Walter first, but he was definitely next. The figure's tiny arms were reaching up in a position to mirror that of its mother. In its proper place in the manger, it was a touching image of the love between mother and child. But now. Leaning against the side of a sheep, one arm stretched out toward Mary while the other lay detached on the hay-covered ground.

"Oh no, oh no," Daniel said. He picked up the arm and tried to fit it back onto its body, but it wouldn't stay. It was a clean break without any jagged edges. Maybe he could shove it in and cover up the break with a handful of hay? No luck. Daniel studied the shoulder hole to find a better angle to wedge the arm in. Something was inside. He brought the figure out into the sunlight. Whatever was inside was dark and appeared furry. He felt with his finger inside. It was soft, what little he could feel of it. A mouse? Daniel jerked his finger out at the thought and nearly dropped the figure. That must be why Sir Walter was rummaging around the manger. He was after whatever had somehow crawled inside the figure and died.

If something had gotten in there, then maybe the broken figure wasn't totally his fault. Maybe he could still get his deposit back. But what to do about Fisher? The poor man had nearly had a panic attack when he'd thought the kirk's nativity display would be without a Mary. How could Daniel tell him it was now missing its Baby Jesus? Daniel got his phone and texted Ellie.

Can we meet at Church St before dinner? Bring glue!

Chapter Thirteen

D aniel Darrow held the arm of the baby Jesus in one hand, and with the other, he cradled the hollow ceramic body that contained what appeared to be a deceased mouse or rat. If Fisher found out the star character in his nativity display was broken, he was sure to have another breakdown. So much for a silent night where all is calm, all is bright. Daniel attempted to ward off the coming storm until Ellie arrived with the glue or until he could think of a better solution. He put the arm down and retrieved his phone. He found Fisher's name and texted: *Nativity looks great! Love the camels. I'm sure everyone Sunday will love it too. See u then.* That wasn't too subtle, was it? Hopefully, Fisher would get the message that he didn't need to stop by the kirk until Sunday. Daniel couldn't tell him outright not to come and risk raising his suspicions. Fisher was already so paranoid about the display. And Sunday morning should be plenty of time to talk to Carmen and get a replacement. It would have to be.

Daniel returned the infant figure to the manger and placed its broken arm near where it should be relative to the shoulder. He grabbed a handful of hay to cover over the break. Try as he may to prop up the arm so that it appeared to stretch out toward Mary like the other, the best he could manage was to keep it from sliding down and looking like a third leg. Daniel stepped back to assess the scene. He nodded. It didn't look half bad. Fisher's extra animals and wisemen certainly kept one's eyes busy. If you didn't look too closely, you might never notice that baby Jesus, instead of reaching out to embrace his mother, appeared to be giving her a high-five.

After a bite for lunch at the café around the corner, Daniel returned to the kirk to finish preparing for Sunday's service. He made a note to move Sir Walter's bowls of cat food and water into his own office that morning and lock him in if he could. On a normal Sunday, Fisher was annoyed by the cat's habit of roaming the pews in search of head scratches and belly rubs, distracting parishioners from where their attention should be – Fisher and the choir. Daniel understood the sentiment, though, at times when his own jokes or remarks fell flat, he was thankful for the feline distraction. But this Sunday, it might be best for Sir Walter to lay low. Just in case, Daniel added a paragraph to his homily about forgiveness and mercy and treating all God's creatures with kindness.

Shortly after five in the afternoon, he called to make a reservation for two at Auld Lang Naan. About an hour later, Ellie texted to say she had arrived at the kirk. "So why are we meeting here instead of at the restaurant?" she asked after Daniel had greeted her outside.

"I have a small problem. Did you bring glue?"

"Oh, all I could find was this," Ellie said. She fished a roll of surgical tape out of her coat pocket. "Who carries glue around with them?"

"Who carries surgical tape around with them?"

"Do you want it or not?"

"Yes, thank you! The patient is out front there," Daniel said, pointing to the nativity display. Ellie gave him an uncertain look. "Did you notice anything odd about it?" Daniel asked.

Ellie shrugged. "A bit crowded, perhaps." Daniel led her to the manger. "Wait, is the baby Jesus trying to give Mary a high-five?"

"Is that not a normal position for a baby?" Daniel said. "Look closer."

Ellie leaned down. "His arm is missing!"

"What? No, it's right...Oh no, where is it?" Daniel touched the place where the broken arm should have been. He couldn't see very well inside the manger as the sun had already set, and the display was lit only by two small spotlights casting their light in from opposite corners. Daniel patted the hay along the side of the figure. Down past its feet, he discovered the missing arm. He held it up and let out a sigh of relief.

"I'd say that's more than a small problem. Does Mr. Fisher know?" Ellie asked.

"It's that bad?"   •

"Well, any normal person would hardly care, but Mr. Fisher? Even I know of his rivalry with the Old High Church. When my da was alive, he used to call it the Christmas holy war. Mr. Fisher once asked him to construct this elaborate lighting display for it. Of course, Da refused. Said it would be a fire hazard with all the hay. Mr. Fisher didn't speak to him till well past new year."

Daniel sighed. "Technically, this is Sir Walter Scott's fault."

"Blaming the cat? Really? I wouldn't have thought you were scared of ol Mr. Fisher," Ellie said with a laugh.

"It *is* Sir Walter's fault. And I'm only a little scared of Fisher." Even in the dim evening light, Daniel could see Ellie's raised eyebrow. "Fine, I'm a lot scared of Fisher. You should have seen him when he was carrying the Virgin Mary's head out of the storage closet."

"He did what?"

"It's a long story. I'm just glad you were able to bring something to stick this arm back on before I can get it replaced."

"You couldn't have walked over to the store for glue yourself?"

"There's another reason I asked you to meet me here," Daniel said. He picked up the ceramic body. "Here, I think this is why Sir Walter was slinking around the manger. I thought it was a mouse that somehow crawled in there and died, but it seems too big."

"So what? Now I'm pest control?" Ellie said.

"You're enjoying my troubles a little too much," Daniel said. He handed her the figure. Ellie peered inside the arm hole, then smelled it.

"It's not a dead mouse. You'd smell it if it was, believe me. Or if it is, it's been in there a long time." She tipped the figure on its side and shook it. Nothing came out. She took it to one of the small spotlights to get a better look inside. "It's too dark to see anything in there." Ellie turned the figure over, inspecting it in the light. "Curious."

"What?" Daniel asked.

"Whatever's in there is too big to pull out of this hole you made, er, I'm sorry, this hole Sir Walter made, but I don't see any other opening big enough for a mouse to get in."

Daniel took back the figure and looked it over. "I've heard mice can squeeze into a space the size of a dime." Ellie raised her eyebrow at him again. "Um, five pence?" he said. He held his finger and thumb apart, estimating the size of the coin.

"So, if there is a wee hole in there that we're not seeing, this mouse squeezed in, grew, and then couldn't get back out?" Ellie asked.

"Whatever happened, I'm worried that after I tape the arm back on Sir Walter will just come back and rip it off again. Do you know any way to keep him away from it?"

"You could sprinkle some hot red pepper around the manger. That should keep him out."

"Be serious.

"I am. Cats don't like red pepper."

"Here, I'll hold it on while you tape it up." When Ellie had finished taping it, Daniel placed the figure back in the manger. "There, good as new. Kind of."

"Can I keep it?" Ellie asked.

"What?"

"The baby Jesus. Can I keep it awhile?"

"Why would you want to do that?"

"You've got me curious about it now. I want to see what's inside. We can't see anything here, but if I brought it back to the clinic, I could get a pair of long tweezers in there."

"But—"

"Don't worry. I'll have it back before Mr. Fisher notices."

* * *

Ellie had traveled to Church Street via city bus. Her vehicle, or rather her mother's, was in the shop again, so Daniel called for a car to take them to the restaurant. "A bit chilly out for such a wee un," the driver commented as

Daniel handed the baby Jesus figure to Ellie inside the car.

"He's right. Daniel, luv, give me your scarf," Ellie said. She wrapped the figure warmly in the scarf. "He's our wee bundle of joy. Couldn't find a sitter, could we?"

Daniel flipped his coat collar up over his now bare neck and got in the car. She really was having too much fun with this. On the drive to the restaurant, the driver commented on how well-behaved the baby was. "Haven't heard a peep from him. Usually, I dread picking up young couples with babes. Always so much crying."

"He's had a big day. His uncles stopped by, all bearing birthday gifts. Then we saw some sheep and camels," Ellie said. The driver gave them a look through the rearview mirror when she mentioned camels.

Daniel rolled his eyes, but couldn't help smiling. "Don't forget the cat. He adores the cat. Yes, quite an eventful day. He's all tuckered out now," he said, finally giving in to the joke.

Ellie smiled and held the baby close to him. "He has your eyes."

In the foyer of Auld Lang Naan, Ellie kept the scarf pulled over the baby's ceramic head. "Perhaps, they'll have sympathy, and we'll get in faster if they think we have a baby," she said.

"I made a reservation," Daniel said.

"Still, it's worth a shot."

They received adoring looks from a few of the other waiting guests, but didn't get to their table any quicker.

"You're not concerned about what people might think if they saw us here with a newborn?" Daniel asked.

"No one I work with likes Indian food. I'd be more concerned about running into someone from Church Street if I were you, Mr. Reverend," she said.

"Oh, I hadn't thought of that. Word would get back to your mother. Could make for an awkward future visit."

"That's unlikely," Ellie said.

"I don't know. Traffic for rumors is pretty high on Church Street," Daniel said with a laugh. "Hey, I'm sorry again about last time."

"No, I overreacted. It's hard seeing Mum in jail, even now. I was already feeling a bit down when you showed up late that morning after admittedly being out the night before with Young Hugh and that Carmen woman. There's something about her, the way all the men in the room look at her, the way she knows it and commands it. And you're different around those two, even if you don't want to admit it."

Daniel looked away. She was right of course. Even in his undergraduate days, he'd never stayed out all night at clubs, not remembering how he'd gotten home the next morning.

"Then her number shows up a million times on your phone."

"Yeah, I need to invest in a new phone case. But, I get it. I would have jumped to the same conclusion if it had been some guy's number all over your screen. Like Cameron," Daniel said. Now it was Ellie's turn to roll her eyes. "I know, I know. Y'all broke up a long time ago. I just don't know why he has to be so handsome."

"He is handsome, isn't he," Ellie said.

"Ha ha," Daniel said, deadpan. "How's the kid?" Ellie looked down at the baby in her arms. She fiddled playfully with the scarf.

When the hostess finally called for them, she looked slightly confused. "No one mentioned a baby on your reservation. I'll go fetch a highchair."

"I thought it'd just be the two of us," Daniel said apologetically.

"We didn't exactly plan for him, but what can you do?" Ellic said. The hostess's eyes widened. Then she nodded and said, "I see."

"Don't worry about the highchair. I'll hold him. He's as serene as a babe in a manger," Ellie said. The hostess shrugged and walked them to their table.

Chapter Fourteen

A winter wind blew in off the North Sea, through the city of Inverness early Sunday morning. It brought a dusting of snow and ice pellets that battered the north-facing windows of the residents of Bellfield Park like the sound of hundreds of moths seeking light and warmth inside. The sun had not yet risen, but Daniel Darrow was already awake. He dressed and passed the closed door of Young Hugh's room on his way to the kitchen. Since his arrest, Young Hugh rarely left his room. Daniel had tried asking him again about the conflicting stories of his alibis, but Hugh refused to engage on the subject. Whether it was out of self-preservation or the pain of his shipmates' betrayal, Daniel couldn't tell.

Not one month ago, Daniel had been perfectly content to live in the flat alone. Though Young Hugh had been there only a couple of weeks and was, in fact, still technically present, the place now felt empty. Was it wrong to miss the company of someone who might be a liar, or worse, a murderer? Daniel felt guilty for not being able to help Young Hugh more. The elder Macphersons had placed such hope in him and, so far, he had uncovered nothing that could help their son. Daniel's interviews and their son's silence only seemed to confirm Young Hugh's guilt.

Daniel felt worse still for Edna, Archie Caird's widow, who had also come to him for help. Here he was, living in the same flat as the man suspected of killing her husband, and he couldn't bring himself to tell her. How was he supposed to choose between the two? Surely, she knew of Hugh's arrest by now. How was he to face her at this morning's service? Perhaps she wouldn't show. It was snowing. What a reverend he had become, hoping people wouldn't come to church!

He looked out the kitchen window. A sheet of white covered the ground. Only a few tall tufts of dormant grass poked through. The sidewalk and road were wet, but remained clear, their stored heat from the day before sufficient to melt the snow for now. Though, Daniel thought, if the snow picked up, it might solve another problem that had kept him from sleeping through these past few nights. He had been unable to secure a replacement for the star figure of the kirk's nativity scene, and he dreaded having to tell Fisher. Carmen Oteiza hadn't returned his calls, and Ellie hadn't yet returned the broken figure. With a little luck and a lot more snowfall, perhaps no one would notice the empty manger. If this were Easter, everything would be fine—the tomb was supposed to be empty. But for Christmas, Jesus was most certainly supposed to be there. Or, Daniel laughed to himself—what else could he do—or, he could mold the snow into a wee baby snow Jesus?

On his way to Church Street, Daniel felt his phone buzz. Ellie had texted him. Had she returned the figure? *Don't be mad*, the text began. Never a good sign. *I need more time with baby J. No worries though, I'm at kirk now w/ replacement.* Before he could respond, she sent another message: *Trust me.* Daniel did trust her, but he also knew from experience that when someone begins with *Don't worry* and ends with *Trust me*, there's more cause for the prior than the latter.

By the time he arrived at Church Street Kirk, a small crowd had gathered out front. Daniel had found Highlanders to be generally more tolerant of cold and dreary weather than his Carolina brethren across the pond. Still, he was surprised to find so many huddled outdoors on this snowy morning, rather than tucked comfortably within the walls of the kirk. Curiosity sometimes trumped comfort, though, and, as he approached, his suspicions were confirmed. They were gathered around the kirk's nativity display. So much for *Don't worry*.

Daniel looked, but he didn't see Fisher in the crowd. He heard some laughter, and from the sound of their voices, they all seemed to be in good spirits. But why? Before he could get in close enough to see for himself, he heard Ellie call his name. "What's all this?" he asked when he found her.

"Seems the display is a success," she said proudly.

"What did you do?"

"Shhh," she said, "Just call it a Christmas miracle." She showed him to the manger. It wasn't empty or filled with a snow-infant. Inside lay a doll, roughly the size of the original ceramic figure. This one, though, had a full head of orange-blond hair, a mischievous expression on his face, and was dressed in a white shirt and black overalls, or dungarees. "Now that's a true Scottish nativity, that is," one parishioner laughed. "Oor Wullie we have seen on high," another sang. Daniel looked to Ellie quizzically.

"Oor Wullie, he's a popular Scottish cartoon character. Kind of like, em, your Dennis the Menis, but he speaks Scots and is way funnier. We had coloring pages and Scots language poems about him in primary school. I found this doll amongst some childhood things Mum had stowed away at the house," Ellie said.

"And this is your *replacement* for baby Jesus?" he asked. Ellie just shrugged. Daniel glanced back at the crowd. The children thought it was hilarious. They giggled and danced in front of the manger shouting words and phrases in Scots that Daniel had no idea of the meaning. Their parents looked on, proud of the kids' newfound interest in both the language and the kirk. Even the older parishioners wore rosy smiles and offered hushed laughter at what they assumed was a teenager's prank. "There's a lad who's proud of his heritage," one elderly man said to another. "Aye, better than the graffiti and gang signs."

Daniel looked back to Ellie and smiled. "A Christmas miracle indeed. I hope Fisher feels the same."

"That truly would be a Christmas miracle. Good luck," she said.

"You're not staying to find out for yourself?"

"I'm not that brave. Besides, I want to take advantage of no one being at the clinic now to take a crack at that figure. Ha! Don't worry. I'll try to not crack it any more than you already did."

"Don't worry, sure," Daniel said. They hugged goodbye.

Inside, Daniel found Fisher, as usual, wrangling his choir into their robes and attempting a warm-up hymn before the service began. Daniel avoided eye contact with the choir director, heading instead to Rev. Calder, who was preparing the scripture reading.

"Reverend Darrow!" Fisher called out. Daniel kept walking. "I said, Reverend Darrow," Fisher called louder. He left his choir to fend for themselves and positioned himself to cut Daniel off. "Are you trying to avoid me?"

I'm evidently not trying hard enough, Daniel thought. "No, sorry, I just have a lot on my mind."

"Well, I'm glad I caught you. I've been wanting to ask you, how's our Young Hugh Macpherson getting on? I haven't seen him since we all went to the loch for Archie's vigil. Though, I understand; I wouldn't want to show my face either if I was accused of what he is. But he did come to the vigil, didn't he? Does that seem odd to you?"

"I haven't known him very long, but he doesn't seem like the type that would be capable of, well, what he's been accused of." Neither one of them could bring themselves to say the word – murder. *Murderer*. "He seems to be taking it pretty hard," Daniel said.

"People are capable of the most extraordinary things, given the right motivation," Fisher said, with an eye toward his unruly choir.

"Should the choir be worried?" Daniel joked.

"What? No, practice is what I meant, practice. Oh, I feel simply awful about this whole mess with Young Hugh and Archie. And then I think of poor Edna. She never misses a Sunday. Always sitting right there. Her eyes so full of sorrow. I feel she's looking right at my soul sometimes," Fisher said. He pointed to a pew near the front.

"It is terrible. I can't imagine what she's going through, or Hugh," Daniel said.

"Should I pop in for a visit? I know Reverend Calder is tending to Edna, but has anyone seen to Young Hugh? Other than you, of course? Not to step on your toes, but I've known the family since I started here at Church Street many years ago."

"I'm sure they would appreciate that. You've got a big heart, Mr. Fisher," Daniel said. He was surprised at Fisher's show of concern, though he knew he shouldn't have been. The Macphersons were long established pillars at Church Street, a family as significant to the kirk as its physical corner stone. Any tragedy that rocked them was sure to be felt throughout the ecclesial body.

"It's no trouble. I certainly have plenty of time on my hands these days," Fisher said.

"Why's that?"

"I thought everyone knew. The Millburn Academy, they've dismissed me. Couldn't even wait until after the holidays. Budget cuts, they said."

"Fisher, I'm so sorry. That's awful."

People began to trickle in now, still full of smiles and hushed laughter. Fisher saw them too. He quickly changed the subject. "Have you seen the scene outside?" Fisher asked. Daniel nodded. "Shameful," Fisher said, shaking his head.

"Your added animals and wisemen really made it something," Daniel said.

"They do look good, don't they? But you know what I'm talking about. Oor Wullie in the manger where our Lord should be!"

"People seem to like it," Daniel said.

"It's shameful, I tell you. I bet it was some cheeky teenagers from the Old High having a laugh at my expense. They just can't stand our display beating theirs this year."

Daniel wanted to tell him that it was absurd to think a rival yuletide gang of teenagers, if such a gang existed, would be so invested in his little Christmas holy war. But, at least as long as Fisher thought that, he and Sir Walter were off the hook. Omitting the truth wasn't quite the same as lying, was it? Daniel thought of Young Hugh Macpherson again.

"You must get that figure back," Fisher said.

"I'll talk to the company and get it replaced as soon as possible. And, well…." Daniel got distracted by the choir, which had also noticed the people entering and had decided to welcome them with song—"Away in a Manger," in their best and loudest Scottish brogue.

Awa in a manger

Nae hoose fur his bed

The wee laird Jesus

Lay doon his sweet heid

Fisher sighed, pulled at his thinning hair, and rushed back to them.

Daniel went over to Reverend Calder, who was now tidying up the altar.

"That nativity display has sure caused a stir. I've never seen Mr. Fisher in such a tizzy," she said.

"The choir doesn't seem to be helping," Daniel laughed.

"Oh, they rarely do!" she said with a wink. "We're all having a good laugh this morning, but you really must mend the situation. I hope you know what you're doing with that company you hired."

"I will. I'll call this afternoon."

Reverend Calder nodded. She finished setting the alter cloths and took her seat. Daniel rushed to the back room to change into his robe before the service started.

Chapter Fifteen

Afte the service, Daniel tried calling Carmen Oteiza again, but again, she did not answer. Well, if she wouldn't answer, he would just have to go see her in person. Daniel donned his full winter garb for the trip: thick puffy coat, gloves, tweed scarf and hat, and the thickest wool socks he could find that still fit in his shoes. Still, he felt chilled out on the Port with little to stop the wind. The sun remained hidden behind a thick, gray sky, its heat unable to melt the snow had accumulated since that morning. Daniel wasted no time in finding Carmen's office.

She looked surprised to see him. Daniel thought for a moment this element of surprise would give him the upper hand in their talk. He intended to get a replacement Jesus figure that day. He would carry it back himself if he needed to. Carmen recovered quickly with, "Reverend Darrow, you are just the man I want to see."

"I've tried calling. Several times, in fact," Daniel said.

"You have," she said. Daniel nodded. She was too smart to play dumb. He took a seat without waiting for her to offer one. He was cold and tired of her avoiding him. "My phone must not be working properly," she said.

"I need to speak to you about the nativity display I ordered."

"Yes," she said. She turned from her computer screen and folded her hands in front of her on the desk. She looked directly at Daniel. "You have a missing piece, I believe."

"Um, yes. How did you know?"

"We do not take kindly to thieves, Reverend Darrow. These statues are our business, and they are expensive."

"Are you suggesting I stole it? I didn't steal it," Daniel said. That was the second time today he had kept back a portion of the truth. Technically he hadn't taken the figure, Ellie had. But he couldn't tell Carmen that.

"I am afraid you will lose your deposit if the piece is not returned."

"I thought you would fix any broken pieces. That's what you told me when I signed the rental contract."

"I cannot fix what is not there," Carmen said.

"What if someone really did steal the figure? Not me, but what if I can't return it?"

"You will lose your deposit."

"And how much was the deposit?" He had already stretched the kirk's budget to rent the display. If he couldn't get at least part of that money back, Fisher wouldn't be the only one angry with him.

"You do not want to lose your deposit," Carmen said. Her voice carried a threatening tone. This was a side of Carmen Daniel hadn't seen before. "I advise you to go now and recover the statue," she said.

"So that's it?" Daniel stood. Now he was the one surprised. This had not at all gone the way he had thought it would.

"We will all be much happier when it is returned," she said. Daniel searched her face for any sign of the old, flirty Carmen that had once been so generous with drinks and dancing. But he saw only the stern and, if he was completely honest, intimidating, business manager. With a flit of her hand, she dismissed him and returned her attention to her computer screen.

* * *

Daniel left Carmen's office confused and annoyed. He had only used her company because Young Hugh had suggested it. Young Hugh insisted they were the best in the business and would make his life easier. But ever since he had signed the contract, it had been one headache after another. When he got back home, he would complain to his flatmate about their terrible customer service. First, though, he wanted to check in on Ellie. He was ready to return the figure and put this whole mess behind him. He retrieved his cell phone to text her. But when he looked at the screen, she had already messaged him. Having turned the phone on silent for the service that morning, he hadn't heard it ring.

Meet me at the clinic. I need to show u something, Ellie's text said.

Daniel took a bus southwest through the city, across the Ness, then the Canal, to the Kinmylies district. Ellie's, or rather her mother's, car was the sole vehicle in the parking lot. Daniel tried the clinic door, but it would not open. Ellie came to unlock the door and ushered him into one of the exam rooms. Posters depicting various animal ailments like heartworm and tooth decay hung on the walls, along with brochures touting their cures. All the exam rooms likely looked identical, though Daniel could swear it was the same room in which he had once taken Sir Walter Scott for his yearly health checkup. The same room where he had first met Ellie.

He remembered her walking through the door that day, wearing light blue scrubs and auburn framed glasses, her hair pulled back in its now familiar ponytail. Struck by her beauty and wit, he had stumbled over his words. He had hardly been able to introduce himself that day much less the yowling cat he had brought her.

"Hello, Earth to Daniel. Anyone home?"

"Sorry, I was just remembering when we first met. I think it was in this room," Daniel said to her.

"Aye, you brought in Sir Walter. And if I recall, you mistook me for my mother."

"Not once I saw you. You have the same name. It wasn't fair."

"How is the ol' kirk cat? Does Fisher suspect him of breaking our wee babe here?" Ellie asked. The broken figure of baby Jesus lay on the exam table in the middle of the small room.

"He thinks it was teenagers. I didn't correct him. Seemed safer that way, for Sir Walter and for me," Daniel said. He picked up the broken ceramic arm. "I see you didn't call me here to say you've found a way to reattach this."

"No, better. Come look." Ellie shined a small light into the arm hole in the figure's body.

"It still just looks like fur or something. A rat?"

"That's what we thought, but then I tried this." She showed him a thick black tube with a light on its end. "It's an endoscope, used to see what's going on inside the body. There's a wee camera on the end." She poked the tube into the hole. A large mass of dark fur appeared on a nearby screen. Using a kind of thumb-joystick, she maneuvered the camera around the mass inside the figure.

"Looks like fun," Daniel said.

"It is."

"So, what are we looking at?"

"I'm not sure, but it's definitely not a mouse or rat."

"No?"

"There's no head or feet or even a tail. It's just fur." She was right. No matter what direction she wound the camera around the inside of the figure, the screen only showed the same dark fur.

"I don't think something crawled in there and died. I think that whatever is in there was put there," she said.

"Wait! Go back," Daniel said. Ellie pulled the camera back. "There. Is that string?"

Ellie nodded. "That's what I wanted you to see. Curious, isn't it."

"Can you get it out?"

She shook her head. "It won't budge. Unless you want me to make the hole bigger?" Ellie pulled out the endoscope. While she put it away, Daniel picked up the figure. Under the bright lights of the exam room, he could see a thin seam running along the midsection of the figure. It reminded him of the mussel Young Hugh had found in the river at Archie Caird's vigil.

"If we could pry this open without breaking it," he suggested, showing Ellie the seam.

"Hmm," she said, "That'll be tricky."

"Let me guess, you'll need more time to work on it?" Daniel asked. She nodded. "Carmen won't replace the figure with a new one until this broken one is returned. I was all set to take it back today and forget about it. But now you've got me curious too. I'm sure I can think of some kind of excuse to buy us a little more time."

"There's always teenagers," Ellie said. Daniel laughed.

"Since we're waiting, do you want to grab an early dinner?" he asked.

"Just let me hide this away and lock up," Ellie said.

* * *

When Daniel arrived home, he was surprised to see a familiar car parked at the curb. He couldn't place where, but he was sure he had seen it before. Likely a member of the kirk stopping by to visit the elder Macphersons. That was it. He'd seen it Sunday mornings parked along Church Street. So why was it now parked in front of his door rather than theirs? Daniel walked the short path through the front garden. His front door was unlocked. Young Hugh, having not left his room in days, had no reason to leave the door unlocked. Daniel put his ear close to the door for a moment, but heard nothing. He slowly opened the door.

"Hello? Hugh?" he said as he stepped inside.

He nearly stumbled back out the door when Mr. Fisher's head appeared from behind the hallway that led to the bedrooms. "Reverend Darrow, hello. Sorry, I didn't mean to frighten you," Fisher said, walking into the living room.

Daniel recovered his composure and shut the door. "Mr. Fisher? What are you doing here?"

"I popped in to see Young Hugh. I told you this morning."

"Yes, I remember. I just didn't know you meant today," Daniel said. He put his coat away and then began filling the electric tea kettle. He smiled to himself as he watched the water fill to the two-cup mark. There was a time, when he had first moved to Inverness, that he would have left his guest waiting in uncomfortable silence for a cup of tea that Mr. Fisher would have been too polite to ask for, and Daniel would have been too ignorant to offer. Now he reached for the kettle as if by instinct or muscle memory. "Milk or honey?"

"Yes, please," Fisher said. He sat down on the couch while Daniel waited for the water to boil.

91

"How did you get in? Is Hugh here?" Daniel asked.

"Hugh, eh, the elder Hugh Macpherson let me in. I hope I'm not intruding, you said you thought Young Hugh would appreciate a visit. The elder Hugh said it won't do any good, though. Young Hugh won't leave his room even to see them, his parents."

"How long have you been waiting?"

"Oh, not long. I just arrived, in fact. I called for Young Hugh, but he didn't answer. That's what I was doing when you came in. I was looking for his room."

"His is the first one down the hall. But I'm afraid Mr. Macpherson was right. I live with Young Hugh, and even I hardly see him."

"He's taking this trouble with Archie Card hard, then?"

Daniel nodded. He pulled two mugs from the cupboard. "It's weird, I don't even know him very well, but I kind of miss him. He has, or had, a very infectious personality. Here, take both of these. Maybe you can bribe him for entrance to his room."

"Thank you. I fear it may take more than a cup of tea, but I'll try. I simply want him to know that he has people who care about him, even in this dark time."

"That's kind of you," Daniel said. He thought of Edna Caird and felt terribly guilty. Yes, Reverend Calder paid her visits, but it wasn't Reverend Calder who she had asked for help. No, Edna Caird had sought him out. Why hadn't he talked to her since that Sunday when she had pleaded with him to find the reason for her husband's death? He had gone all over the city searching in vain for an alibi for Young Hugh, but Edna? He had avoided her like the plague. He knew he needed to talk with her, find out more about Archie, if he was to help her. He also knew, in those quiet moments when he couldn't busy himself with other distractions, that getting too close to the Cairds might mean uncovering things about Young Hugh that he would rather leave covered. He feared that he would be unable to help one of them without inevitably hurting the other.

Chapter Sixteen

F lett divided his men into two groups: riders and mourners. He told the four riders to meet him at MacKenzie's stable outside the town of Inverness tomorrow at daybreak. The mourners were to meet at the nearby kirk. After his last job, he had to be extra careful. Up and down the coast, excisemen were on high alert for smugglers. Particularly, bearded pregnant women smuggling brandy. After Flett had beaten and left for dead one of their own, the lawmen were out for revenge. Everything had to be planned to the tee this time. Flett had managed to persuade the local reverend to aid him on this latest endeavor. The clergyman's presence would add an extra air of believability to the procession. This would be Flett's most daring and, if successful, most lucrative job yet.

With his men dispersed to their respective sites, Flett rode off to meet his supplier near Loch Ness. It was late afternoon by the time he arrived at the man's house. It was more a hovel, dug out of the hillside, than a wood or stone house. The man's wife opened the door a crack and peeked out. When she saw who it was, she motioned for him to tie his horse around back and to hurry inside. Her husband met him at the door. "Were ye seen?" he asked.

"Have the English outlawed simple visits between friends now?" Flett said.

"Your nerves is made of stronger steel than mine is, Mr. Flett. Come on to the back," the man said. Flett followed him to a backroom, the entrance of which was around a corner, hidden from view of the main room. Though the whole place had such an odor, no one would be surprised at what went on there. Flett had to stoop so as not to hit his head on the low ceiling. The odor of whiskey and smoking wood and peat were stronger back here. The room was lit only by the fireplace, roughly cut into one wall. On top of the fire, sat a very large copper pot with metal tubes sticking out. Smoke hung like a blue-gray cloud on the ceiling, causing Flett to cough and stoop lower. He knew that if the room had better ventilation, a second chimney in addition to the one in the main room, it might draw unwanted attention. Such illegal whiskey stills were common across the Highlands. Many poor crofters would starve without the extra money this illicit trade provided them. Such stills were also commonly destroyed by police or customs agents. So far, this one had eluded detection.

Flett sat on a bag of grain to catch his breath. The man examined the copper pot and added another log to the fire. "Yer ankers is there, all ready," the man said, pointing to several small wooden casks, about a fourth the size of a full barrel, stacked along the opposite wall.

"Perfect," Flett said. "My man with a wagon should meet us after the sun is set. Has Mrs. Ross finished with my, em, riding partners?"

"Aye, she has. Tis quite a order you give us, Mr. Flett. I wish I could be there to see you pass through Inverness town!"

"It will be a sight, though the fewer that truly see it, the better," Flett said.

Flett and the man left the still room and met his wife in the main chamber. "Show Mr. Flett what ye made him, luv," the man said. The woman pulled a plaid blanket off a wooden chest. She opened it and ushered Flett over.

Flett peered inside. "There's four in there?" he asked. She nodded. "Perfect." Flett pulled a small leather pouch out of his coat pocket. It jingled with gold coins. He handed it to the man. "As promised," he said.

"Thank you, Mr. Flett. You be careful," the man said.

"And you, my friend," Flett said.

* * *

Flett was already waiting at MacKenzie's stable when his four riding men arrived in the still dark morning hour. He showed them to the horses he had secured. "You two men hold the horse. Keep her calm. You two help me with this," Flett ordered. He opened a wooden trunk and pulled out its contents. One of the men jumped back.

"You said we's carrying spirits, no bodies," the man said.

"Shut up and grab an arm," Flett said.

The man slowly stepped forward and grasped the limp figure's arm. He looked to Flett in surprise. The arm was much lighter than it should have been. He squeezed it. It contained no flesh or hard bone. Only a cloak stuffed with wool. The man pulled the figure's head up to get a look at its face. A lightly tanned leather ball with a stitched-on nose and painted-on eyes stared back at him. The man nearly dropped the body. "What's this?" the man asked Flett.

"That's your riding companion. Get him up there behind your saddle," Flett said. The man lifted the stuffed figure onto the nervous horse.

"He won't sit right, Flett. He's no got a belly."

"Had to leave room for his spirit, didn't we," Flett said with a laugh. He rolled an anker over to the horse. The two men heaved the small cask of whiskey onto the cushion behind the saddle and strapped it in place with a leather lashing. Flett then opened the riding companion's cloak and buttoned it around the cask so that the cask formed the fake rider's torso.

Flett and his men stood back to admire their work. One of the men slapped Flett on the back and said, "Flett, I do believe this is your best idea yet!" They quickly loaded up the other *riders* and left for the kirk. They received a few glances from people on the street as they rode past, but none attempted to stop them. It was not uncommon to see people riding double as they were. Most who took notice, mumbled something about the poor state of affairs in Scotland that would drive so many men to such poverty that they would have to ride pillion. Most pedestrians averted their eyes, feeling it impolite to stare at the misfortune of others. Flett kept his head down and his hat lower until they arrived at the kirk.

He tied his horse loosely outside and met the reverend at the door. "We're all set," the reverend said. Flett nodded and entered. The rest of his men were waiting inside, dressed in mourning clothes. Flett walked the center aisle of the kirk to inspect the coffin. It was a simple wood construction, wider at the front and tapered toward the end. He opened the lid and brushed aside the top layer of straw. Inside he saw several additional ankers in a row, two abreast where the coffin widened to accommodate a body's shoulders. He nodded approvingly and replaced the straw and lid.

With the funeral procession ready, Flett led the way, followed by the reverend, the mourners and coffin, and finally, his four pillion riders. They proceeded straight down the main road toward the Inverness docks. Pedestrians on the street bowed or crossed themselves and stepped aside as they passed by. Flett suppressed his urge to smile at the success of his plan.

Then he saw a customs agent. The agent was dressed in a long cloak common to his station. He stepped out of the way of the funeral procession, stopped, then walked toward them. Flett got the reverend's attention and nodded toward the agent. The holy man understood and began loudly reading from the bible he held. The reverend stepped out of the procession and paused near the agent and several other townsfolk who had stopped to watch. He began reciting a prayer for the dead and indicated that the onlookers should bow their heads and join him in the prayer. Flett cracked a smile and kept the procession moving.

* * *

William MacCrivag's little green car pulled up to the curb at Bellfield Park in front of a house with one red door and one blue door. From behind the blue door, Reverend Daniel Darrow heard a car horn. He took a last gulp of coffee and grabbed his overnight bag. He thought of shouting a goodbye to Young Hugh Macpherson but didn't. Young Hugh hadn't left his room in days, not even to visit with Mr. Fisher. Nothing more than a quick trip to the toilet or to grab a bite from the kitchen. He wouldn't notice if Daniel was gone or still there. When Daniel opened the door and stepped outside, he could see his breath in the frigid morning air. White smoke poured from the waiting car's exhaust. The back windows were fogged up and frosted around the edges. William MacCrivag got out and opened the trunk, or boot. Daniel placed his bag next to the two already in there.

"Hello, Reverend, happy you could join us," Philip Morrison said from the front passenger seat once Daniel had gotten into the back. "It's been, what, a year since you were in Stornoway?"

"Yes, I think that's about right," Daniel said. He thought back to his last visit to Philip Morrison's home in the seaside town of Stornoway on the Hebridean Isle of Lewis and Harris. He had accompanied Mr. MacCrivag on an impromptu trip to restore a missing bottle of rare Scotch whiskey. That trip had given Daniel the chance to escape Inverness for a time and put some distance between himself and a particularly embarrassing incident. Now, Daniel was again looking forward to a few days' respite from his responsibilities in Inverness. He felt pulled in so many different directions, from Edna Caird, to Young Hugh and his parents, to Fisher. Not to mention Carmen Oteiza and the threat of losing the kirk's sizable security deposit. Ellie wanted a few more days to investigate the mysterious creature inside the baby Jesus figure before he returned it to Carmen. So, when William MacCrivag asked if he wanted to accompany him as he drove Philip Morrison back home, Daniel jumped at the chance to get away. He could take care of any urgent kirk business virtually, assuming he could find a wifi signal.

The little green car sputtered and shook with effort to pull away from the curb. "You certain this'll get us all the way to Lewis?" Philip Morrison joked.

Mr. MacCrivag did not find his friend's slight against his beloved car amusing. "She simply needs to get warmed up, then she'll purr like a kitten. These Scottish winters are hard on the ol' lass," Mr. MacCrivag said, patting the steering wheel affectionately. He drove them north, toward the Moray Firth. As the car crossed the Kessock Bridge out of Inverness, Daniel gazed out the window. He felt his troubles evaporating like the mist that hovered over the icy waters of the firth below. "Brrr," Mr. MacCrivag muttered as he cranked up the car's heater. The engine revved, then settled down to a steady chug. "Easy there," he said, patting the dashboard.

"You're awfully quiet back there, Reverend," Philip Morrison said.

"Oh, I was just thinking about everything going on back home. Young Hugh Macpherson and all," Daniel said.

"'Tis a sad story that. To think the very lad responsible for poor Archie's death came along with us to his vigil. Ironic, I would say," Philip Morrison said.

"I cannae believe Young Hugh would do that. I've known him his whole life. He's a good lad," William MacCrivag said. "What's your theory, Reverend?"

"I wish I had one. Mrs. Caird asked me to discover her husband's killer, but the police seem to have beaten me to it. Only I wish they hadn't. Or I wish they'd found someone else besides Young Hugh," Daniel said.

"Well, you've got plenty of time to ponder. It's a five-hour drive to Ullapool, then just as long on the ferry. Might be six the way Willy drives," Philip Morrison said.

"I drive better in the summer. We mustn't make a habit of these winter trips," William MacCrivag said. Then, looking at Daniel in the rearview mirror, he added, "I tried to keep Philly in Inverness until warmer weather, but he insisted. The Island calls, he says."

"It's in my blood. You know this," Philip Morrison said. "But enough talk of murder and cold weather. I want to hear about the Reverend and young Miss Elspeth Gray. Willie tells me there's talk around town of a baby?"

Daniel turned abruptly from the window. "What? No, no. That was…that's a long story."

"We've a long trip," Philip Morrison said.

Attempting to change the subject, Daniel answered, "What I want to know is what adventure you have in store for us? The last time I visited, you promised us a hike up Mount Roineabhal."

"I did, didn't I? But in warmer weather," Philip Morrison said with a wink toward William.

"My vote is for sitting by a warm fire and enjoying a bottle of good whiskey. Perhaps your famed Dochgarroch?" William MacCrivag said.

Philip laughed and shook his head. "He's always trying to get a crack at that bottle. It's the only one in existence, as far as I know. Passed down to me from my father from his father, back to my ancestor, Flett Morrison, the famed free trader."

Chapter Seventeen

Daniel Darrow, William MacCrivag, and Philip Morrison arrived in Stornoway after the sun had set. Stornoway, Philip Morrison liked to boast, was "the largest town on the largest island" in a string of islands known as the Outer Hebrides, which crowned the north of Scotland. To which William MacCrivag liked to counter, "The whole of the island's population wouldn't fill half of Inverness!" Daniel Darrow snickered at both of them, "What is Inverness, forty-eight, fifty thousand? Raleigh's ten times that at least."

"Quality over quantity, lads. Quality over quantity," Philip Morrison retorted.

They pulled up to a shop for a takeaway dinner of fish and chips. At Philip Morrison's house, Daniel and Mr. MacCrivag laid out their spread of fried fish and potatoes on the kitchen table while Philip worked on starting a fire. One whole wall of the living room was constructed of stone. He knelt and stacked small sticks for kindling in the hearth, which was carved out of the middle of the stone wall. "She'll take a bit to get going. I've been away too long. The chimney's gone cold," Philip Morrison said. The glow of the budding fire against his beard and mane of speckled white and orange hair gave him the appearance of a lion lying in wait behind a campfire.

William MacCrivag removed his wool hat, revealing his complete lack of hair. He quickly pulled it back on. "We'll eat with our coats on if we must. I cannae wait much longer. I'm starving!" William MacCrivag said, his accent adapting to the colder northern clime more quickly than his body.

"Do you need a hand?" Daniel asked Philip.

"No, no, I'll just have tae keep an eye on her," Philip Morrison said as he stood up to join them at the table, his own accent catching up with MacCrivag's. He sat angled with an eye toward the fire. Daniel chuckled to himself, wondering how long it would be until he couldn't understand more than a few words either one of them spoke.

"This is good," Daniel said, crunching into a fillet that was more fried breading than fish.

"Not bad. Not as fresh as I'd like," Philip Morrison said.

"Philly, you recall the summer we caught those massive salmon, up near, where was it, Uig?" MacCrivag asked.

"That was a proper fish fry!" Philip Morrison said. He glanced at the fire, then down at his plate. His face sullen.

"What is it?" MacCrivag asked.

"It's nothing. Just reminded me of Archie Caird for some reason. That was a fellow that knew how to fish," Philip Morrison said.

"I should hope so, was his livelihood, wasn't it," MacCrivag said.

Philip Morrison looked back at the fire. "I should put on another log," he said. He left the table to tend the now healthy flames. The fire had done its job, heating the small living room and attached kitchen. Enough for the men to remove their coats and William MacCrivag his wool hat.

When Philip Morrison returned to the table, Daniel asked him, "You knew Archie Caird well?" Philip Morrison nodded.

"Philly earned a wee commission on Archie's Hebridean tours. Needed a local to show folks around, didn't he," William MacCrivag answered.

"Have you spoken to Mrs. Caird since, well...." Daniel asked.

Philip Morrison shook his head. "Only briefly. At the kirk with Willy, to express my condolences."

"Does Young Hugh Macpherson still live with you, Reverend? I haven't seen hilt nor hair of him since his arrest," William MacCrivag asked.

"Yes. he can't leave Inverness until there's a trial—a condition of his bail. I guess after he got fired from the shipping company, the judge doesn't consider him a flight risk. I think his parents might have some influence too," Daniel said. Philip Morrison stared at him as he spoke. Daniel couldn't make out the expression that had settled on his host's face. It was disapproving or solemn, certainly not smiling. "But I rarely see him," Daniel added quickly. "He hardly ever leaves his room, much less the city."

"Guilty conscious," Philip Morrison mumbled.

"I've known Young Hugh since he was a babe. I'll admit he has earned himself a reputation for getting into trouble, but it's hard for me to believe he's capable of doing what he's been accused of. At least not intentionally," William MacCrivag said.

They ate in silence for several minutes. Finally, Mr. MacCrivag succumbed to the rising heat from the now roaring fire or the unpleasant turn the conversation had taken. He took a final drink from his beer and slammed the can on the table in a decisive manner. "Let's go fishing tomorrow. Up to Uig, in Archie's honor," he said.

"Wrong season," Philip Morrison said.

"Well, we can at least have a nice walk along the shore. It'd do us good. Fresh sea air, take in the beauty of Lewis. What do you say, Reverend?" MacCrivag asked.

"Sure, sounds fun," Daniel said.

* * *

The next morning, Daniel awoke with a pain in his neck. He slowly sat up and stretched his stiff limbs. Philip Morrison's couch was a relic from a time before Daniel was born. It creaked and offered uneven support as a place to sit. It was even less hospitable as a bed. It had Daniel eyeing the cold wooden floor with envy.

He listened for sounds of movement in the rest of the small house. Silence. Strange, he thought. The last time he had visited, Philip Morison had been up by dawn with a pot of coffee and baked beans heating on the stove. Daniel pulled a quilt around his shoulders and walked over to the hearth. He wondered how hard it would be to get the fire going again. He didn't have much experience with starting fires. He had never needed to back home in the States, and the fireplace in his current flat at Bellfield Park had been replaced with an electric unit. All he had to do there was flip a switch, and flames would appear like magic from somewhere inside the faux-wooden logs. He felt suddenly foolish and inept at his inability to perform such a basic task. Making fire was one of the few skills that separated humanity from the other animals. It had been a driving force of civilization for millennia. And here he was, a young college-educated man, shivering under a quilt for lack of a flint and steel or two sticks to rub together or whatever it was one used to make a fire.

A beam of early morning light shined through a part in the window curtains, glinting off something on a shelf on the far side of the stone wall, away from the hearth. Distracted, Daniel gave up his search for a fire starter. The shelf held a few books, a trophy depicting a man with a fly-fishing pole, and a rectangular wooden box a little over a foot in length. The box had a smooth, polished finish and a brass clasp on one side. It was the clasp that had caught the light.

"Careful there. That's my prize possession."

Daniel turned around, surprised to see Philip Morrison standing at the far end of the room, fully dressed in brown slacks and an oatmeal-colored knit sweater. "I wasn't going to touch it. I was just trying to see what it says," Daniel said.

Philip Morrison walked over to the shelf and took down the box. He cradled it like an infant. "This has been passed down in my family for three generations. Back to my most famous relative, or infamous depending on who's telling the story, Flett Morrison. Here," he said, unhooking the latch with one hand. The inside was padded with a velvety cushion, like a tiny coffin. Philip Morrison gently pulled back a second cloth to reveal a dark glass bottle wrapped in a tattered, yellowed label with a hand-written inscription – Dochgarroch Whiskey, 18—. The inscription was thin and faded. Daniel couldn't make out the last two digits.

"Is this the bottle Mr. MacCrivag was talking about yesterday?"

"Aye, sometimes I wonder if his visits aren't simply a ruse to get at this."

"It's that good?"

"I dinnae kin, never tasted it. You can see it's rather old. Likely worth a small fortune if I were to sell it, but I never would. No, this bottle is my heritage. Willy will simply have to do with a bottle of Lewis's finest Abhainn Dearg."

"Um, where's Mr. MacCrivag?"

"We'll let him sleep a bit longer. Long drive yesterday must've worn him out," Philip Morrison said. He put the protective cloth back around the bottle, closed the box's lid, and returned it to its place on the shelf.

"I didn't know your family were distillers," Daniel said.

"Not distillers quite. Come to the kitchen. I'll put on a pot of coffee and tell you about ol' Flett and the family, eh, business. Do you know how to fry an egg?"

Daniel followed him to the kitchen. Philip Morrison rummaged through the cupboards. He handed Daniel a frying pan and placed a can of ground coffee, followed by a can of baked beans, on the counter. "Flett Morrison was what we in Scotland used to call a *free trader*," he said.

"A what?"

Philip Morrison handed Daniel a few eggs then returned to the coffee pot. "A smuggler. In the nineteenth century, further back really, the English leveled heavy taxes on Scotland to pay for its wars with the French. They taxed many goods, but particularly spirits – French brandy coming in, Scotch whiskey going out, anything they could. Got so the common crofter could hardly make enough to feed his family, and many couldn't. Those that did had to find ways around the crown. Illicit whiskey distilleries popped up along every burn and glen in the land. It was risky, but a man has to eat."

"So, your relative was a bootlegger?" Daniel asked.

"Keep listening. The poor crofters were good at making the whiskey, but it was too dangerous to move. That's where my great, great grandfather came in. Flett smuggled the illegal whiskey to eager buyers in the south. That bottle on my shelf was one of them. He sailed from Inverness to Stornoway to the Baltics, back to England. A roundabout circuit, but still cheaper than paying the massive taxes. He had to be inventive, didn't he, to evade the police and taxmen. Oh, he thought of the cleverest of tricks." Philip Morrison told Daniel of the belly canteens designed to look like pregnancy bumps, the ankers dressed up as pillion riders, and the fake funeral processions. Daniel could hardly believe the stories; they were so fantastic. "Gospel truth," Philip Morrison insisted.

By the time they were through with their eggs and into their second cups of coffee, William MacCrivag walked in groggily from the hall. He was dressed, as Daniel still was, in a t-shirt and sleeping trousers, all tied up in a large robe. "Knew I smelled something cooking in here. I see you couldn't be bothered to wait for me?"

"We saved you some on the stove," Philip Morrison said, pointing to the leftover eggs and warmed beans. "Reverend here's quite the cook."

"It was just eggs," Daniel said.

William MacCrivag piled the remaining food onto a plate and joined them at the table. "So, what's the story? What've I've missed?"

"Mr. Morrison was telling the most incredible stories about his great, great grandfather," Daniel said.

"Ah, the Dochgarroch," MacCrivag said, a twinkle in his eye.

"Don't get any ideas. We're just telling stories, no tasting," Philip Morrison said.

William MacCrivag shook his head in disappointment and cut into the fried egg. The yolk oozed out, mixing with the baked beans. Daniel grimaced. He would never get used to this particular breakfast pairing.

"Did you tell him how they used to stuff bottles inside geese to hide them?" Mr. MacCrivag took note of Daniel's frown. "I shouldn't think you'd be alarmed, Reverend. Tis a rather American thing to do, isn't it? Stuffing things up birds' arses? You have a whole holiday to celebrate it."

Daniel laughed. "Fair enough. But I can still find it a little weird. Also, um, haggis?"

William MacCrivag simply shrugged and continued eating.

"When you two are finished sharing culinary oddities, I suggest you get dressed. It'll be cold today. It's not the season for salmon, like I told Willie, but there's other wildlife to see if you know where to look," Philip Morrison said. He stood and took his plate to the sink.

William MacCrivag leaned in close to Daniel. "I knew a wee trip outdoors would brighten his spirits. He's so predictable."

"I heard that," Philip Morrison said from the other side of the room.

Chapter Eighteen

Daniel Darrow, William MacCrivag, and Philip Morrison loaded into Mr. MacCrivag's little green car. Daniel sat in the backseat alongside a tacklebox and two fishing poles that Mr. MacCrivag had insisted on bringing despite Mr. Morrison's objection that it was the wrong season for fishing. They drove west toward Uig Bay, nestled on the opposite coast of the Ilse of Lewis.

"Hey, look," Daniel said as they passed through the center of town. Both men in the front of the car looked in the direction he pointed. William MacCrivag veered dangerously into oncoming traffic as he did.

"Eyes on the road, Willie!" Philip Morrison shouted.

"Sorry," William MacCrivag said, jerking the car back into its proper lane.

"You nearly killed us, Reverend. What's the worry?"

"Sorry, I just noticed that kirk there. It has a nativity display like the one I got for Church Street. It might even be the same one."

"That one may look similar, but it's not the same as ours," William MacCrivag said.

"Road, Willie!"

"Right, right. I'm watching the road. We're past it now anyway."

Daniel turned back in his seat to get another look out the back window. "You don't think so?"

"No, that one had a proper baby Jesus and less wildlife."

"Just focus on driving," Daniel said, shaking his head.

Though Stornoway was the largest town in Lewis, it was still quite small and within a few minutes, they'd left it behind. The view outside of

Daniel's passenger window transformed from seaside harbor town to rugged, windswept country. Nearly treeless with grey stone tearing through the thin carpet of grasses and pocked throughout with small lochs interconnected in a spider's web of streams and narrow rivers, the landscape of the island was severe in its beauty.

Phillip Morrison appeared to know the names of every loch on the island, and as they passed one, he shouted it out. "There's Loch Cnoc a' Choilich." "Loch Breugach." "Thota Bridein." He was clearly showing off, though he could have been making it up for all Daniel knew. He could have been simply growling out gibberish syllables, and the poor Reverend would have been none the wiser.

"Mr. Morrison, I was thinking about the stories you told of your great, great grandfather Flett and I was wondering," Daniel said.

"Yes?"

"I was wondering why he and his men didn't just take their, um, contraband south over land into England? Hidden it in wagons or something? Wouldn't that have been easier and faster than sailing all over Scotland and Scandinavia to get there?"

"I dinnae ken faster, but it would've surely been more dangerous. Easier for soldiers and taxmen to watch the old roads than the open seas. And horse carts weren't as quick as our modern motor vehicles," Philip Morrison said, patting the dashboard of the little green sedan with a wink toward its driver.

"She's plenty quick," William MacCrivag said. "I drive the speed limit. We can't all be criminals now, can we."

"How much horsepower does she have? Fifty? Sixty?" Philip Morrison asked mockingly.

"Fifty or sixty more than your naught."

"Ah, you've got me there," Philip Morrison said. He nodded toward Mr. MacCrivag's side window. "There's Loch Ceann Hulabhaig."

"What about sailing down the Ness River or the Caledonian Canal?" Daniel asked.

"Eh?"

"Why didn't Flett sail his goods down the river or canal?"

"Why it wouldn't've been as much fun, would it? Couldn't've played dress-up," William MacCrivag said with a laugh.

"Wouldn't have been possible either. The river leads straight into the port, which was heavily monitored. Legal trade only. And the canal wasn't yet built," Philip Morrison said.

"Are you sure about the canal?" Daniel asked.

"You're questioning Philly about his famous ancestor? Careful, Reverend. Philly knows more on that subject than the good Lord himself," William MacCrivag said.

"No, it's just that Ms. MacGillivray, Eliza, she mentioned the Caledonian Canal in one of her *prophesies* to me a few weeks ago. I think I told you. Something about fully rigged ships sailing up it. The way she said it, I assumed she was talking about old sailing vessels."

"Aye, and Tomnahurich, the faerie hill. I remember. Another one of her prophesies borrowed from the true Brahan Seer. Now for him, it really was a prophecy. Like Flett, he lived before the canal was built."

"But no large sailing vessels ever used it, if I recall correctly. By the time it was completed, we'd all moved on to motorized shipping, and most of those were too big," Philip Morrison said.

"Young Hugh, um, Carmen Oteiza's company," Daniel said, quickly correcting himself after remembering Philip Morrison's reaction to hearing Young Hugh's name the night before. "They told me they were planning on using it to ship their holiday displays across Scotland."

"They've opened the canal up to more than touring boats over the past few years – small freighters and the like, to save on petrol and emissions. Everyone's trying to be more eco-friendly," William MacCrivag said.

They drove on until the green and gray flecked landscape turned to white sand and blue-green ocean. William MacCrivag parked the car, and they got out. They zipped their coats tight to brace against the wind and walked down the unpaved path that led to the beach. Philip Morrison told Mr. MacCrivag he needn't bother with the fishing poles or tackle box, but William insisted on hauling them along. The beach was deserted on this overcast, December morning. And Daniel was under no illusions as to why. The hills surrounding the sandy cove provided little protection from the wind. The cold brought a tear to his eye and made him squint.

"Ah, this is what we needed, lads," William MacCrivag said. He had on his black and white puffin coat and a thick wool cap. He inhaled deeply and stared out at the sea. Philip Morrison nodded approvingly and put his arm around MacCrivag's shoulder. "Breath it in, Reverend. There's nothing like this island air," Philip Morrison said. Daniel took a deep breath, too enthusiastically. The cold stung his throat and lungs. He coughed while the two older men laughed. Philip Morrison turned his back to the wind and pulled a cigarette and lighter out of his pocket. Every time he flicked the striker, the wind blew it out. But he was persistent and kept trying, as persistent as William MacCrivag had been with his fishing poles.

"Philly, look there!" William MacCrivag said, pointing to the far side of the cove. Philip Morrison cursed quietly at his lighter but ignored Mr. MacCrivag. "You see it, don't you, Reverend?"

Daniel didn't see anything. A small log bobbing in the water?

"Would you put that daft thing away and look? You'll miss it," William MacCrivag said.

Philip Morrison stuffed the lighter and unlit cigarette in his pocket. "What are we looking at?"

"An otter. Just there. That is an otter, right?" Mr. MacCrivag said.

"An otter?" Daniel asked. He peered more closely at the bobbing log and noticed that it did indeed have eyes, a tiny doglike snout, and whiskers. It slid out of the water, ran across the sand, and hopped onto a kelp-covered rock. It made a squeaking noise and leaped behind the rock.

The three men watching from the other side of the cove didn't make a sound. They stood perfectly still, forgetting the cold and the wind and the lack of nicotine. A second later, two otters flew out from behind the rock, tumbling over one another, play fighting like puppies. One chased the other back around the rock, then across the sand into the water. They slipped gracefully in and out of the waves. One dove and resurfaced with something dark between its paws. It flipped and floated on its back, munching on whatever it had captured. The other swam up and tumbled over it. Then they both swam off out of sight.

The three men stood silent for several minutes longer, staring in the direction where the two otters disappeared. Reverend Darrow broke their silence. "That was amazing! I've never seen an otter before."

"It was, wasn't it," William MacCrivag said.

"I didn't know Scotland had otters," Daniel said.

"We should count ourselves lucky to have spotted them, especially this time of year. They aren't as plentiful as they once were," Philip Morrison said.

"No? I remember seeing loads of them when I was young. The family would take short holidays to Skye," William MacCrivag said. He stared off into the horizon for a while longer. "Well, let's get off this frigid beach and find someplace with food. By the time we do, it'll be lunch." He gathered his unused fishing poles and box.

"So, what's happened to the otters?" Daniel asked on their walk back to the car.

"Same thing that happens to most of God's wild creatures, I suppose. Habitat loss, poaching, and now changing climate," Philip Morrison said. "We lot have a real way of upsetting things. You know this whole island used to be full of trees, a massive forest. But then the Vikings arrived and needed lumber for their ships."

"But that was a long time ago, literally ancient history," Daniel said.

"Aye, it was. The history of this land and its people are inseparable. We've shaped one another, some for the better, some for the worse."

"Philly, food!" William Morrison shouted. He was waiting impatiently on a short hill several yards ahead of Philip and Daniel, between them and the car.

"And some only care about their bellies," Philip Morrison said. "We'd better pick up the pace before he digs into the bait in the tackle box."

* * *

As they were finishing up lunch at a small restaurant near the beach, Daniel felt his cell phone vibrate. It was Ellie. "Excuse me," he said. He stepped out on the patio.

"Hello, Ellie?"

"Where have you been? I've tried to get ahold of you all morning," Ellie said. Her voice was faint, fighting through static.

"I'm in Lewis with Mr. MacCrivag and Mr. Morrison. We were driving. I guess the reception wasn't great. I can barely hear you," Daniel said. He walked along the patio in search of a stronger signal.

"That's right, I forgot. Well, a lot's happened since you've been away."

"It's not even been two full days."

"I could tell you now or wait till you get back."

"Mr. MacCrivag and I aren't driving back until the day after tomorrow."

"I'll tell you now, then. First, Young Hugh. It's worse than we thought. He could really use a good alibi about now. He—" Ellie's voice cut out.

Daniel walked back a few feet to when her voice had been the clearest. "Ellie? Are you still there? We couldn't find a solid alibi. What's wrong now?"

"Daniel, you're breaking up. Can you hear me?"

"Yes. What's going on with Hugh?"

"There you are. Well, when the police searched your flat, they must've found something. No one knows what exactly, but they've announced they've stopped pursuing other leads. Must be pretty sure they've got him," Ellie said.

"Wait, they searched the flat? That does sound bad. If Hugh really did kill Archie Caird, maybe I shouldn't be in a rush to get home," Daniel said, only half joking.

"Perhaps, but there's more."

"More?"

"I've found out what was stuffed in your baby Jesus figure. And you simply won't believe it. I –" Static then silence.

"Ellie, are you there? Ellie?" Daniel looked at his phone's screen. He had no signal. He held his phone out above his head and paced up and down the patio. Nothing. Daniel went back inside.

"You looked like E.T. trying to phone home out there," William MacCrivag laughed.

"It was Ellie. Do you know where I can get a decent cell signal?" Daniel asked.

"I'm impressed you got anything at all out here," Philip Morrison said. "Come on, Willie, let's get back on the road. The Reverend seems impatient to restore his love connection."

William MacCrivag made exaggerated kissing sounds with his lips.

"It's not that, it's, oh never mind," Daniel said. There was no point in trying to argue with those two when they got going. As much as Mr. MacCrivag loved gossip, Daniel knew that this was not the time to tell him about any developments in Young Hugh's case. Besides, the less objection he raised, the quicker they could get back to Stornoway, and he could call Ellie back.

Chapter Nineteen

After Ellie's call on Wednesday, Daniel wanted to get back to Inverness as soon as possible. Unfortunately for the Reverend, William MacCrivag hadn't wanted to cut his stay with Philip Morrison short just so Daniel could, as MacCrivag had mocked, "rush home when his lady friend came a calling"—more kissy noises. So, Daniel left them on the island and headed home alone. But it wasn't just Ellie that he was impatient to see. Since his arrest, Young Hugh had transformed from happy-go-lucky socialite to sullen recluse. Daniel could only imagine how he was now dealing with the surprise police search of their shared flat. Of course, Daniel couldn't mention his concern for Young Hugh to Philip Morrison. So, he had simply played along with Mr. MacCrivag's game and let them believe his affection for Ellie was his only motivation.

The earliest ferry from Stornoway to the Highlands with a bus connection to Inverness was the following morning. When the bus let him off at Inverness bus station, Daniel hopped on another that would take him back across town to the Kinmylies district. Daniel arrived at the veterinary clinic a few minutes before it closed Thursday evening. He held the door as an elderly woman exited the clinic. She carried a crate that held a yowling cat. He offered her a sympathetic smile, knowing all too well the joys of taking an unwilling feline to the vet. He batted a loose string of garland from the doorway when he entered. With Christmas only one week away, even the veterinary clinic had joined in the general festive spirit of the city. The outside windows were painted with scenes of cats and dogs wearing Santa hats and reindeer antlers. Inside, the receptionist, also wearing a Santa hat, seemed quite perturbed when he asked to see Ellie.

"Doctor Gray is with a patient now. Actually, her last scheduled patient of the day. It's nearly five, and we close up at five. Is it an emergency, or would you like to make an appointment for tomorrow?"

"No, don't worry, I'm not here for an appointment," Daniel said. He held open his hands as proof that he carried no leash or small animal crate. "I'm her—" Daniel paused. He didn't know what to call himself. He and Ellie had been on many dates. Yes, they were definitely *dating*, but had they ever actually called themselves boyfriend and girlfriend? Did adults even use those terms? The receptionist clearly didn't recognize him, despite his many visits to the clinic, most of them without the kirk cat in tow. He didn't want to cause Ellie undue blethering at the office, by using the bf-label. He'd certainly endured enough of that recently from Mr. MacCrivag, however good humored. Ellie hadn't seemed too concerned to be seen in public with him and a baby. She'd even used the opportunity to try and get quicker seating at Auld Lang Naan. Still, he decided to err on the side of caution and settled on simply *friend*. "I'm her friend," he told the receptionist.

The receptionist nodded and motioned to an empty seat next to a man with a cockatoo on his shoulder. Daniel sat and stared absently at the various promotional posters for pet foods and medicines hung on the walls. The cockatoo pecked at his hair. He shooed it with his hand and leaned away from it. The bird stretched toward him, its large head feathers in full bloom. "Should old acquaintance be forgot. Should old acquaintance be forgot!" the bird shrieked. The man upon whose shoulder the bird perched shot a glare toward Daniel. *Hey, the bird started it,* Daniel wanted to say. Instead, he slowly stood up and walked to the other side of the room, pretending to be interested in a display of specialty canned dog food.

After several long minutes of reading and rereading dog food labels and trying to ignore shrieked verses of Auld Lang Syne, Daniel finally saw Ellie and her patient exit the door that led from the examination rooms to the main lobby. "Come back in two weeks, and we'll see how she's getting on," Ellie said to the woman holding a small fluffy dog. "Ah, Mr. Boyle," she waived to the man with the cockatoo. "I see Robert Birds is doing well. I could hear his lovely singing all the way in the back. Did Dr. Patel get you sorted?"

The man blushed and nodded. "Thank you, yes. Just waiting on our prescription."

"Daniel, I have your, eh, test results in the back," she said, motioning for Daniel to follow her. To the receptionist, she said, "We'll just be a minute. You can go when you're done with Mr. Boyle. I'll lock up." The receptionist raised a suspicious eyebrow but was more interested in the prospect of clocking out early than questioning Doctor Gray.

Daniel followed Ellie back to the same examination room where she had first shown him the furry insides of the broken nativity figure. "Close the door," she said. She then unlocked a cabinet and brought out the baby Jesus swaddled in a spare doggie blanket. She laid the figure on the exam table along with a small plastic bag.

"What's this?" Daniel asked.

"That's a piece of what was inside our wee babe here," Ellie said.

Daniel opened the bag and held a piece of furry hide cut roughly an inch in diameter. "Some kind of animal skin?"

"Aye, but what animal?" Ellie asked. The tone of her voice told him that she knew the answer, but she wasn't ready to tell just yet.

He inspected the piece of hide, rubbed it between his fingers. The fur was short, but quite thick. "It's too soft for cow hair. Rabbit?" Daniel guessed.

"Close," Ellie said.

Daniel gave it another look. Its color was dark brown, almost black. "Mink?" he guessed. He'd never held mink before, but he'd heard it was soft and often used for clothing.

"Now you're on the right track," Ellie said. She took the piece of hide. "This is otter."

"Otter?"

Ellie nodded. "The more I examined it, the more I thought it might be some kind of weasel. You see how thick the fur is and its coloring. I couldn't get the whole thing out without breaking the figure further, and I know you didn't want to do that. So, I figured out a way to cut off two small pieces.

I kept one and sent the other to one of my professors in Edinburgh. He's an expert in small animals, particularly those in the weasel family. He rang me back yesterday confirming my suspicions, definitely family Mustelidae. I didn't expect him to then say otter. It's hard to tell exactly which species without seeing the whole hide, but he assured me this is from an otter."

"Huh, that's so weird. I just saw an otter the other day, two, actually. On a beach in Lewis. O...something; what was it called? We passed a giant statue of a Viking chess piece on the drive there."

"Uig," Ellie said.

"Yes, that's it. We only saw them for a few minutes. They were super cute, running around and tackling each other. Mr. Morrison said they were endangered in Scotland?"

"Around the world. People hunted them nearly to extinction. You can see why. They've the densest fur of any mammal, completely water resistant. But otter fur has been banned for over a hundred years. My professor was quite astonished to see a piece of otter pelt. Perhaps that's why he contacted me so quickly. He wanted to know where I'd gotten it."

"What did you tell him?"

"I told him I would have to get back to him."

"Good."

"Good? Whoever put this in there knows it's illegal. They went to a lot of trouble to hide it. What will they do if they find out we have it? I think we should give it to the police."

"We will, but not just yet," Daniel said. He unwrapped the ceramic infant figure and held it up. He tried to look in the broken arm hole, but couldn't see anything without a light. "Free traders," Daniel said. Ellie gave him a blank look. "Smugglers."

* * *

The sun had nearly set over Inverness and the temperature was rapidly dropping. Daniel Darrow imagined the ceramic baby Jesus figure that sat in his lap must be quite warm, wrapped in its fleece blanket. The colorful doggie bone pattern didn't exactly fit the yuletide season, but on a night like this, no one would care. Ellie drove them through the city, across the Caledonian Canal, across the Ness River, to Bellfield Park.

"Are you certain you want me to come in with you?" Ellie asked.

"I haven't seen Hugh since the police search. I don't know what his state of mind is, or what he's gotten himself caught up in. But you know, safety in numbers," Daniel said.

Ellie shook her head, "That doesn't make me feel better."

When they opened the door, the flat was dark except for a dim light coming from the hall that led to the bedrooms. "At least we know he's home," Daniel said. He turned on the lights in the living room and kitchen. "Stay here with this. I'll see if he's up for a chat." Daniel left Ellie with the blanketed ceramic Jesus and went to knock on Young Hugh's door. No response. He heard music thumping from inside the room. He knocked louder.

"Hugh, buddy, I'm back from Lewis. You won't believe what I saw there. Come out, and we'll have a chat." Still nothing. "I heard about the police search."

The music stopped. Daniel heard a rustling around inside. He stepped away from the door, so Hugh wouldn't catch him with his ear pressed to it. Hugh opened the door. He had on sweat pants and an old Scotland rugby hoodie with a rip along the shoulder seam. His black hair stuck out in several contrary directions, though the bags under his eyes gave the impression he hadn't slept soundly in days. He followed Daniel to the living room where Ellie was waiting on the couch. When Hugh saw her, he immediately looked away and made a futile attempt at taming his unkempt hair.

"Sorry, I forgot to mention we have a guest," Daniel said.

"Let me put on some tea," Ellie said and headed to the kitchen.

When her back was turned to them, Hugh jabbed Daniel in the stomach with his elbow. Daniel winced and held up his hands. He mouthed *Sorry*. He knew it was a pathetic apology, and he felt embarrassed for Hugh. But he worried that if he had told Hugh that Ellie was there too, Hugh would never have left his room.

"So, you went off to Lewis, did you?" Hugh said. He sat down on a chair beside the couch. "Must be nice. Judge changed the terms of my bail. I can't even leave the flat now."

"I'm so sorry," Daniel said. He didn't imagine the judge's order would make much of a change in Hugh's routine as he'd rarely even been out of his room in days. "Well, you didn't miss much. It was even colder up there than here if you can believe it," Daniel said, taking his place on the couch beside Ellie's coat and the bundle of dog blanket. Hugh simply shrugged, as if to say, *What did you expect?*

"Oi, Ellie, you can come back. Your idiot boyfriend's pathetic excuse to get me to socialize worked," Hugh said.

"Great, because I have no idea where you boys keep your tea," Ellie said. She joined Daniel on the couch. "You'll have to excuse him. He didn't run his brilliant plan by me first. I hope I'm not imposing."

Hugh shook his head, *no.*

"Tell us about the police search. Are you okay? What did they find?" Daniel asked.

Hugh shrugged again. "Not much to tell. Two officers came in unexpected. Said they had a new tip. They looked over the whole place. Even your room. I told them it wasn't mine, but they didn't care."

"A tip?" Ellie asked.

"That's what they said," Hugh said.

"What were they looking for?" Daniel asked.

Hugh sighed and rested his chin in his hands. He closed his eyes for a moment and then shook his head.

"What?"

"I didn't do it. I didn't kill Mr. Caird," Hugh said.

"Hugh, what did they find?" Daniel asked.

"A wristwatch. It belonged to Mr. Caird," Hugh said. Daniel and Ellie stared at him, shocked into silence. "I don't know how it got here, I swear!"

Neither Daniel nor Ellie spoke. They could think of nothing to say.

"Why *would* you believe me? No one else does. Everyone's always said I'm no good, irresponsible, the black sheep. Now I'm a murderer too, I guess!" Hugh said, nearly shouting. He stood and shoved the chair. It slid across the hardwood floor, slamming against the wall with a loud thud. Hugh stomped to the kitchen. "I'll make the damn tea."

"Hugh, come back! That's not what we think," Ellie said. Hugh rummaged through the cupboard, ignoring her. "It isn't, is it?" she whispered to Daniel.

Chapter Twenty

While Young Hugh waited on the water to boil, Daniel took the pause as an opportunity to develop a more compassionate approach to a conversation that seemed to have devolved rather quickly from polite small talk to full Spanish Inquisition. He righted the chair that his flatmate had shoved against the wall. He recalled the trial of Susanna, the story Reverend Calder had told him. Susanna's accusers had put her on trial with only their own lies and false evidence to make a case that the townspeople had been all too eager to believe. Daniel hoped that his own desire to believe Young Hugh wasn't equally as rash.

Hugh returned to the living room with three mugs filled with black tea. He still appeared irritated by the unexpected, and unwanted, socializing. But the ritual of making tea had calmed him sufficiently for him to at least return to the same room as Daniel and Ellie. Hugh sat down and breathed in the steam from his mug, the liquid inside still too hot to drink. "I mean, why would I steal the old man's watch? I guess it looked expensive, but it was ancient. And I have my own," Hugh said. He held up his wrist showing a sleek black smartwatch. Its electronic screen face illuminated with the upward motion of his arm. "There's no way that old thing could send a text or map his GPS. It didn't even have real numbers."

"Wait, did you have that on the night Caird was killed? If your watch has GPS, couldn't it tell the police that you weren't anywhere near Loch Ness that night?" Daniel asked.

"I thought of that too. They said I could have taken it off before I went to the loch," Hugh said.

"I have a friend at uni that had one of those. She's always bragging about how it tracks her workouts—calories burned, resting heart rate, all that. She's actually quite annoying about it. We get it, you work out, you look amazing," Ellie said, rolling her eyes with great exaggeration. She took a sip of her tea. "What I'm getting at is, Hugh, could your watch have recorded that kind of data? And if so, could we correlate that with the GPS data?"

"Oh, that would prove he was wearing it *and* not at the loch!" Daniel said.

"Thanks, Sherlock, that's what I was about to say," Ellie said sarcastically.

"Sorry, continue," Daniel said. He took a sheepish sip from his mug.

"No, that's all I had," Ellie said.

"I don't know. I've never used any kind of health app. Never had a need to. My job keeps me pretty fit, or it used to," Hugh said.

They sat for several minutes, sipping their teas, thinking. Eventually, Daniel broke the silence. "Hugh, I've been wondering – ever since I heard about the search—why did the police search the flat now? You mentioned someone tipped them off? Do you have any idea who?"

"I never said *someone*. The police just said they received a new tip. But now that you mention it, someone did stop by to see me earlier that day. Allen, a mate from work. You've met him," Hugh said.

"That big, surly guy that shouted us out of the warehouse?" Daniel asked.

"No, that's Luka. The only reason he'd come calling is if I owed him money. Allen works with us on stocking and deliveries. Maybe you didn't notice him over Luka. Allen's okay. He wanted to know how I was getting on. Said he wanted to check in earlier, but they've been so busy. Always are this time of year. I didn't think anything of it. We had a few beers, played some Call of Duty, talked about old times. It was actually the first time I've had a little fun and felt almost normal since everything happened. But a few hours after Allen left, the police showed up. You don't think he—? He wouldn't, would he?"

Daniel put his mug down and thought for a moment. "Did you ever leave him alone while he was here?"

"You think he planted the watch?" Ellie asked. Daniel looked at Hugh.

"We were together the whole time."

"Are you sure?"

"Yes. Well, I didn't follow him to the toilet, but... can't believe Allen would set me up. We've worked together for over two years. He showed me the ropes when I first started working for Carmen. He's my friend," Hugh said.

"How much do you know about Carmen Oteiza? I mean, what kind of business she does?" Daniel asked.

"Huh? We set up holiday displays. It's not very complicated or glamorous, but it pays. And I get to travel, all over, the EU, Scandinavia, we set up a cracking display in St. Petersburg last Christmas. It was massive."

Daniel looked to Ellie and then the bundle that lay on top of her coat. She picked it up and handed it to Hugh. "So, you don't know anything about this?" she asked him.

Hugh eyed the dog blanket and then her apprehensively. "What's this?" he asked. He unwrapped one end. "A ceramic baby? Wait," he unwrapped it more. "This is one of ours. The model you ordered for Church Street, right? It's broken."

"Look inside," Daniel said.

Hugh held up the figure and peered into the shoulder hole. "Is there something in there? I always assumed they were hollow."

"Here, I took this sample," Ellie said. She pulled the small patch of otter pelt from her coat pocket.

"You carry that around with you?" Daniel asked. She shrugged and handed it to Hugh.

Hugh turned the fur over in his hand. "I don't understand," he said.

"It's otter," Ellie said. The confused expression on Hugh's face remained unchanged.

"Otters are endangered. Selling their pelts is illegal," Daniel said.

"I know that. We learned about otters in primary school. Native to the Highlands, nearly went extinct. But what's an otter doing in this?" Hugh held up the figure again and tried to see inside it.

"We think Carmen isn't simply in the holiday display business," Ellie said.

"That's just a front. She's a smuggler," Daniel added.

"Wait, let me see if I understand you," Hugh said. He looked over the sample of hide, then the ceramic figure. "Carmen is smuggling illegal otter pelts inside these baby Jesus's? That's absurd."

"We don't have any proof yet, other than this one broken figure, courtesy of Sir Walter Scott," Daniel said. Hugh gave him a truly confused look now. "The kirk cat," Daniel said. Hugh nodded as if he understood, then appeared even more puzzled. "It's a long story. But think about it. The company's a perfect cover. You travel all over the world. You set up these displays, full service, so no one except you ever has to mess with them. All these illegal goods hidden right out in the open. Who would ever expect it?"

"I need something stronger," Hugh said. He handed the baby Jesus back to Ellie and walked to the kitchen. Daniel heard him rummaging through a cupboard. Hugh returned with a half-empty bottle of Scotch. He poured some in his former tea mug before offering the bottle to Ellie and Daniel.

"I'm driving," Ellie said. Daniel also declined.

Hugh shrugged and emptied his mug in a single gulp. He poured another. "So what if Carmen smuggles stuff in these displays. What does that have to do with me?"

"I don't know yet. But it can't be a coincidence that the police showed up with new evidence only hours after one of her men stopped by," Daniel said.

"You think she had something to do with Archie Caird's murder?" Ellie asked.

"Maybe he was working for her, you think? Like a secret contact? Or a supplier? He was a wilderness guide. If anyone knew where to find endangered animals to smuggle, it would be him," Hugh said. He took another gulp from his mug excitedly. "I bet he got a guilty conscience and was going to rat her out. Or maybe he wanted a bigger cut of the profits. Either way, she had him taken out. And she had me take the fall for it, the new guy, the one everyone already knew was bad news." Hugh poured another dram from the bottle. "Let's go tell the police!"

"Hold on," Daniel said, "we don't know all that. The only definitive thing we know is that someone put an illegal otter pelt in that figure. If it was Carmen, she obviously has a pretty sophisticated operation, and if she did have Mr. Caird killed, we don't know of what else she's capable. I think we need to find out more before we go to the police."

"That's easy for you to say. You're not the one accused of murder. I think you just don't want another Bonfire Night episode," Hugh said.

"You heard about that?"

"When you accused those boys from your own kirk of burning down the old Broonburn House last year? Called the police to arrest them in the middle of the bonfire celebration because you thought they were going to strike again! Yes, I heard about that. Inverness is a small town at heart, and word travels fast, especially when some cocky American comes in and mucks things up so spectacularly."

"Alright, it's possible I'm still a little gun-shy when it comes to talking to the police. But I really do think we should find out more about Carmen's operation first. And I have a plan to do just that."

* * *

The next morning, Daniel took a bus to Church Street. It would have been a fine morning for a lazy walk. The freezing winter winds remained off in the North Sea, and the forecast called for partly cloudy skies with no measurable precipitation all day. The more optimistic citizens preferred to think of such a day as partly sunny. There was a chill in the air, but that could not be helped, and it was nothing a few layers or a well-insulated coat could not handle. Overall, a pleasant December day in the city of Inverness.

But Daniel Darrow was in a hurry. He'd gotten off to a later start than he'd wanted. After Ellie had left the night before, he and Young Hugh had stayed up finishing off the bottle of Scotch and telling stories of faraway places. Young Hugh, of France and Norway, and Poland. Daniel of the US, the Carolinas. Young Hugh did most of the storytelling and most of the drinking. But Daniel had had enough to sleep through his alarm this Friday morning. When he arrived at Church Street Kirk, he headed straight to the nativity display in the lawn on the front side of the building. He was about to look in the manger when he heard someone call his name. Eliza MacGillivray and Edna Caird were walking down the sidewalk toward him.

"Good morning, ladies. How nice to see you both. What are you up to this morning?" Daniel said.

"Tis such a lovely day, we thought we'd have a wee walk and visit the shops. Before they get too crowded on the weekend," Eliza said. She pulled the collar of her long black and white checked coat closer to her neck, covering the donut-shaped seeing stone she always wore on a thin gold chain. One of the eldest members of Church Street Kirk, Eliza MacGillivray was also one its most active. She was constantly walking one place or another throughout the city. Daniel rarely saw her sitting still. Even during Sunday services, she fidgeted in her pew like a small child.

"And where's your furry friend? I don't know that I've ever seen you without him," Daniel asked. As if on cue, the large black handbag that she carried began to shudder.

Eliza MacGillivray unzipped the bag, and out popped two rabbit ears, then two black eyes and a twitchy nose. Daniel reached gently to pet it, but before he could touch it, the rabbit ducked back inside the bag.

"He's not on a leash this morning?"

"He's hurt his foot. Hopped on a piece of glass the other day. So now I must pamper him." She pulled a biscuit out of her coat pocket, broke a piece off, and held it just above the top of her bag. The rabbit reappeared, sniffed the treat, and greedily snatched it from her fingers. "I think he's being dramatic about the whole thing. Taking advantage of my soft heart. I see you've got your own pet," she said.

Daniel looked down at the bundle of dog blankets he was carrying. "No, it's not a dog or anything. It's a, well, it's a long story. Pretty boring, really. Mrs. Caird, how are you?" Daniel asked, turning to Edna and hoping to change the subject. She hadn't said a thing this whole time and pretended now to ignore his greeting.

"I'm sure it's not my place, but Reverend, you truly should know," Eliza MacGillivray said. Daniel looked at her, surprised. "You're still staying with the Macphersons? With their boy?"

"Oh," Daniel said, understanding. "Yes, that's where I live."

"Mmhmm," Eliza muttered.

"Mrs. Caird, Edna, I haven't forgotten about what you asked me two weeks ago. I've looked into it as best I can. I talked to some people and—"

"Have you?" Edna Caird cut him off. "The police have already arrested that boy for…" she paused, pulled a tissue from her pocket, and dabbed her eyes. "And you don't appear to care in the least. How can you live in the same house as him? After what he did to my Archie? I've heard of the people you've *talked* to, as you say. You're only trying to defend that boy." Her voice was faint but hard. She dabbed her eyes again and looked away.

"That's not true. I haven't forgotten about Archie," Daniel said. Though, he knew in his heart there was some truth to what she said. He had gone out of his way to defend Young Hugh Macpherson, even before he'd had any reason to believe him. Daniel wanted to justify himself—say something about not rushing to conclusions or prematurely judging people. How did the story go that Rev. Calder had told him, about the woman falsely accused? Did he truly believe it applied here, or was he just hoping so because he liked the Macphersons?

"I trusted you. I thought a reverend was supposed to be like a shepherd, caring for *all* his lost sheep. But you prefer the company of wolves," Edna Caird said. "Come, Eliza." She pulled Eliza MacGillivray's arm.

"Mrs. Caird," Daniel said, but she ignored him.

"Ships shall sail eastward and westward by the back of Tomnahurich," Eliza said. She touched the spot just below her neck where her seeing stone lay then allowed Edna to take her away.

Daniel felt terrible, but he knew that his best chance of helping Edna was by helping Young Hugh. He also knew that there was no way he could explain that to her, not yet. He turned his attention to the nativity display. Oor Wullie was still tucked away in the manger, Mary and Joseph gazing down adoringly at their adopted Scottish child. Daniel unwrapped the ceramic Jesus he had brought with him from the dog blanket and returned the wee holy babe to its rightful place. He placed the broken arm as close to its shoulder as possible where it wouldn't fall out. He took a quick look around the barn scene for Sir Walter Scott and then bundled up Oor Wullie in the dog blanket. Before heading inside the kirk, he dialed Carmen Oteiza's number.

"Ms. Oteiza? Yes, this is Daniel Darrow. Great news, I've found the missing nativity figure! It was hidden behind the manger under some hay. It must've fallen out. I've put it back, but it got broken somehow. An arm fell off. Can you replace it? By the end of the day? Yes, that would be perfect. Thank you."

Chapter Twenty-One

Daniel Darrow waited in the café at the corner of Church Street. He snagged a table by the window with a view of the kirk. The view was partially obstructed by passing vehicles and the angle of the café's window, but he could still see most of the front of the building and the nativity scene. He could certainly see if anyone were to go into it and switch out any ceramic figures. Carmen Oteiza hadn't said when someone would stop by, only that he would have a new baby Jesus by the end of the day. He was surprised to hear that she could get a replacement out so quickly. That's good customer service, considering the hostile tone she'd taken when he'd first mentioned that the figure was missing. But, then, given the contraband hidden inside the figure, perhaps it was not so surprising that she would be eager to get it back.

As Daniel waited at the table with a view out the window, he ordered a steady stream of coffees and pastries. Enough to keep the café manager happy about his taking up the valuable seating. After about two hours, his bladder and the responsibilities of his day job forced him to admit defeat. Reverend Calder had wanted to meet before noon to go over preparations for Church Street Kirk's Christmas services. Besides Easter, Christmas was the biggest draw on the kirk's calendar. And with Christmas only a few days away, they had a great many preparations to talk through.

He stopped by the nativity scene before entering the kirk. Everything was just as he'd left it. The broken figure was tucked away in its manger. He hadn't missed the exchange. Before he met with Reverend Calder, he called Young Hugh Macpherson. He hoped that Hugh's desire to clear his name would overpower his reluctance to leave his bedroom. Somebody still needed to keep an eye on the manger.

An hour into his meeting with Reverend Calder, Daniel's cell phone rang. It was Young Hugh Macpherson. Reverend Calder was in the middle of telling him how she'd arranged for a Gaelic language vocalist and flute player for the upcoming service. "Mr. Fisher may not like sharing the musical spotlight, but I've been trying to get this duo to come to Church Street for a while now. I heard them at my friend's kirk up in Cromarty two years ago. I think the congregation will enjoy the performance. Many folks know a smattering of Gaelic. It will be good to hear some traditional hymns sung in the traditional language. Eh, do you need to answer that?" she asked Daniel.

His phone buzzed again. "Sorry, would you mind?" Daniel pulled out his phone. This time it was a text. *Where r u? Truck just pulled up.* He glanced at the time. Surely it was time for a break. "Actually, how would you feel about taking an early lunch?"

"We still have much to discuss," Reverend Calder said. Daniel glanced at the text again. His boss sighed. "I can see you'll be distracted if I say 'No.' I should know by now I cannot compete with young people and their mobiles. Bring me back something sweet if you're going out," she said.

"Sure thing!" Daniel said, already halfway out the door. *Where r u?* Daniel texted as he made his way through the back garden and around the side of the kirk.

Across the street. In my parents' car. Hurry.

Daniel rounded the outside corner of the kirk. He could now see the nativity display and, parked with two wheels on the curb, a white truck with the words *Highland Removals* printed across the side. Daniel was surprised to see a man stooped over the manger. He was expecting Carmen, though now he wasn't sure why. Of course, she wouldn't come herself. He hurried toward the man. "Hello. I'm Daniel Darrow. Are you here to replace my broken figure?"

The man stood up with a jump. He clearly wasn't expecting to be disturbed. "Yes, eh, I've got the replacement in the truck. I was just inspecting this one."

Daniel recognized him immediately as one of the two men who had originally set up the display. What had Young Hugh said his name was? Allen? The same man who visited their flat the morning before the police had also paid a visit. That rather glaring coincidence gave Daniel pause. Still, he was relieved Carmen had not sent Allen's brutish partner, Luka. She wasn't attempting to intimidate him, which meant that she did not suspect he knew anything about the contents of the figure.

"It's broken," Daniel said.

"I can see that. It was intact when we set it up. How did this happen?"

"I don't know. I found it there on the ground covered in hay. Maybe someone bumped into the manger and knocked it over?" Allen looked where Daniel had indicated. The spot didn't appear any different than the surrounding ground. Daniel wished he had thought to make an indention earlier or kick the hay around a little.

"You really shouldn't let people get that close. These are expensive and rather delicate figures," Allen said. He picked it up, turning it over and sideways to examine it. He didn't make a point of looking inside, but Daniel noticed Allen pausing for a brief moment at the shoulder hole. "Is there anything else I should know? Carmen mentioned it had gone missing?" Allen asked.

"No, that's all. I thought it was missing, but it must've just fallen out and gotten buried under the hay on the ground like I said. It kind of blends in," Daniel said. Other than its anachronistically blond hair, the infant figure did not blend in with the hay at all. Daniel was having trouble believing his own story. He could only imagine what Allen was thinking.

Allen glanced at the spot on the ground again. He gave the manger a shake. It hardly moved. "Must've been quite a bump."

"Yeah, must have."

Allen stared at Daniel with narrowed eyes for a solid minute. But Daniel was sticking to his story. What else could he do? He certainly couldn't admit that he was, in fact, the one who'd broken the figure, stolen it, and discovered an illegal otter pelt inside it. "You said you have a replacement?" Daniel asked.

"Just in the truck," Allen said. He took the figure and held it upside down.

He found the serial number printed on the heel of one of its feet. "Inventory," he said. He typed the number into a spreadsheet on an iPad he had with him. He then took the broken figure to the white truck that was parked halfway up the curb and returned with another. He recorded its serial number too and placed it in the manger. "Try to be more careful with this one."

Daniel nodded and waited until Allen got into the white truck before he dared glance across the street. The Macphersons' vehicle was easy to spot—a silver 2000s-era Land Rover. Daniel walked across the street as casually as he could manage. Passing the Land Rover, he spied Young Hugh slunk down in the driver's seat, trying to remain out of view from the front windows. Once Allen's tuck was about half a mile down the road, Daniel quickly doubled back and hopped into the passenger seat. "Driver, follow that car!" Daniel said,

"Huh?"

"Sorry, I've always wanted to say that."

Young Hugh simply shook his head and started the engine. He kept a car or two between them and Allen. "He shouldn't know this car, but better to be careful," Young Hugh said.

Daniel nodded. "So where do you think he's headed?"

"Back to Carmen's would be my guess." Young Hugh followed the white truck north toward the harbor. When they hit the Shore Street roundabout, a small Nissan cut them off. Young Hugh cursed and slammed on the breaks. Luckily Allen's moving truck was neither quick nor difficult to see amongst a street of otherwise smaller vehicles. Hugh sped through traffic to catch up. The gas gauge in the old Land Rover visibly ticked backward toward empty. When they reached the now familiar warehouses by the harbor, Hugh slowed down. The white truck pulled into the warehouse where Carmen kept her inventory. Before he was out of view, Allen stuck his head out the driver's side window and looked back. Hugh ducked and turned his face away. He drove on past the warehouse.

"Do you think he saw me?" Hugh asked.

"I don't know. You said he wouldn't recognize this car?" Daniel asked.

"Hope not. I'm not supposed to leave the flat, remember. I hope this plan of yours is worth it. Let's circle around and park across the road to be safe."

They parked and waited. Several minutes passed. "Do you think we missed him?" Daniel asked. Hugh shrugged. They could make out the shadow of the moving van inside the open warehouse door. Daniel glanced at the clock on his phone. Reverend Calder hadn't given him a specific time to return, but he didn't want to test her generosity. Several more minutes passed. "How long should we wait?"

"What were you expecting to see?" Young Hugh asked.

"I don't know. More than this. Maybe this was a dumb idea. He was just doing his regular job. Picked up a broken figure, replaced it with a new one. Nothing unusual." Daniel sighed. A stakeout had seemed like a good idea when he'd suggested it. Now he wondered if the plan's supposed brilliance hadn't been simply the influence of the late hour and half a bottle of whiskey. Daniel glanced at his phone again. He had wasted his lunch break, and they were still no closer to discovering the truth about the nativity displays.

"Hold on," Young Hugh said. He ducked and pointed out his window. Daniel leaned over to see. A man walked out of the warehouse's side door.

"Is that Allen?"

"Aye. Can you tell what he's carrying?"

They were parked too far away to be sure, but whatever he was carrying appeared to be the same size as the baby Jesus figure. Another person appeared from around the corner. They met, and Allen handed off the item.

"Is that Carmen?" Daniel asked.

"No one else would be wearing a skirt."

"Kilt?"

Young Hugh shook his head. He and Daniel watched as Carmen and Allen talked. Carmen held up the figure, inspecting it.

"You think she knows what's inside?" Hugh asked.

"I wish we could hear what they're saying," Daniel said. "Wait, they're leaving."

Allen followed Carmen to the water where a large ship was docked. They exchanged a few more words before Allen returned to the warehouse. Carmen took the baby Jesus figure onboard.

Young Hugh sat up and gave Daniel a puzzled look. "That's odd," he said. "What?"

"Why would she take that busted piece onboard? We unloaded all the cargo into the warehouse when we first arrived. And the repair workshop's set up in there too," Young Hugh said. Daniel remembered seeing it briefly when Hugh had showed him around. "If a display is broken, that's where it should've been taken. Luka fixes them. And if he can't, there's a bin we toss it in, but he's very good at fixing things."

"Could he have already repaired it while we were sitting here?" Daniel asked.

Hugh shook his head. "Not with the whole arm broken off like that."

"So, what's on the ship?"

"Nothing. It often doesn't even stick around. The captain will let us unload at some port, load someone else's cargo and take them wherever they're going, then return to pick us up later when the holiday season's over."

"So why is it still here?"

"We do a lot a of business in the UK during this time of year. Christmas is our busiest season, actually."

"Mine too," Daniel agreed.

"Well, when we first arrived, we unloaded all we thought we could sell here in Inverness. Then we sailed up the canal renting out displays along the way. Now that Christmas is nearly here, it won't be long before we, er *they*, must go back and retrieve everything. The captain may not have had time to make another shipment before then."

"The Caledonian Canal?"

Hug nodded.

"Huh," Daniel said.

"What?"

"Something Eliza MacGillivray said to me. About fully rigged ships sailing past Tomnahurich Hill."

"The Brahan Seer's prophesy, right? So what?" Hugh asked. He peered out his window again. "She's still in there."

"That prophecy seems to fit our situation pretty well, don't you think?

You, with a fully rigged ship, sailing that same canal."

"I suppose. But you can make those prophesies fit nearly anything if you wring 'em tightly enough."

"Hmm," Daniel muttered, but his mind was already elsewhere. He was trying to remember the second prophecy Eliza MacGillivray had given him. In his mind, he saw her. She stood on the sidewalk outside Church Street Kirk, bundled in her long black and white checked coat. She rubbed the smooth round stone that always hung from her neck between her bony forefinger and thumb. Her eyes clouded over as if they'd just experienced an inexplicably sudden onset of cataracts. He recalled images of pearls and blood. What had she said exactly?

"Rev"

"Huh? What?"

"I said there she goes."

"Who?"

"Carmen. Who you do you think? Are you even paying attention?"

"Yes, sorry," Daniel said. He leaned over to look out Hugh's window. Carmen Oteiza had just stepped off the railed gangway connecting the ship to the dock. "She doesn't have it."

"That's what I said. She left the broken figure on the ship. Why would she do that?" Hugh asked.

"I wish we could see what she did with it. I have a suspicion that's not the only one."

"We could, you know," Hugh said.

"What?"

"We could see what she did with it."

"How?"

"Stay in the car. I'll be right back," Young Hugh said with a mischievous look in his eye. He pulled the hood of his jumper over his head and opened the door.

"Wait, what are you doing?" Daniel asked.

"You were just wanting to say thank you for their excellent customer service." Hugh stepped out and shut the door softly.

CHAPTER TWENTY-ONE

"What?" Daniel asked. But Hugh was already gone.

Chapter Twenty-Two

Daniel watched as Young Hugh sprinted across the road. Hugh stopped two warehouses from Carmen's. He glanced quickly around the corner of one. Daniel looked to Carmen's warehouse. No one had come back outside. Hugh snuck around to the next building. Still nothing from inside Carmen's. *What was Hugh up to?* Hugh looked back to the car. He held up his arm. Was he waving? Did he want Daniel to join him?

Before Daniel could speculate any further, the car's alarm sounded. The horn honked, the lights flashed. If his seatbelt hadn't held him in, Daniel would have jumped out of his seat in surprise. He searched frantically for an off button. The dashboard held controls for the stereo and climate control, but no alarm. Daniel unbuckled his seatbelt and crawled over into the driver's seat. He felt around the steering wheel. The key was missing from the ignition. He looked out the window. Young Hugh was still standing, hidden against the back of a warehouse. Elsewhere, though, he saw plenty of movement. The car alarm had attracted the attention of half the port. Workers from every warehouse in sight, and even two nearby ships, peeked out to see what was causing all the commotion. But Daniel's eyes were fixed on only one warehouse where two men had just exited and were now walking toward him.

Daniel patted around and behind the steering wheel for the key. It was still missing. He opened the compartment in the center armrest. Nothing but old receipts and cassette tapes. *Who had cassette tapes anymore?* "Not important. Focus!" Daniel told himself. But it was hard to think straight with the deafening noise. He glanced back outside to Hugh, but his flatmate was gone. And Allen and Luka were only steps away from the car.

Daniel ducked under the steering wheel to search the floormat. Nothing.

Knock, knock. Daniel's head shot up, banging on the bottom of the steering wheel. Luka tapped on the driver's side window with his massive fist. The fist was so close, Daniel could see the hairs on his knuckles.

"Reverend Darrow?" Allen shouted over the car alarm.

"Your alarm," Luka shouted.

Daniel threw his hands up in an exasperated surrender. "I'm sorry, I can't turn it off."

"What are you doing here?" Allen shouted.

Daniel glanced toward the warehouse. Carmen had stepped outside and was now walking toward them. Luka grabbed the door handle and pulled. The door was locked and didn't open, though the entire car shook with the force of Luka's attempt. Where was Hugh?

Then Daniel remembered what Hugh had said before he left. "I was just wanting to thank you for your customer service," Daniel shouted through the glass.

"What?" Allen said.

"Your excellent customer service. I wanted to say thank you," Daniel shouted. "For replacing the nativity figure so quickly." Before Daniel could finish his sentence the alarm quieted. Luka pulled at the door again, and this time it opened. He stuck his large head inside, only inches away from Daniel's.

"You do not need to be here," Luka said. Daniel could smell his breath. Pickles and fish.

Daniel leaned back as far as he could. "I'm sorry about the alarm. I couldn't figure out how to turn it off. I must have dropped the key," he said. Daniel made a show of looking for the missing key. He could tell the two men were getting impatient. "Hold on. I'm sure it's here somewhere."

"Is there a problem, boys?" Carmen asked, more an accusation than a question. She was at the car now, standing between Allen and Luka. Luka pulled his head out of the vehicle.

"He says he cannot find his key," Luka said.

"Sorry, I'm always doing this. Butterfingers. Let me check under the seat," Daniel said. He didn't know how much longer he could keep up the show.

"Reverend?" Carmen said.

"Yes, hold on, I think I might see it," Daniel said. He ducked and reached under the seat.

"Said he wanted to thank us for replacing that broken figure so quickly," Allen said to Carmen.

"Next time, just call," Carmen said. Daniel could hear the eye roll in her voice. "Let's go. We have work to do."

Daniel continued pretending to search for the ignition key for another minute. When he no longer heard voices, he slowly leaned up and looked out the window. Carmen and the two men were back across the road and headed toward their warehouse. Daniel leaned back in the seat and breathed a sigh of relief. He closed his eyes for a moment to calm down. He opened them again with a jolt when the passenger door opened.

Young Hugh crawled inside, careful not to let anyone see him. He leaned his seat back as far as it would go, nearly horizontal. He tossed the car's key to Daniel. "Drive!"

"Wait, what?" Daniel stammered. Hugh gave him a forceful look and pointed forward. Daniel put the key in the ignition and started the car. He drove a few blocks away and pulled into a petrol station. He stopped the car. "What just happened?"

"I needed a distraction."

"The alarm?" Daniel paused. He removed the key and looked at the key fob that was attached to the ring. The fob had three buttons on its face: unlock, lock, and alarm. "You had this the whole time? You caused the alarm!"

Hugh just smiled.

"That was really dumb. What if you'd gotten caught? You'd be breaking your bail."

"Don't forget, you're the one who smuggled me out of the flat, Rev. Don't worry, though. No one saw me. Besides, that's not the only key I got," Hugh said. He pulled a set of keys out of his pocket and dangled them from his finger. The keyring had a clip with a decorative ship's anchor engraved on it. "I hope you didn't have plans for tonight."

* * *

Reverend Calder, for all her general compassion and geniality, was also quite fastidious. When she set an agenda for a meeting, she saw it through to the very last point. No early lunch breaks or late returns would deter her. So, when five o'clock rolled around, and she and Reverend Darrow still had to discuss the scripture readings for the kirk's two Christmas Eve services, the beneficiaries of their annual Christmas charity donation, and whether to include a full reading or simply an excerpt of Sir Walter Scott's poem—the man not the cat—*Old Christmastide*, she continued on as if it were still midafternoon. "The poem is rather long, isn't it," she said. "But some in the congregation do love it so." Hoping to avoid a recitation of the rather long poem and to end the rather long meeting, Daniel moved to include an excerpt. Reverend Calder nodded in agreement. "But then which part?"

When Daniel Darrow finally left Church Street Kirk, the sun had long set, and most restaurants had already served their first and second dinner rushes of the evening. Daniel grabbed a takeaway falafel wrap and finished it before he was halfway home. He arrived to an empty flat for the first time in weeks. He pulled back the curtain from the front window. The light was on in the twin front window of the elder Macphersons' side of the duplex but their silver Land Rover was not parked out front in its usual space. That meant Young Hugh still had it. Had he already gone back to the port? Daniel glanced at his phone. No messages. He went to his room to retrieve the pocket notebook he'd left in his jacket. He flipped to the page where he had recorded Eliza MacGillivray's prophesies.

Strange as it may seem to you this day, the time will come, and it is not far off, when full-rigged ships will be seen sailing eastward and westward
by the back of Tomnahurich, near Inverness.

That was the Brahan Seer's original prophecy. The notion of a ship sailing from

139

Inverness eastward across the Highlands must have seemed quite strange indeed back in the seventeenth century, nearly two hundred years before the Caledonian Canal was built. The prophecy seemed to Daniel to have an eerie parallel to Carmen Oteiza and her company's current presence in Inverness. Though, as Young Hugh had pointed out, a prophecy could be made to fit most any future interpretation if the interpreter was willing to wring it tightly enough. Still, that fact hadn't stopped the people of Church Street from believing with full confidence in Eliza MacGillivray's other visions.

Daniel turned to the second prophesy she had given him that day—the one that had preoccupied his thoughts since he had left Young Hugh at the Inverness port. The one that had caused him to hear only half the words Reverend Calder had said in their meeting. As far as he could tell, this one was an Eliza original.

The time has come, tis already past when,
through a fog on the silt muddled burn,
a pearl from white to blood red shall turn.

It sounded more like a memory than a prophecy. A warning? *Burn.* Was she predicting another fire, like the infamous Broonburn House fire? Perhaps it wasn't a fire at all. The prophecy's other imagery implied water rather than fire. Fog, silt, pearl. *Of course!* Daniel thought. How could he have been so obtuse? *Burn* didn't mean fire. Eliza had used the old Scots word, *burn,* meaning stream or river. But what did a muddy river have to do with a pearl or blood?

Daniel dropped the notebook. He recalled the day he had gone with several other men to Loch Ness. Mr. Tweed had led them, in a morbid sort of way, to the very spot where Archie Caird's body had been found—near the mouth of the Moriston River as it emptied into the loch. Daniel remembered Young Hugh, apart from the group, kneeling at the shoreline. He remembered Philip Morrison reaching into the water and pulling out a mussel, then prying it open just wide enough to glimpse the white pearl inside. Daniel picked up the notebook and read the prophesy again. Was he reading into it what he wanted to see? Was he wringing it too tightly?

He felt a sudden buzzing in his pocket. A text from Young Hugh: *R u coming?*

Daniel looked at the time. It was too early. *I thought we were meeting later?* *Come now*, Young Hugh texted back.

Daniel closed his notebook. Prophesies would have to wait. He changed into a pair of dark blue jeans and a black hoodie. The hoodie had writing on the front, so he turned it inside out before putting it on. He found a pair of nearly new running shoes in the back of his closet. They had been an impulse buy at a time when he thought he might take up jogging to stay in shape—before he realized he hated jogging. He had tossed them in the back months ago because, as irrational as he knew it was, he felt that they were silently judging him every time he passed them over for a pair of loafers. Tonight, though, they might get a second chance to prove their worth.

* * *

The carpark outside the Inverness Port was nearly empty when Daniel arrived. He pulled his hood over his head and buttoned the collar of his heavy coat. Stuffing his hands in his pockets for warmth, he paced the sidewalk. He heard the distant sounds of machinery and a few shouts from men working the night shift. Further still, he could hear the noise of traffic and Friday night pub crawlers. Daniel's phone buzzed. *To your left.* He looked left to the chain link fence topped with three strands of barbed wire that surrounded much of the port's warehouse district. A few cars were parked in the mostly barren lots, but otherwise no signs of life. *Your other left*, his phone buzzed again. Daniel turned. Two headlights flashed once at him from across the road. He hurried over and got into the silver Land Rover.

"Brrr, why isn't the heater on?" Daniel asked.

"The only car sitting here with its engine on would draw attention," Young Hugh said. He was bundled up in a thick coat, gloves, and black beanie-style hat.

"I thought you were going to pick me up?"

"Couldn't leave my post, could I. Might miss something." Hugh pointed toward his old ship and handed Daniel a small pair of binoculars.

It was too dark to see much. The few scattered street lamps seemed only to intensify the shadows. The ship had small safety lights on its bow, stern, and bridge. "You couldn't have parked any closer? I don't see anything," Daniel said.

"I think this car might be a touch recognizable—after this morning," Hugh said with a wink. "I texted as soon as the last man left."

"Are you sure it's empty?"

"I've been sitting here a long time, mate. She's empty," Hugh said. "Here." He handed Daniel a black cloth.

"What's this?"

"Put it on," Hugh said. Hugh pulled down the rolled edge of his beanie to reveal a ski mask with slits for eyes and mouth. Daniel held up his own mask. "Don't tell me you're getting cold feet now."

Chapter Twenty-Three

"I'm not sure about this," Daniel said. He held the black ski mask in his hands.

"The stakeout was your idea," Hugh said.

"Watching, yes. But breaking in?"

"You can't always sit on the sidelines, Rev. Sometimes you have to lineout." The look of incomprehension on Daniel's face was visible even in the low light. "Scrum?" Hugh said. Daniel shook his head. "I've got to take you to a rugby match when this is all over. Let me put it in terms you might understand. Even Jesus broke into the ol' Temple and trashed the place when he had to. I didn't sleep through every sermon as a kid."

"I don't think this is quite the same," Daniel said.

"Sure it is. Besides, we're not really breaking in. I've got the keys, remember," Hugh said. He dangled the stolen keys in front of Daniel as if he were trying to entertain an infant.

"You don't think Carmen will have noticed that her keys are missing?"

"This is a spare. They keep it in the warehouse workshop. Won't be missed."

"Are the masks really necessary?" Daniel asked.

"Just a precaution. I've spent a night in jail, and I don't fancy going back. Do you?"

Daniel sighed and pulled on the mask. It was tight, and the eye holes were a little too wide, but at least his head would be warmer. "I can't believe I'm doing this," he said. He should be putting on an Advent stole and setting out a chalice of wine and loaf of bread, not donning a black ski mask in preparation to sneak aboard a smuggler's ship.

"Leave your coat here. It's too bulky," Hugh said. He took off his own coat and opened the door. "Let's go."

Daniel followed Hugh across the street and into the main grounds of the cargo port. Hugh kept to the shadows as they made their way to the ship. He darted across the brief spaces illuminated by lampposts. He paused, hunkered down, or flat against a wall, when a distant voice sounded not quite distant enough. For a man who, until last night, had become a recluse in his own house, Young Hugh moved now with great agility and purpose. He was like a gymnast running through a familiar floor routine. If they had not been wearing masks, Daniel was certain he would glimpse a wide grin on Hugh's face.

Between the cold and his nerves, Daniel struggled to keep up. He felt stiff and light-headed. Instead of adrenaline heightening his senses, he felt them dulled, or at least confused. He jumped at all the wrong sights and sounds—a trash bag blowing past, the flicker of a lamppost, the sound of his own shoes crunching on a piece of broken glass. By the time they reached Carmen's warehouse, Daniel was a complete wreck. He lifted up his mask, struggling to catch his breath.

"What are you doing? Pull that back down. Are you that out of shape?" Hugh said in a loud whisper.

"I'm sorry, I—" Daniel took several deep breaths. "I've never done anything like this before."

"That's not what I've heard," Hugh said. Daniel looked at him blankly. "Last year. Didn't you and Ellie Gray sneak into the morgue at Raigmore?"

Hugh was right. They had snuck into the records room of the hospital's morgue to glimpse the file of the poor young man who had died in the Broonburn House fire. But they'd had no other choice then. They had to see that file. It was the only thing that could clear Ellie's mother's name. And they'd nearly gotten caught in the process.

"That was different," Daniel said.

"Why? Because that breaking and entering was for your girlfriend?"

"No, it's not that."

144

"It's exactly that. I have a reputation for getting into trouble, not being reliable. I know that. And I'll admit, some it is deserved. But I didn't kill Archie Caird. That's not me. But if Carmen's company *was* somehow involved and seeing what's on that ship can prove it, we've got to try. I've got to try." Hugh paused and put his finger to his lips. He nodded over Daniel's shoulder around the corner of the building.

Daniel froze. He didn't hear anything. He pressed his back against the wall, wishing, like a chameleon, he could change the color of his black hoodie to match the off-white building. His ears twitched. He definitely heard something this time. A scratching or shuffling along the floor. Someone moving a box or crate? He stood, holding his breath, trying not to make a sound, not even to blink. The noise got closer. He dared not turn his head to see.

Daniel jumped when Hugh touched his shoulder. Hugh muffled his laughter with his free hand. "Look," Hugh said, pointing. A large rat sat at the corner of the building. When it noticed Hugh pointing, it hurried back inside. "Maybe you should go back and wait in the car."

"No," Daniel said. He took a deep breath to calm himself. "I said I would help you, and I will." He pulled his mask back down. "Let's go."

He followed Young Hugh to a storage building at the edge of the complex. Only open air now lay between them and Carmen Oteiza's ship. Young Hugh peeked around the corner of the building. "It's clear. Ready?" he asked. Daniel nodded. They sprinted across the open space. A single chain covered the entrance to the gangway. Hugh ducked under it and climbed the shaky stairway up to the ship's main deck. Once on board, he directed them away from the safety light that illuminated the entrance.

"Now what?" Daniel whispered.

"Now we find out what's really going on aboard this ship," Young Hugh said. He led Daniel to the ship's stern. "This is the bridge. If the captain keeps any records, they'll be in here." Hugh checked the door. Locked. He pulled a keyring out of his pocket. "I hope one of these works," he said.

"You *hope* they work?" Daniel asked.

"Shhh," Hugh said. He put a key in the lock, but it didn't turn. He tried another and another. Click. The handle turned, and the door creaked open. "You should have more faith, Rev."

Daniel sighed and followed him inside. The room was wide and narrow. The entire wall opposite the door was lined with a row of large windows that sat above another row of consoles and computer screens. The screens were all dark. The room was illuminated only by the faint light that made its way from the shipyard through the windows.

"Where do we start?" Daniel asked.

"I don't know. I never had much reason to be in here," Young Hugh said. He scanned the bridge. "You start on that side, and we'll meet in the middle. I didn't bring a torch. We'll have to use our mobiles for light."

"Won't someone see that?" Daniel asked, pointing to the windows.

"You're right. Keep low and try to shield it from the windows." Hugh turned on his phone and partially covered it with one hand, so the light was directed down. Daniel did the same. He made his way to the side of the room Hugh had indicated and began searching for anything that might be helpful. Without access to the ship's computers, the various screens were useless. Daniel searched in every drawer and cabinet he came across. It was slow going, hunched down as he was to avoid the windows and make use of the small light his phone provided.

Daniel wasn't sure exactly what he was looking for, but he felt certain he would recognize it when he saw it. Something to explain the contents of the baby Jesus figurine. Something to connect Archie Caird to Carmen Oteiza. He found a clipboard with dates and corresponding ports—a record of the ship's travel history. Daniel snapped photos of the most recent few pages so they could review them in more detail later. One drawer held nautical maps, another was stuffed full of receipts and cargo manifests. The most recent one was for Carmen Oteiza, but it didn't list anything unusual—a number of crates with contents described vaguely as *outdoor displays*. If they were transporting anything illegal, it wouldn't be on any official documents. Still, Daniel took a photo of it just in case.

"Did you find anything?" Hugh asked when they both reached the center console.

CHAPTER TWENTY-THREE

"Not much. Some maps, dates. Nothing that seemed unusual," Daniel said.

"Same," Hugh said. "Perhaps we'll have better luck elsewhere."

Daniel looked at the time on his phone.

"Don't worry. No one will be on board for hours," Hugh said assuredly. He ushered Daniel out of the bridge, but the caution he took opening the door and scouting the upper deck betrayed the confidence in his voice.

The air outside the bridge felt colder than Daniel remembered. As his adrenaline from sneaking through the shipyard and then onboard began to wane, he suddenly felt very tired. But there was no time to rest. Young Hugh dashed across the main deck. Daniel followed. They passed several large metal containers. "Wait," Daniel called.

"What?" Hugh said. He stopped and looked around them nervously. "Did you hear something?"

"No. I was just wondering," Daniel said. He paused for a moment to catch his breath. That was part of the reason he'd stopped. The frigid air. The unexpected sprint. His lungs weren't ready for it. But he dared not admit that to Hugh. "What about these containers?"

"I doubt we'd find anything in these. Whatever we're looking for wouldn't be up here so readily open to routine inspections. And besides," Hugh felt down the short side of one of the containers. "I don't have the key to these. They're not all Carmen's," he said, holding a heavy metal lock in his hand. "No, we need to get below deck." He took another quick glance around them, then dashed off again.

Daniel followed him to another locked door. Hugh tried one of the keys from his stolen set. "Hard to tell which one in the dark," he said. He tried another. "Got it!" The door opened to a narrow stair that led down to a dark hallway. Dim red safety lights spaced far apart on the ceiling provided the only light. The hallway smelled of diesel fuel, rust, and cigarette smoke. But it was warm. A little too warm. Daniel pulled his mask up off his face and unzipped the top third of his hoodie. He followed Hugh down the hall.

Their footsteps were louder here than above, on the main deck. They echoed off the walls and down the hall in either direction. Hugh pulled on a door handle, but it wouldn't budge. He tried various keys. "I can't see," Hugh whispered. Daniel held his phone's light over the door handle. Hugh tried the remaining keys. Daniel gave him a questioning look. Hugh shook his head. "Might not work down here."

"Did you try them all?" Daniel whispered. Hugh held out the keys. Daniel pushed them back. "No, I'm sure you did. What now?"

"There's more doors," Hugh said, nodding down the hall.

"Do we have time?"

"We better."

They slowly made their way down the hall, trying each door along the way. Daniel held his phone out for illumination while Hugh ran through the keys. None of the keys worked, but they tried them each time anyway. Two of the doors were already unlocked. One was a small cleaning closet. Buckets, mops, rolls of paper towels, and bottles of cleaning supplies. Behind the other unlocked door was a vast, seemingly empty cargo space. When they entered, the door slammed shut with a deafening bang. The noise echoed like a gunshot ricocheting off every wall. Without the dim hallway safety lights, the room was pitch black. Daniel held out his phone for light. Hugh did the same. The lights narrowly illuminated their faces, casting shadows that caused their features to appear severe and ghoulish. It reminded Daniel of boys sitting around a campfire telling ghost stories.

They followed the same strategy in this room as they did when searching the ship's bridge. Daniel did not encounter a single obstacle along the entire length of his wall. "You find anything?" he asked Hugh when they met in the center of the far wall. Hugh shook his head. "Why would this huge room be empty?"

"Cargo must've already been unloaded. Nothing to replace it with yet. It'll likely be full again after Carmen, and the rest of the crew pack everything up at the end of the season," Hugh said.

"Where would they have put our old baby Jesus?"

"It's got to be on board somewhere. I never saw it come off the ship."

"It's getting late," Daniel said, looking at his phone. "Or early. Either way, we shouldn't stay here too much longer."

"Let's get on with it then. There's only a few more doors to check on this deck," Hugh said. He retraced his steps along the side of the room. Daniel followed him. Neither wanted to chance crossing the center of the cavernous room. With the light from their phones only illuminating a couple of feet ahead, locating the single exit door was a tedious task.

Back in the hallway, they continued their search. Two more locked doors. Only one door left before the hall ended at another stairwell leading back up to the main deck. Hugh put his hand on the door handle and was about to turn it when Daniel stopped him. "Did you hear that?"

"What?" Hugh asked.

"A bang or something above us. Like something hitting metal."

Young Hugh shook his head. "These old ships like to creak and moan," he said. He turned the handle. Unlocked. The door opened to another dark room. Hugh stepped inside while Daniel searched the wall beside the door for a light switch. When the lights came on, both men stood frozen – partly because of the sudden brightness and partly because of what their squinted eyes gradually revealed.

The room was larger than the cleaning closet but much smaller than the empty cargo space they'd explored earlier. This room, though, was not empty. Wooden crates, haphazardly staked, lined one wall. Shelving covered the opposite wall with each shelf holding row after row of ceramic baby Jesuses.

Chapter Twenty-Four

"What is this? Some kind of creepy nursery?" Young Hugh asked. Daniel picked up one of the figures. It felt heavier than the one he and Ellie had wrapped in a dog blanket and carried around Inverness. He laid it back down and picked up another. This one was lighter.

"Where are the other figures? The wisemen, the animals?" Young Hugh asked.

In the far corner of the room, Daniel inspected a large, open crate. "If you thought the babes on the shelves were creepy, have a look at this," he said. Hugh joined him and looked inside. Broken limbs, torsos, and ceramic heads filled the crate—enough parts for dozens of complete figures. On top of the pile lay a figure with a missing arm. Daniel picked it up. The top half disconnected from the bottom. He looked inside. Empty.

"Is that it?" Hugh asked.

Daniel held the two pieces together. With a twist, the top half connected to the bottom. The seam was so well hidden in the folds of the infant's ceramic swaddling clothes it all but disappeared. No wonder he and Ellie hadn't found a way to open it before. He looked the figure over closely and nodded. "Looks like the same one from the kirk. The break in the arm is the same. But then, all these figures look alike."

"I knew it was still on the ship!" Hugh said.

"So, where's the otter pelt that was inside it?" Daniel asked.

They both looked to the wall with the stacks of crates. The lids were nailed shut. "See if there's a hammer or something that can open this," Young Hugh said, nodding to one of the shelves. Daniel searched through the pile of tools: a hacksaw, bottles of glue, screwdrivers, wrenches, box of nails, and a hammer. Beside the hammer lay a small crowbar. Daniel grabbed both.

Hugh used the crowbar on one of the lids. "Help me with this," he said after he'd loosened the nails on one side. Together, he and Daniel pried open the lid. "Straw?" The crate was filled to the brim with straw.

"Like what they use to line the manger?" Daniel asked.

Hugh held up a handful of it. "Looks like. But why store it like this? The stuff we use for the displays is shrink-wrapped in plastic—compressed twenty-kilo bales."

Daniel buried both hands in the straw. Nothing but more straw. He dug deeper, down to his elbows. The straw poked and scratched his hands and arms, even through the thick sleeves of his hoodie. He felt something hard and solid. The bottom of the crate? It was too shallow for that. Looking from the outside, the crate appeared at least twice as deep. Daniel pulled out armfuls of hay until a plywood bottom was revealed.

"Look," Hugh said, pointing to two notches on either end of the board. The notches were wide enough for three of four fingers to grasp, like handles. He and Daniel each took one and lifted. "A false bottom!"

They sat the plywood aside to reveal layers of furs stacked in neat rows. Daniel held one up. The pelt was dark brown, turning to light tan along the edges where its stomach and arms would have been. It brought to mind the otters he had seen playing on the beach in Uig.

"This is incredible," Hugh said. "I never knew about any of this."

Daniel dropped the pelt and turned to Hugh.

"I heard it too," Hugh said.

"The boat creaking?" Daniel asked.

They both rushed to the open door and peeked out. A high moan came from the far end of the dark hallway. Rusty door hinges ground open. A stream of light poured in.

"Oi, who's there!" a voice called out.

Daniel looked at Hugh, eyes wide. He ran back to the open crate and began throwing hay back into it. Hugh, still at the door, whispered, "Rev, we've got to go!"

"They'll know we were here," Daniel said, frantically shoveling in hay. He glanced at the floor, panicked. There was no way he would be able to put back all the hay. Not without more time and perhaps a broom. In his haste, he had forgotten to replace the plywood false bottom.

"There's no time!" Young Hugh said.

"Luka? That you?" the voice from the end of the hall shouted.

Daniel gave up his efforts with the crate and returned to the door. "Wait," he said, retrieving his phone from his pocket. "Evidence." He pushed the unlock button to take a picture. But instead of a camera app, the home screen showed a red low battery button, then went dark. Daniel tried again. The phone didn't react at all. He sighed. "Battery's dead."

"We might be too if we don't get out of here!" Young Hugh said.

"But—" Daniel protested.

"Fine," Young Hugh said. He pulled out his own phone and snapped a picture. "Now, let's go!" He shut off the room's light and grabbed Daniel's arm. He led Daniel down the hall, away from the open door. In a few yards, they ran into another door. Footsteps originating from the open door at the other end of the hall echoed toward them. Hugh tried the handle. It was unlocked. He swung the door open and practically pulled Daniel up the stairwell.

It was still dark outside and cold. A few persistent stars shone through patches in the otherwise cloud-covered sky. Daniel saw his breath in thick, quick puffs. On any other night, he might have enjoyed the brisk sea air after being confined in a stuffy, windowless room. On any other night, he might have been tucked away safely in bed in his cozy flat on Bellfield Park, far from the Port of Inverness. But tonight, he had no time to dream or savor the calm winter night. He closed the door behind him that led to the lower deck. He glanced around, tried to get his bearings. He and Young Hugh stood at the far side of the ship from the gangway where they had first snuck aboard. The bridge light was illuminated.

"You said no one was on board," he said to Young Hugh.

"No one was."

Someone exited the bridge door. It was too far and still too dark to identify who.

"Do you think they saw us?" Daniel asked. The person from the bridge began walking quickly toward them.

"I'd say so," Young Hugh said.

"What do we do?"

The person from the bridge was now at the gangway. A loud, metallic bang sounded from below them—a door slamming shut.

"What do we do?" Daniel asked again. But Young Hugh was frozen. "Hugh!" Daniel said. No response. "Is there another way off the ship?" Young Hugh took a step toward the gangway, then a step back. He shook his head.

"I don't want to go back to jail," Young Hugh whispered.

"Who is there?" The man from the bridge shouted. Daniel could tell from the voice it was a man. As he got closer, Daniel could see he was a *big* man. And he was carrying something. A stick? He held his arm up and shined a light at them. Daniel winced and looked away. Young Hugh stood frozen like a deer before the man's one headlight.

Daniel pulled his mask back down over his face. He grabbed Young Hugh's arm and ran. He didn't know where he was going, but he knew where he couldn't go. They reached the end of the ship and stopped. A single rail stood between them and the water. Shipping containers lined the center of the deck, leaving only two paths on either edge to walk. One was blocked by the man with the flashlight. "We can go around," Daniel said. He and Young Hugh ran to the opposite side of the ship, hoping to double back down the other path and reach the gangway before their pursuer realized where they were headed. As they turned the corner, Daniel looked back just in time to see the door to the lower deck open.

The second pursuer, from the lower deck, saw them and, realizing their plan, raced to a tight space between the center row of containers. They only made it a few yards before Daniel saw the second man emerge from between two containers. They were now cut off from both paths. "Oi, stop!" the man shouted. He ran toward them.

Daniel turned back. He wasn't thinking now, just fleeing. He ran until he reached the railing again. The flashlight bobbed up and down, closer with each footstep of its holder. The second man shouted again, his voice louder now. Daniel felt suddenly claustrophobic. He couldn't breathe. He looked out past the rail. The lights of another cargo ship on the other side of the port shined as brightly as the stars, and beyond that, a cluster of private boats docked in the marina. Then the Kessock Bridge and the dark, open waters of the Moray Firth. He looked down at the water below and felt dizzy.

"We have to jump," he said.

"You daft? The water's freezing!" Young Hugh protested.

Daniel glanced back to the center of the ship. He could now clearly see the two men approaching, covering their only exit. Was one of them Allen? It didn't matter. The men would be upon them in minutes. "We have to," Daniel said.

Young Hugh leaned over the rail. "It's too far. And how would we get to land? The dock's too high."

"There, around the corner," Daniel pointed. "Looks like a rocky incline. We'll have to swim for that."

"I don't-"

But Daniel was already climbing over the rail. Hugh followed. Their pursuers were running toward them now. Seconds. Daniel looked Hugh in the eye, took a deep breath, and jumped.

The fall felt longer than he'd imagined it would be. Between the dark, cloudy night and the water, like black ink, he had no frame of reference to judge either his speed or his progress. A monochromatic void. Only the rush of air told him he was falling. Then the splash. Or more like crash. He hadn't thought to dive off the ship's bow—kneel over, press his hands together over his head like an extended prayer. He had simply leaped. And now his feet slammed into the water. Hard. Painful.

But he had no time to focus on the pain of impact. The shock of the freezing water shot through him like a bolt of electricity, knocking the breath out of him. His extremities became immediately numb. His arms and legs flailed, fighting against the water for something solid to grasp. How deep had he sunk? His lungs burned. He wanted to open them, suck in air, but he knew he couldn't. Not yet. His mind had only one thought—*UP*. He had to keep moving up. He struggled, thrashed against the water. Propelled himself up, up. His lungs felt like they were about to implode, desperate for oxygen.

He breached the surface, gasped, choked in air. He was dangerously close to the ship. The waves threatened to smash him against its hull. He turned toward the dock. Young Hugh was right. Its sheer concrete walls were far too high to climb out of the water. Where was the rocky slope? It had been clearly visible from the atop the ship, but now it was gone.

Daniel heard a gasp to his right. Young Hugh burst through the surface, splashing wildly. Daniel swam to him, but not too close. He didn't want to get hit or accidentally pulled back under. He located the end of the dock's concrete wall. Beyond that corner would be their way out. He grabbed the top of Young Hugh's hoodie and pulled.

"I'm okay, okay," Young Hugh said after a moment. His panic subsided, Daniel let him go.

"This way," Daniel said. He swam toward the shore. His arms and legs felt like logs, heavy and stiff. He swam on. Past the high concrete corner, he saw the rocky slope. He swam harder. The freezing waves slapped against him. He swallowed as much saltwater as air.

A solid pressure hit Daniel's leg. The leg was too numb for him to tell for sure what it was, but given his proximity to the shore, that had to be it. It was a manmade, steep slope constructed of boulders rather than a sandy beach. Daniel walked as best he could on the slippery rocks, worn smooth by decades of waves and covered in algae. When the water was shallow enough, he fell to his hands and knees. Young Hugh was right behind him. Together they scrambled up the small hill of boulders.

At the top, on the flat concrete, Daniel fell to his back, exhausted. Only now did he realize he was shivering. He ripped the ski mask off his head. No wonder it had been so hard to breath in the water. Little ice crystals had already begun to form on the frayed bits of fabric. He tossed it into the water and lay back down. He looked over to Hugh, also maskless, also laying spread out on the concrete. Daniel wanted to say something to him. He wanted to laugh or cry. But his teeth were chattering too much. His eyes wanted to freeze shut.

"Over there!"

Daniel heard shouting from the ship. He saw the bright flash of the light the big man carried, now attempting to pinpoint their location. No time to rest. He leaned up, patted his arms and legs to try and get the blood flowing. "We've gotta get out of here," he said to Young Hugh. Hugh nodded and stood.

"This way," Young Hugh said after scanning the area. He led Daniel away from the shore, back through the Port, past stacks of shipping crates, piles of massive offshore wind turbine blades. They progressed at a fast walk, too exhausted and cold to muster the energy for another sprint. Hugh gave the warehouses a wide berth, in part because of where they had swum ashore and in part because of a strong desire to avoid another potential confrontation with more of Carmen's men.

When they reached the Land Rover, they were still sopping wet. The elder Macphersons would not be happy about the puddles left behind on the leather seats, but that was a concern for another day. Young Hugh started the ignition, cranked the seat warmers, and blasted the heater. He sped away from the Port at a speed that in the daylight would certainly have earned him a traffic ticket. But at this hour, the roads were deserted. Daniel watched the city lights stream past. Neither said a word. Only when they were safely parked in front of their flat did Daniel feel he could relax a bit. "That was too close," he said, breaking the silence.

"Aye," Young Hugh agreed.

Daniel exited the car, careful not to let the door slam and alert the elder Macphersons or anyone else of their late arrival. Inside the warm flat, Hugh walked straight to his bedroom. "Hugh," Daniel said. Hugh paused, his hand on the doorknob. "I think we've been going about this all wrong."

"Yeah?" Hugh said.

"Yeah. All this sneaking around," Daniel said, shaking his head. "I think we need to confront Carmen head-on."

"Whatever you say. But it'll have to wait. Right now, all I want to do is get out of these wet clothes, wrap in at least three blankets, and sleep the entire day!" Hugh said. He entered his room and shut the door before Daniel could respond.

"Sounds like a plan," Daniel said.

Chapter Twenty-Five

Daniel Darrow sat on the number 12 bus, clutching his satchel in his arms. At the Shore Street stop, a woman boarded. She was bundled in a puffy coat and red tartan scarf. Daniel smiled at her as she approached. She sat in the row across the aisle from him. He didn't know her, but it was the polite thing to do. A simple courtesy, acknowledging another's existence. So often, people sat with hoods up or earphones in, eyes locked on phone screens. Daniel was not innocent of such antisocial behavior. To avoid other commuters, he'd buried his nose in a book or popped in earbuds, even with no audio pulsing through them. He'd even been known to place his coat and bag on the seat beside him to make it look as if it were already occupied. Sometimes a bit of space and solitude were good for the soul. Sometimes it was base self-absorption, plain and simple.

But this morning, the bus was crowded, and Daniel was feeling gregarious. So he smiled, made eye contact. Perhaps he had yet to fully come down from last night's adrenaline high. Young Hugh Macpherson did not have the same problem. When Daniel had knocked on Hugh's bedroom door, asking if Hugh was joining him, Hugh failed to answer. When Daniel knocked again several minutes later, Young Hugh mumbled through the closed door, "Best if I stay here." Daniel still wondered what exactly his flatmate had meant. Was Hugh afraid of confronting Carmen Oteiza face-to-face after being fired and accused of a murder they were both sure she had some part in? Or did he simply want to catch a few more hours of sleep after a very long night. Either way, Daniel knew that no force on earth could rouse Young Hugh from bed if he was set on staying in. So, Daniel had left without him.

The woman on the bus did not return Daniel's smile. He didn't mind. She was, after all, under no obligation to reciprocate. They didn't know one another. But Daniel did not expect the look she did give him. It was a raised eyebrow look of incredulity, almost a sneer. Come to think of it, this was not the first strange look he had received this morning. Daniel turned from her. He patted down his hair. It was still a little damp from the hot shower he had taken this morning. He had had to get the salty sea smell off of him. And the hot water had felt so good, he had stayed in longer than usual. He felt rushed after, though now he couldn't think why. It's not like he would be late; he hadn't made an appointment.

Then he noticed it. A pink ceramic arm sticking out from the top flap of his bag. Its tiny fingers were opened as if it were trying to claw its way out. *Well, that explains the funny looks*, Daniel thought to himself. He tried to stuff the figure further into the bag, but its life-sized bulk and stiff posture made it difficult. He managed to get the arm in, but just barely.

He had brought along the figure on a whim. He had intended only to talk to Carmen – ask her straight out what was going on. Let her know he'd figured out her smuggling ring and hope that the shock would catch her off guard. Surprise her into connecting the dots between Archie Caird's murder, Young Hugh, and whatever illicit game she was playing at. Daniel had read such confessional scenes in countless books. He simply had to get her to think that he already knew the answers to his questions. He was merely there to give her a chance to explain her side of the story.

This was assuming there were dots to connect. But there had to be. After all, he'd been through with Young Hugh, he couldn't believe Hugh could kill someone. Gamble away his money—sure. Sneak aboard someone's ship and riffle through their things—obviously a possibility. But murder—no way. When confronted by Carmen's men, Young Hugh had frozen. He didn't have a killer's instinct. He barely had a flight instinct, much less fight. Still, there were crimes of passion. But Young Hugh said he hardly knew Archie Caird. What would lead him to kill a man he hardly knew?

No, Carmen had something to do with it. Young Hugh's sudden firing, her man Allen's surprise visit to their flat just before new evidence was uncovered, the otter pelt hidden inside the nativity display he had ordered from Carmen. But how did Archie Caird fit in? As far as Daniel knew, Carmen had less of a connection to Caird than Young Hugh. Daniel could see all the pieces, but he couldn't yet fit them together. With any luck, his own surprise visit to her office this morning would make it all clear.

He was running the scenario through his mind half an hour earlier when he'd passed Church Street and seen the nativity display. He'd stopped and pretended to admire it. Then, as discretely as he could, he'd swiped the baby Jesus out of its manger, stuffed it in his bag, and walked quickly to the nearest bus stop. He was counting on luck, but a little insurance couldn't hurt.

* * *

When the bus arrived at his stop, Daniel exited without making eye contact with anyone. The bus pulled away, leaving him at the Port of Inverness. It looked different somehow, in the morning light. The warehouse buildings, the docked ships, the piles of wind turbine blades, and other materials too impracticable to store indoors—they were all still there. The place was the same, but different. Or perhaps it was Daniel that was different. Having been there at night, seen the shadows and shadow cargo, he observed it now with new eyes.

He walked straight to Carmen's warehouse. There were fewer workers about than at the other times Daniel had visited the Port. That was to be expected on a Saturday morning. Those that were there eyed him suspiciously as he made his way to the part of the building that held Carmen's office. He looked at the ground or straight ahead, ignoring their stares. He couldn't risk losing his nerve now.

Daniel didn't bother knocking when he reached the door. There was no room for politeness if he wanted the element of surprise on his side. Carmen was sitting behind her desk. She was typing with one hand while the other held her phone to her ear. When Daniel burst in, her typing hand froze. She stared at him for several seconds before speaking. "Ya tebe perezvonyu," she said to the phone, then hung up. *What language was that?* Daniel wondered.

"Reverend Darrow, yes? I was not expecting you," she said.

Good, she was surprised, thought Daniel. "We need to talk."

"Un momento," she said. She continued typing. "We had a break in last night," she said.

"A break in?"

"Yes, two men trespassed on the ship. You would not know anything about that, would you?"

"What? No. Why would I?" Daniel stammered. *Did she know? How could she?* They'd worn masks. "Did you contact the police?" *Why did he ask that?* He certainly didn't want the police involved.

"Not yet. I have my own ways of dealing with such people. I am still determining if anything was taken."

"Your own ways?" Daniel asked. He could feel his palms sweating. He unbuttoned the top two buttons of his coat. He didn't recall the heater being this efficient the last time he was here. He was supposed to rattle her, not the other way around.

"What do you need? You can see I am very busy this morning," Carmen said.

"Right." Daniel shook his head and took a deep breath to regain his confidence. "I know what you're doing. The displays, smuggling, firing Hugh Macpherson. And I won't let you get away with it. You need to come clean."

"What is this? I am sorry I had to fire your friend, but I cannot have criminals working for me." Carmen said. She stopped typing and locked eyes with Daniel. "You are becoming a very difficult client, Reverend Darrow. Unless there is anything wrong with your display, I must get back to my work."

"Don't play dumb, Ms. Oteiza. I know about the displays. It's all a front for you to smuggle illegal goods! Do you have anything you want to say for yourself?"

"That is nonsense. You should go," Carmen said. She waved him away with the flip of her hand as if he were nothing more than an irritating fly.

She returned her focus to her computer screen.

"Fine, I didn't want to do this, but you've forced me." Daniel took the infant figure out of his bag and held it up. He hurtled the figure to the ground. It shattered, making a loud crash, like a dropped dinner plate or vase. Now he truly had surprised Carmen. She jumped and gasped. "How do you explain this?" Daniel said triumphantly. He pointed an accusing finger at the floor.

Carmen did not respond. She simply stared with wide eyes at the pieces scattered across her floor.

"Well?" Daniel said.

Carmen, now standing, looked at Daniel. She nearly shouted her response. "Explain what? Why would you do this?"

"To prove...." Daniel looked down. Empty. He saw nothing but broken ceramic pieces. No rolled-up otter pelt, no bundle of illegal goods, nothing. The figure had been empty. "I don't understand. There should be something inside it. You're using the figures to hide illegal...." Daniel's voice trailed off into silence.

Carmen picked up her phone and dialed. "Come to my office. Bring a spare infant figure, lot N3, and a broom. Oh, and bring Luka." She put the phone down and returned her gaze to Daniel. "Reverend Darrow, my man is coming to replace what you have broken. This is the last replacement you will receive. And," she glanced down at the mess of ceramic on the floor, "your deposit has expired."

Daniel responded with a simple nod. He had arrived with such confidence and hope. Now his emotional state, not to mention his plan, lay shattered on the floor. An awkward silence consumed the room while they waited. After several long minutes, the door opened. Allen walked in. Allen, who had visited Young Hugh at their flat, who had replaced and questioned Daniel about the original broken figure. Allen glanced at the floor, then to Daniel and Carmen. He shrugged and handed the replacement figure to Carmen.

"I see why you asked for a broom," he said as he began to clean up the mess. "Now where's the, ah here you are," he mumbled to himself as he swept. He picked up a broken, though still mostly intact ceramic foot. Turning it over, he found a series of numbers printed on its heel. "N312," he mumbled, unlocking the iPad he had brought with him. He typed the number into a spreadsheet and then tossed the foot onto the other pieces he had swept together in a small mound.

"I also asked for Luka. Reverend Darrow needs someone to show him out," Carmen said.

"Luka's off this morning. After last night, I gave him the morning off. I should have run it by you first."

"That's okay. I know the way out," Daniel said. He took the replacement baby Jesus and stepped past Allen.

"Wait," Allen said. He took the figure and held it up to see its foot. "N319," he said. He handed it back to Daniel and typed the number into his iPad.

Before he could leave, Carmen called out to him. "Reverend Darrow, I do not expect to see you here again." Daniel nodded and made his escape.

Chapter Twenty-Six

"Are you certain you can handle this by yourself?" Reverend Calder asked. She smoothed out the wrinkles on the decorative alter cloth.

"Yes. Finish putting this out, water the flowers. Everything's pretty much done already. I'll mainly be double checking," Daniel said.

"This is our biggest night, and you've seemed," she paused, thinking of the right word, "distracted lately. I'd ask you to pick them up, but—"

"But I don't have a car. Besides, you booked these musicians. They're probably expecting you to greet them when they arrive. Maybe you can have a singalong on the ride to their hotel," Daniel said.

"Oh, do you think? That would be a treat, wouldn't it!" she said in a tone that was serious and hopeful and not at all joking. Daniel smiled and chuckled to himself. For his boss's sake, he hoped these Gaelic singers would be as big a hit with the rest of the congregation as they clearly were with her.

"Don't worry about me. This has my undivided attention. Now go. You don't want to leave them waiting," Daniel assured her.

"Mr. Fisher should be along in a while to help. He's promised a surprise for this eve. See if you can get out of him what it is. I'd prefer not to be surprised on a night like tonight," she said. She left the alter cloth and gave one more glance to the materials for that evening's Christmas Eve service. "Right, I'm off then. You're certain—?"

"Yes," Daniel said, waving her off. She nodded and left him alone. He finished drying a large silver chalice, one of the kirk's more valuable possessions. It was only brought out for the major ecclesial holidays like

Easter, Pentecost, and Christmas. He then retrieved his phone from his pocket. No messages. He tapped the phone's news app. It opened to the last article he had read. He scanned the story again. It was a local newspaper; an opinion article posted the day before. *Loch Ness Murder Accomplice?* the title read. The gist of the article was that Archie Caird's murderer had to have had an accomplice. And if Young Hugh Macpherson was the prime suspect, then the police should be paying more attention to people that are close to him: friends, flatmates. Without naming Daniel specifically, the piece noted that Hugh's flatmate has a clear connection to the Caird family.

The author of the opinion piece was anonymous, but claimed to have intimate knowledge of the investigation. Daniel had his own opinion of who the author might be. The timing of its publication, the day after he had confronted Carmen Oteiza, and its clear implication of himself made it obvious to Daniel, who had written the article. Its purpose was also clear—stop poking around into Carmen's business. Daniel was convinced now more than ever that Carmen was somehow involved in something illegal, possibly deadly. But he was equally perplexed as to the means. For all his speculating, planning, and sneaking around, he was no closer to the truth. So, if Carmen wanted to threaten him, she could go ahead. He needed a break. He wanted to help Young Hugh, he truly did, but he was exhausted from banging his head against the wall.

Tonight's service and Christmas Day tomorrow would provide a welcome distraction. More than a distraction—his job. Reverend Calder had noticed him slipping in his ministerial duties. This was one of the biggest seasons in the kirk's calendar, and she was right. It did need his full attention. So, let Carmen think she had won. Let her think she had intimidated him into leaving well enough alone. He needed some distance and time to clear his head. Then, after Christmas was over, he would look at the case again with fresh eyes.

* * *

The service went off smoothly, beautifully even. A few parishioners jokingly lamented the absence of Oor Willie in the manger display, but all were happy with the festive decorations both inside and out. Daniel had to admit Church Street Kirk did appear especially lovely at this time of year, with the greenery and holly showing off their lively colors against the kirk's yellow-gray stone walls. Fisher and the choir led the congregation in hymn singing. They seemed more put together, less haphazard than usual. Daniel attributed this to the fact that everyone already knew all the traditional Christmas songs, so less practice had been needed. They ended with a rousing medley of hymns in Scots before ceding the stage to Reverend Calder's special guest musicians. That was the surprise he'd promised her – a subtle challenge to her Gaelic singers. Mr. Fisher would not be upstaged.

Mr. and Mrs. Macpherson were present, though Young Hugh was not. That was just as well, given the requirements of his bail and Edna Caird's prominent place in one of the front pews alongside Eliza MacGillivray and her pet rabbit. All the glad tidings and goodwill of the season could not thaw the ice that would have been created from the two of them being in the same room. Ellie was missing as well. She spent the evening with her mother at the Inverness Prison's holiday service. Daniel asked her to send her mother the kirk's love. He missed seeing her, but knew he would be too busy to spend much time with her that day anyway.

They met later on the morning of December 26th at the café on the corner of Church Street. The same café Daniel had sat in days earlier, watching for someone to come switch out the broken baby Jesus figure in the kirk's nativity display. A stakeout that so far had led him to an ill-advised nautical trespass, a midnight jump into the icy waters of the Port, an embarrassing confrontation with Carmen, and a second broken baby Jesus—but no closer to the truth.

This morning, Ellie wore a blue sweater or jumper with a knit snowflake pattern across the chest. Her cinnamon hair was down but mostly covered by a fuzzy, white beanie. When he saw her, Daniel felt self-conscious. They hadn't seen one another in several days, and here she was, beautiful as ever, festive even with her white gloves cradling a bright red mug, steam wafting out the top. He glanced down at his own shirt, a wrinkled button-down.

Between the breaking and entering and Christmas services, he'd had no time to wash a load of laundry. Before he had left that morning, he grabbed the least wrinkled shirt he saw, sprayed an extra puff of cologne, and rushed out the door. He now buttoned his coat to cover the shirt.

They embraced, then Daniel ordered a coffee for himself and joined her at her table.

"How was the service?" Ellie asked.

"It went really well. Record attendance. Reverend Calder's Gaelic singers were a hit," Daniel said. He laughed, "I heard several folks ask why we got rid of the Oor Willie in the manger. I think you might have hit upon a new Church Street Christmas tradition!"

"Ha, and you doubted me!" Ellie said triumphantly. She sipped from her mug. "I wish my mum could've been there. The Christmas service was always her favorite."

"Yes, we missed you both."

"I'm more of a Hogmanay girl myself—more festivity less ceremony."

"How is your mother?" Daniel asked.

"She's...." Ellie nodded but didn't continue. She smiled a close-lipped smile then sighed. "I know it's been over a year, but I'm still not used to seeing her there, in that drab uniform they make the prisoners wear. My mum, a prisoner—it just doesn't fit. I don't know that I'll ever get used to it."

"I don't know that you're supposed to," Daniel said.

Ellie nodded. They each sipped their drinks in silence, watching out the window at the cars driving past. "Speaking of prisoners," Ellie finally said, "looks like Mum might have company soon if things don't progress better for Young Hugh. How is he?"

Now it was Daniel's turn to sigh. Ellie listened with rapt attention, eyes as big as half-pound coins, as he recounted the past few days' exploits.

"Why Reverend Darrow, I'm shocked. I didn't know you had it in you. What happened to the mild-mannered American I knew that was once too scared to even try haggis?"

Remembering it all out loud, Daniel surprised himself. What *had* gotten into him? "I don't know. Must be spending too much time with the likes of you and Young Hugh."

"I don't know if I should feel insulted or flattered," Ellie said.

"Let's go with flattered. And since I'm clearly listening to bad influences lately, do you have any ideas? I can't just give up on Hugh, but I...I'm stuck. Maybe Allen showing up at the flat really was just a coincidence. I think Carmen is a dead-end. Even if she is up to something shady, I can't seem to link her to Hugh or Archie Caird," Daniel said.

Ellie thought for a moment. She gazed out the window again.

"Well?" Daniel asked.

"I'm going to need a refill," she said. "To get my little grey cells firing."

"Poirot?" Daniel asked. He had several of Agatha Christie's Poirot novels on his shelf at home, next to St. Augustine and Wendell Berry. Ellie nodded. "Was he a coffee drinker?"

"Only if it was fully caffeinated," Ellie said with a smile.

Daniel left the table to order her another cup. When he returned, she had her coat on. "You should put that in a takeaway cup," she said.

"Why?" Daniel asked.

"We're going on a trip!"

"We are? Where?"

"Back to the scene of the crime. Back to Loch Ness."

Chapter Twenty-Seven

Once they got out of Inverness, traffic was light on the A82. Ellie sped along at a pace that allowed her to easily overtake the few vehicles that ventured out that morning. On a drive that should have taken at least forty-five minutes, they traveled the length of Loch Ness and arrived at the village of Invermoriston near the loch's far northwestern shore in just over thirty. They stopped for an early lunch at a small café. It had rough white walls and a dark roof in the style of many of the buildings in the village. After lunch, they headed back toward Inverness.

"Does any of this look familiar?" Ellie asked after about a mile.

"I don't know. I thought I'd recognize it on the way down, but then we hit that little village and, well, I don't know," Daniel said.

"I'm not complaining. I was hungry, and the scenery is nice, but the plan didn't include driving up and down the loch all afternoon."

"It can't be too far. It was near the mouth of a river," Daniel said. He stared past her out the driver's side window. Trees and water rushed past. "Wait, slow down. I think this is it."

Ellie slowed and searched for a place to pull off the road. The shoulder was narrow, taken up by either guardrail or trees. She eventually found a place past the guardrail where the foliage wasn't too thick. The ground sloped steeply, so she was not able to get as far off the road as she preferred to avoid traffic. "Are you sure? This isn't exactly a proper parking space," she said after they exited the car.

"Yes, back that way. I remember that little cottage," Daniel said. He jumped back from the road as a car sped past, honking.

"Be careful! They almost hit you."

"I'm okay," Daniel said

"I was talking to my car," Ellie said. She opened the door and switched on the hazard lights.

"Ouch," Daniel said, holding his hand to his heart. "Coming out here was your idea, remember."

"One I'm beginning to regret."

They walked back past the cottage Daniel had remembered seeing the first time he'd been there. Though it had only been a couple weeks, it felt like ages had passed since that day when he had joined Young Hugh and a few other men from the kirk for their private memorial for Archie Caird. Daniel led Ellie across the road, through a line of trees, and down the hill to the loch. The water was calm, with few boats out. Its deep blue surface reflected the gray clouds overhead, giving the water a silvery hue. Daniel looked up and down the shore, trying to get his bearings. He heard the rush of the River Moriston opening into the loch and headed in its direction.

He couldn't find the place where the youth's campfire had been. He stopped at a spot that felt familiar, but he couldn't be sure. Enough time had passed for the fire's ashy remnants to have washed away. Daniel and Ellie progressed on toward the mouth of the river. On another day, in the summer, with a clear sky and bright sun and small tour boats crisscrossing the loch, this would have been a pleasant, relaxing walk, romantic even. They could have strolled hand-in-hand, stopped and tossed small stones into the water, or spread out a picnic on the soft green turf. Today, they walked stiffly along the rough line where the dormant grass met the rocky, sandy shore, careful not to step into a freezing puddle or slick patch of mud. Their hands shoved deep inside their respective coat pockets for warmth.

They stopped when they reached three large, oblong rocks that formed a line pointing toward the center of the loch. The farthest of the three appeared shorter, deeper, though there was no way to tell its true size from the shore. Gentle waves lapped against it and left a wide crown of ice on its surface.

"Is this where they found him?" Ellie asked.

Daniel nodded. He imagined Archie Caird's body, the waves pushing and pulling at him, though never able to dislodge him from the crevasse between the two nearer rocks. His body held in a kind of purgatory between the land and the loch. Daniel walked around to the other side of the nearest rock. He wasn't sure exactly what he was looking for—something the police investigators might have overlooked, some key that might unlock the mystery of Caird's death and save Young Hugh. But the rocks revealed no secrets. They stood, silent, as they had for centuries, unmoved by all the unrest around them save the gentle steady crash of waves against their weathered edges.

"Anything?" Ellie asked. She joined Daniel by the nearest rock. The wind had picked up since they first reached the shore. She stood close to him. He put his arm around her and shook his head.

"Looks like a normal lake to me. I don't know what we were expecting to find. If the police did miss something, it's probably washed away by now," Daniel said.

Ellie's gaze followed the three rocks out to the center of the vast loch. The water stretched northeast back toward Inverness as far as her eyes could see, meeting the horizon, seemingly without end. "Let's keep looking. We already made the drive out here," she said. "What else are we going to do?"

"Go back to that warm little café for some hot chocolate?" Daniel said. Ellie smiled. She rested her head on his shoulder in a kind of embrace that allowed her to keep her hands inside her coat pockets.

"Come on," she said, nodding toward the rocks. They approached as close as they dared, not wanting to get their shoes wet. It would be a long drive home with wet, frozen feet. Neither Ellie nor Daniel saw anything of note, so they expanded their search. They walked up and down the rocky, sandy shore. Daniel wished he had worn rubber boots rather than his thin-soled sneakers. His toes were going numb. They searched the grassy area between the shore and the tree line. Nothing.

"Okay, I'm ready for that hot chocolate now," Ellie said.

"Giving up?" Daniel asked.

"Coming here was a long shot. You were right. It was daft to think we could find anything the professionals couldn't."

Daniel nodded and sighed. "What are we going to tell Young Hugh?"

Ellie shrugged. "Perhaps we can regroup at your flat and come up with something. Three heads are better than one."

"Are they, though? So far, our three heads have only gotten me jumping into a freezing ocean and now trudging around a frozen beach," Daniel said.

"Perhaps we need more than three. Any chance you've made any detective friends at Church Street?"

Daniel thought of the most likely candidates: Mr. Tweed with his connections to the movers and shakers of Inverness, Eliza MacGillivray and her uncanny prophecies, William MacCrivag and Philip Morrison. They all seemed to favor the late Archie Caird over Young Hugh. Even Mr. MacCrivag, who had liked Hugh as a youth, had finally come around to accepting his guilt. *No*, Daniel shook his head. No help for Young Hugh would come from Church Street.

He picked up a pound coin-sized stone and tossed it into the loch. The ripples circled out from where it impacted the water, but were quickly overtaken by the waves. Daniel turned and started up the hill.

"Wait," he said.

"Did you see something?" Ellie asked.

"No, but I just remembered something from the last time I was here. Not quite the cuddly animals you're used to at the clinic, but I think you'll like it."

Ellie gave him a suspicious look.

"It's cool, really. Should be just over there," Daniel pointed with his chin. He led Ellie back to the edge of the water. They walked a few yards past the three rocks, toward the mouth of the River Moriston. Daniel got as close to the water as he could without actually stepping in. He squinted, peering through to the bottom until the incline became too steep and the water too dark. "I remember them being somewhere here," he said. He walked on another couple yards.

"What are you looking for?" Ellie asked, not venturing as close to the frigid water.

Daniel leaned toward the water and looked. He stood and scratched his head. "I could have sworn they were here," he said. He looked down the shore. "This is too far. Maybe I missed it." He walked back slowly, splashing through the edge of the water, his gaze focused several feet out.

"Daniel, what are you doing? Come back. You'll catch a cold or frostbite out there!" Ellie said.

Daniel ignored here. He continued, ankle deep in the water, until he reached the three rocks. "Where are they? I don't understand," he said.

Ellie reached for his arm and pulled him back up the shore. "Where are what? What are you looking for?"

"The mussels. They're gone."

"Mussels?"

"There was a whole colony of them. Colony—is that what it's called? Anyway, a bunch of them, just past these rocks. I saw them when I was here last with some men from the kirk. Young Hugh found it actually. He'd wandered off from the group, and we found him staring into the water. Mr. Morrison reached in and grabbed one. He pried it open just a sliver, and you could see a tiny pearl growing inside. It was really interesting. I wanted to show you," Daniel said.

"Mussels in freshwater? Those are fairly rare, endangered in Scotland. You're not supposed to disturb them," Ellie said.

Daniel grimaced. "Oh, he tossed it back. I guess it was okay, because they seem to have all swam away now."

"Mussels don't swim away. They're filter feeders. Once they're settled into a spot, they stay there," Ellie said.

"So?"

"So, if you saw a colony of mussels, they would still be there."

"But they're not. Unless... Do you think someone would take them?"

"That would be illegal." Ellie shrugged. "You said you saw a pearl inside one? People have been known to do worse things for a lot less."

"Like murder?" Daniel asked. He heard Eliza MacGillivray's scratchy old voice in his head: *The time has come, tis already past when, through a fog on the silt muddled burn, a pearl from white to blood red shall turn.*

Chapter Twenty-Eight

Ellie drove up the A82 back toward Inverness. Daniel sat in the passenger seat. Shortly after they'd started back, after the car had heated up, he took off his shoes. He pressed his wet feet close to the floor heating vent. His toes tingled as warmth began to return to them.

"And you are certain mussels wouldn't just swim away?" he asked.

"No way," she said, shaking her head.

"So, someone had to have taken them. Sometime after Archie Caird was killed, after our little memorial even." Daniel sighed. He stared out the window as they sped past the length of Loch Ness. The sky had turned a darker shade of gray. He wondered if it might rain soon, or snow.

"He must have known," Daniel said.

"What?" Ellie asked.

"Archie Caird. He must have known about the mussel colony and the pearls, and that's why he was killed."

"You really think so? Seems a bit of a stretch," Ellie said.

"He was a wilderness guide, right? That's how he made his living. If anyone knew about the mussels it would be someone like Caird."

"Okay, I'll give you that. He could have known about them, but how do you get from a wilderness guide knowing about some small part of the wilderness to him being killed?"

"Maybe he was in debt and needed some quick cash. He could've tried to sell the pearls," Daniel said.

Ellie considered Daniel's theory for a moment. They had traveled about half the length of the loch. She saw a sign for Urquhart Castle. "Look," she said, nodding to the window. "Do you remember?"

Daniel smiled. How could he forget? The ruined castle perched on the edge of the loch had been the site of their first kiss. He thought back to that afternoon over a year ago. The sky was clear, but a wall of dark clouds sat ready on the horizon. They had met only a few times previously, and their introduction had not gone so well. Sir Walter had yowled and hissed the entire trip to Ellie's clinic, and once there, Daniel had stumbled over his words and managed to turn a compliment into an insult. Still, for some reason he had yet to fully comprehend, Ellie had agreed to see him again and later invited him out to Loch Ness. Perhaps it was only sympathy or hospitality toward one recently immigrated. Daniel remembered walking with her through the broken stone outlines of the castle's once grand halls and rooms. The storm clouds steadily advanced and then let loose their store in a sudden downpour. Daniel and Ellie took refuge under the half-exposed castle tower. He was soaked and cold but full of nervous energy. Their bodies were so close, holding on to one another out of surprise and for warmth. Their hands met, then their eyes, then lips.

"Should we pull in and have another visit? Looks like it might rain," Daniel said.

Ellie laughed. "I don't know that it would even be open today. Besides, it's too cold. I thought you wanted hot chocolate."

"You're right. Who needs a romantic kiss under the shelter of an old castle? Hot chocolate would be way better."

"Ha ha. Perhaps you should give up the preaching gig and go into comedy," Ellie said. She gave Daniel a playful jab in the arm. They drove on for several more minutes. "I don't know," she said.

"Huh?"

"About what you said earlier. About Archie Caird selling the pearls. Not every mussel has a pearl inside it. There could've been loads there, or you could've seen the only one. It's certainly not a sure way to make money. And even if he did find enough pearls, how would he sell them? It's not exactly legal."

"Well, I do know someone who deals in illegal animal products," Daniel said.

"Of course! Carmen Oteiza. Did you see any pearls on her boat when you and Young Hugh snuck onboard?"

"No, but then we didn't have a lot of time to look around," Daniel said.

"But why would Carmen want to kill Caird if he was her supplier?" Ellie asked.

"Maybe Caird and Carmen had a falling out and when Carmen needed him out of the picture, she set up Hugh to take the fall?"

"You think she could kill someone? She seemed a bit of a tart when we met her at the pub, but a killer?" Ellie asked.

"She puts on the charm at first, but believe me. She can be, well, scary. If she couldn't kill someone herself, I could see her ordering someone else to do it."

Ellie looked at Daniel with wide eyes, "You're still assuming Young Hugh was set up. She could have ordered him to kill Caird."

"No, surely not," Daniel said. "Anyway, Hugh wouldn't do that. He may not have the best reputation, but we know Hugh; he's not a killer."

"How well do we know him, though?"

"You really think he could have killed Caird?"

Ellie turned her eyes back to the road. "No, I suppose not. This is all just speculation. We don't even know if Caird and Carmen knew one another. All we know for sure is that there was a colony of mussels near where his body was found, and now there's not."

"I agree. We need to find out more about Caird's business. Was he doing okay? Did he need to supplement his income with a little under-the-table help from Carmen?" Daniel retrieved his mobile phone from his pocket. He held it up to the car window. "Not the best reception out here."

"Who are you calling?"

"Someone I should have called a long time ago."

* * *

Ellie stopped in front of a one-story house on the western side of Inverness.

176

The house was on their way, near the A82, giving its residents easy access to the wilder parts of the Highlands. "Are you sure you don't want me to come with you?" she asked.

"No, this is something I need to do alone. Besides, I don't want any hostility toward me deflecting onto you. My last encounter with her wasn't exactly, how would you put it? Cordial?" Daniel said.

"Are you good to get home?"

"We passed a bus stop not too far back," Daniel said. He gave her a quick kiss goodbye and exited the car. He walked up the sidewalk to the front door, turned around, and waved.

Ellie mouthed, *"Good luck,"* waved, and drove away.

Daniel pressed the doorbell. He waited, shivering in his still damp shoes. He did not expect a warm welcome. Edna Caird opened the door. She wore a dark green dress and a plaid wool shawl around her shoulders. "Reverend, do come in," she said. She ushered him down a short entry hall and into her living room. Two plush armchairs sat beside one another opposite a flatscreen television. A bookshelf stood against another wall. Daniel glanced at its contents. *Top Highland Hill Walks, The Great Glen Way: A Guide, Birds of Scotland.* Various other travel and nature books lined its shelves. Mrs. Caird motioned for him to sit. "Will you be staying long enough for tea?" she asked. Daniel nodded. "Milk, sugar?"

"Um, yes, thank you," Daniel stammered. He was thrown off by her hospitality. He didn't expect her to leave him out in the cold, but neither did her presume this. He wondered if she was being genuine or simply playing the expected role of courteous host.

"I was surprised to receive your call," she said as she walked into another room, presumably the kitchen.

"Yes, I should have stopped by much sooner. I'm sorry it's taken me this long. It was—" Daniel stopped. He realized he was talking to an empty room and unless he wanted to shout, he should wait until she returned. He felt strange sitting alone in someone else's living room. He glanced around absently at the bookshelf and the framed photographs on the wall. Most contained images of Edna and Archie standing together in front of some dramatic nature scene—a waterfall, mountain summit, or deep valley. Daniel fidgeted in his chair. When was she coming back? He felt like a naughty kid waiting outside the principal's office. Was she trying to make him nervous?

After several minutes, she returned with two cups of tea. She gave one to Daniel and took the other to her seat in the chair next to him. "You were saying you should have popped in earlier?"

She has sharp ears, Daniel thought. "Um, yes. You came up to me after church weeks ago, asking for help, and, well, I feel like I've let you down."

"Humph," Mrs. Caird nodded. "So, you've finally come to your senses about the Macpherson boy?"

"Not exactly, though I did think about telling you that I had. I thought it would make this easier. But I figured you'd see through that, and it wouldn't be right to lie to you," Daniel said. He looked away, tested his tea. It was still too hot. He really had considered lying to her about Young Hugh. But if Hugh truly was innocent, then enough lies had already been spoken about him; one more wouldn't help.

"The truth is, Mrs. Caird, I still believe, or hope at least that Young Hugh is innocent. But that's no excuse for how I've avoided you lately. If I'm being completely honest, I've been afraid to talk to you. Afraid that if we talked in any depth, that you might confirm beyond a doubt what everyone else has already concluded about him—that he is guilty. Still, I shouldn't have let my affection for Hugh stop me from being there for you. Especially after you'd asked me for help."

Daniel tried his tea again. It scalded his tongue, but he took another sip anyway. He needed the distraction.

"I'm here now, though, and I can only hope I'm not too late. I hope that you can be a bigger person than I could," he said.

Edna Caird considered his words and nodded. "I must say I do not appreciate being forced into a position of being the better person. That really should be your job, Reverend." She sighed. "The kirk does teach forgiveness, so I suppose I must try."

"Thank you," Daniel said. He wondered if her charitable spirit might extend to Young Hugh as well, but he decided not to press her. "As long as

I'm on an honest streak here, I have one more confession. I just came from Loch Ness."

"Because of Archie?"

Daniel nodded. "It was a Hail Mary pass to try and help Young Hugh. I thought maybe I could discover something that might lead to another reason for Mr. Caird's death."

"Hail Mary, Reverend?" Mrs. Caird asked.

"Oh, sorry, like in football, um American football. It's a last hope kind of play."

"And did Saint Mary answer? Did you find anything?"

"Yes, well, maybe. It's more like I *didn't* find something," Daniel said. Mrs. Caird frowned and sipped her tea. Daniel explained the disappearance of the mussel colony. "Do you think Mr. Caird would have known about them? The colony, I mean. Not their disappearance. That would've happened after...."

"After he was killed," Mrs. Caird finished Daniel's faltering sentence. Daniel nodded. "If anyone would have known about them, it would be my Archie. He knew these hills like the back of his hand. His last tour was around Loch Ness. Did you know that?"

"I didn't. How *was* the wilderness guide business, if you don't mind me asking? I know that can be a touchy subject for people, but with Mr. Caird's passing, I mean, the kirk can help out a little," Daniel said.

"Oh, no. It's kind of you to offer, but I'll be fine. You know I'm not too proud to ask for help," Mrs. Caird said with a wink. "Archie had a rather good insurance policy. And before, business was actually booming. Archie was even talking about hiring another guide to expand."

So, Archie Caird didn't need to steal the pearls, Daniel thought. *But if he didn't need them, who did?*

"You said his last tour was at Loch Ness?" Daniel asked.

"Aye. Not quite one of his most exotic adventures, but then not too many people want an exotic adventure this time of year. At least not in the Highlands."

"Do you still have any information about that trip?"

179

"Still trying to save the Macpherson boy?"

Daniel shrugged.

"Dear Saint Jude," Mrs. Caird said, shaking her heard.

"Who?"

"Patron saint of lost causes," she said. "Let me check Archie's desk. He kept all his files there." She stood and left the room. She returned several minutes later carrying a file folder. She handed it to Daniel.

December, Loch Ness, Day Tour, Daniel read on the title tab. He opened the folder. It contained a map with a highlighted route over the north side of the loch, including Urquhart Castle and the Invermoriston Falls. Daniel noted the spot where the River Moriston emptied into Loch Ness. Archie Caird's tour would have passed right by the mussel colony, right by the place his body would later be found. Daniel flipped to another page: the itinerary noting the start and end of the tour and the times spent at various points of interest along the way. Daniel quickly scanned the page. There it was! Just before the stop at the Falls. 2:00 pm *Unique Flora and Fauna of Loch Ness: Scotch Pines, Deer, Red Squirrels, Golden Eagle, Freshwater Mussels, Nessie?* Daniel turned to the next page: *Tour Manifest.* He held the page, looking over the names. He now had a list of suspects with their respective contact information, neatly typed and alphabetized. One name near the top of the list stood out to him.

"Can I keep this?" he asked Mrs. Caird.

Chapter Twenty-Nine

Daniel Darrow sat near the front of the Number 19 bus headed toward the Inverness City Center. He held the Tour Manifest page of the file that Edna Caird had given him. The list consisted of couples, family groups, and a few singles. Altogether, ten adults and four children had been with Archie Caird on his last wilderness tour. Daniel dismissed the names with non-UK contact information: a family of four from the US, a Korean couple, and one German. While not inconceivable, Daniel figured they would have had the least opportunity to return days after Caird's death to retrieve the mussels. Of the seven remaining names, two were children. Strike those. Five names were left. Five people with a connection to Caird and potential knowledge of the mussels. But which of those five also knew Carmen Oteiza?

Daniel was currently on his way to see the first of the five. *I might as well mark one more off the list before getting serious about the final four*, he thought. The bus let him off on Church Street. He found Mr. Fisher outside of the kirk, fumbling about in the nativity display. "Mr. Fisher," Daniel called. "I was hoping I'd find you here."

"Reverend Darrow?" Fisher said, surprised. He stepped out from behind a sixth ceramic wiseman. *Had he added another since Christmas?* Daniel had lost count. With such a crowded menagerie, who could tell?

"Fisher, what are you doing back there?"

"Ah, just checking on my figures. Some are loaners, and I want to make certain they're all in good order," Fisher said. He squeezed past two camels.

"But Christmas is over. This whole display should be coming down soon."

"Exactly! And when that company you hired—Oteiza, right? When they pop by to take it all away, I don't want them taking more than what's theirs. With the trouble we've had over those teens stealing our infant Jesus, I had to double-check my own pieces, didn't I."

"We don't know it was teenagers that took the figure," Daniel said, feeling a twinge of guilt for allowing some nonexistent *teenagers* to take the blame for his own theft. "But it all got resolved. We got the replacement before Christmas. I take your point, though. How can you tell which ones are yours? Besides the obvious ones?" He nodded to a plastic donkey wearing a colorful Mexican blanket on its back.

"The ones you ordered all have these codes on 'em," Fisher said. He picked up a sheep and flipped it upside down to reveal the small string of numbers on its belly. Daniel nodded. He'd seen that before in Carmen's office—right after he'd smashed the baby Jesus figure to pieces. He wished he could forget it. "Mine don't have those, but I'm making a list of what's mine just in case. One can never be too careful," Fisher said. He returned the sheep and began looking over one of the cows. "Did you need something? I'll have Sunday's music list to you and Reverend Calder by Friday. I want to review a couple hymns tonight at practice first."

"Oh, that'll be fine," Daniel said. He hadn't even begun making notes for a sermon yet. "I actually stopped by to ask you about something else. You went on a tour with Archie Caird before he died, right?"

"Huh?" Fisher was on his hands and knees, trying to get a look at the underside of the ceramic camel.

"Loch Ness?"

"Aye, that's right. A good man, Archie."

"Can you tell me about the tour? Did you notice anything unusual about it? Or the people?"

"People are always a bit unusual, aren't they, Reverend," Fisher said. He grunted as he stood. He leaned on the camel's back. "The tour itself was normal I suppose. We all met at the carpark near Tomnahurich, you know, the auld cemetery hill. Archie loaded us up in his tour van and drove down the A82 to Loch Ness. We lunched at Urquhart Castle, had a wee boat ride round the castle searching for Nessie. The usual tourist stuff."

Daniel thought of Eliza MacGillivray's prophesy, the one she'd appropriated from the ancient Brahan Seer: *The time will come, and it is not far off, when full-rigged ships will be seen sailing eastward and westward by the back of Tomnahurich, near Inverness.* A tour bus wasn't exactly a full-rigged ship, but there was that name again – *Tomnahurich.*

"Why did you go on that tour? Surely you've been to Loch Ness before," Daniel asked.

"Archie and I had a wee bet over a rugby match. He never liked wagering actual money, so I took my winnings in the form of a free day tour. It'd been ages since I'd been to the loch, and without my job at the school, I had nothing better to do. I got two free meals out of it, didn't I."

"Mr. Caird pointed out the local wildlife too. Did he show y'all that colony of freshwater mussels?" Daniel asked.

"Mussels? Aye, Archie pointed them out. Not that interesting if you ask me. We spied some red squirrels and a golden eagle. Now that was a sight! Golden eagles are quite rare. But no Nessie. I recall Archie mentioning something about the water being too muddy or murky that day."

"Was it the same colony of mussels that Hugh Macpherson found near the shore when we went for Caird's memorial?"

"Is that what this is about? You're still trying to clear Young Hugh? I like the lad, and I'd be the first to come to his defense, if I thought he had a defense. But you've got to look at the facts, Reverend. I'm afraid he's a lost cause," Fisher said.

That's what everyone keeps saying, Daniel thought. "The mussels are gone now."

"Huh," Fisher thought for a moment. "Fish are prone to swim around. I wouldn't think they'd stick to one place for too long."

"Mussels aren't fish, though. They don't swim off. They should still be there."

Fisher shrugged. "This marine trivia is fascinating, Reverend, but I must be getting back to cataloguing my animals here. I want to have it done before Oteiza comes to pack it all up. Do you know when that might be?"

Daniel shook his head. He thanked Fisher and started the walk down Church Street toward his flat. One more complication added to his plate. Carmen Oteiza would be packing up and leaving town soon. If she was involved in Caird's death, as he suspected, and she left before he could figure out how, Young Hugh would be lost for sure.

* * *

Ellie met Daniel and Young Hugh at their flat in Bellfield Park. She carried two bags with *Auld Lang Naan* printed across their fronts. Daniel opened the door for her and led her inside. Young Hugh was already seated at the table with fork and knife in hand. When the bags were opened, the room filled with the scents of fried rice, cardamom, turmeric, spicy peppers, and of course, hot buttered naan. Young Hugh greedily scooped rice and two different curries onto his plate. "Mmm, cheers. I forgot how good that place is," he said to Ellie through a mouthful of naan. He swallowed. "I feel like this is a kind of last meal for me."

"With any luck, that's what we're trying to prevent," Daniel said.

"Scotch is in the cupboard there," Young Hugh said.

"None of that tonight. We need our wits about us," Ellie said. "If you recall, your last whiskey-fueled plan did not go so well!"

"But, my last meal?" Hugh said sheepishly.

"She's got a point. I don't fancy another midnight jump into the harbor any time soon," Daniel said.

"Fine, then let's get to it. What's our next move?" Hugh asked.

"Here's what we've worked out so far," Daniel said. "Fact one: Carmen Oteiza's holiday display business is a front. What she's really selling is illegal animal products. Which, come to think of it, should make her display rental fees much cheaper, but I digress. Fact two: Archie Caird was an expert in Scottish wildlife. If anyone could supply her with illegal trade, it would be him."

"But he was murdered," Hugh said.

"Which brings us to fact three," Ellie said. "Caird's business was in wilderness tours, so any of his clients could be a suspect. They would know what he knew."

"Caird's tours were popular. Half of Scotland would be suspect," Hugh said.

"Ah, but we don't need to question half of Scotland. We just need to talk to those that went on his last tour," Daniel said.

"Why them?" Hugh asked.

"Because they were the only other ones who would have known about the freshwater mussels," Ellie said.

"Okay, I follow you, but how are we supposed to know who was on Caird's last tour?" Hugh asked.

Daniel held up his finger as if to say, "Hold that thought." He stood and walked to his bedroom. He returned a minute later carrying a manilla folder. He moved a bowl of curry over to make room on the table and pulled out the Tour Manifest page.

"What's this?" Hugh asked.

"Take a look," Daniel felt like Santa passing out presents on Christmas morning. Hugh and Ellie leaned in to examine the paper.

"Is this what I think it is?" Ellie asked. Daniel nodded proudly. "How'd you get this?"

Daniel told them about his conversation with Edna Caird and Mr. Fisher.

"Great, one down, only four more names to go. Looks like two of them don't live in Inverness. It could take some time to track them all down," Hugh said. He ripped off another piece of naan for himself. He chewed the corner, thinking. "If we're right about Carmen's involvement, we might not have that much time. With Christmas over, she's sure to be off soon. I'd be surprised if she hasn't already started taking down the larger displays around town."

Daniel nodded. "So whatever we're going to do, we need to do it soon." On his earlier walk home from Church Street Kirk, he had hatched a plan. Or at least incubated one. "Have you ever heard of the trial of Susanna?"

Ellie and Hugh shook their heads.

"Well, I think it's time we set our own trap."

Chapter Thirty

"Set a trap?" Young Hugh asked.

"Yes," Daniel said. "On my way home this afternoon, I called Carmen to see when she would be taking down the nativity scene at Church Street. And you're right, Hugh, they've already started on some of the bigger displays across the city. But as you know, they're a small operation, and we have a fairly small display, so we're farther down on their priority list. She couldn't give me an exact date, but she said it would definitely be by the end of next weekend. Today's Wednesday, so that gives us just over a week, possibly less."

"That's not much time," Ellie said.

Daniel nodded. "It would be hard enough tracking down all the names on Mr. Caird's tour manifest in that amount of time. And even if we could, it's doubtful one of them would just come out and confess to killing Caird and smuggling freshwater pearls to Carmen. But...." Daniel paused for dramatic effect. Ellie and Hugh had stopped eating to hear him continue. He took a drink. He felt he had a clever plan, or at least the beginnings of one, and he wanted to enjoy the suspense for a moment. Ellie sensed this and allowed him a second drink, before tilting her head and giving him a stare that told him he'd indulged himself long enough—*get on with it already*.

"Okay, we can't get to all these people one at a time, but what if we could get them all together in one place at the same time?" Daniel finally said. He waited for his friends' wide-eyed acknowledgment as the brilliance of his plan dawned on them. Instead, he got scrunched brows and head-scratching. Hugh stood up to get a glass of water from the kitchen.

"How are we going to do that?" Ellie asked.

"I'm still working on that part," Daniel admitted.

"So that was the whole plan? Get them together somehow?" Ellie asked. Daniel shrugged and chewed on a piece of naan so he wouldn't have to continue.

Young Hugh returned and sat down. "Too bad ol' Mr. Caird isn't still around to put on another tour for them. But I suppose if he were, then I wouldn't be in this mess."

"Hugh, you're a genius!" Daniel said.

"Huh?"

"Another tour! That's how we get them all together in one place. We know they like wilderness tours. That's the one thing they all have in common," Daniel said.

Hugh returned a puzzled look. Daniel's fledgling plan had yet to convince him. "But Caird is dead. How can he give another tour?"

Ellie put her silverware down and leaned back in her chair. Hugh opened his mouth to speak, but she held up her finger. She had the seed of an idea that she did not want to lose. "Archie Caird can't give a tour, but that doesn't mean *Caird Highlands Adventures* can't," she said.

"How do you mean?" Daniel asked.

"Mrs. Caird told you Archie had been thinking of expanding, right? Well, what if *we* were that expansion? It would look suspicious if some random reverend or veterinary student or, no offense, Hugh, suspected murderer, invited these people back together. But if Caird Highlands Adventures sent out an invitation...."

"Like a promotion? A free day tour to past guests to get the business going again after Archie's death," Daniel jumped in.

"Exactly!" Ellie said.

"But you're both overlooking one thing," Hugh said. "None of us are wilderness guides. I can't even leave this flat. Even if I could, I wouldn't know the first thing about showing people wildlife."

"Most of the animals that I see are domestic. And I don't have to go out and find them. They come to me," Ellie admitted.

"I may know someone who can help us in that department," Daniel said.

* * *

Daniel and Ellie sat in a rented passenger van near the back of a mostly empty carpark. Tomnahurich Hill loomed behind them, mossy brown with a veil of lingering snow on its top. "It's quite pretty in the spring and summer," Ellie said, looking out the rearview mirror.

"Hmm?" Daniel asked. He was looking at his phone, checking and rechecking the recent calls.

"The hill there. When it's green, it's really quite pretty."

"Mmhmm."

"Are you even listening to me?"

"Yes, sorry. The hill?" Daniel said.

"Mr. MacCrivag's not exactly known for his punctuality. Are you sure it was a good idea enlisting him? Young Hugh's fate is on the line here and, well—"

"They're here!" Daniel said. He nodded toward the entrance of the carpark. A little green sedan pulled in. Daniel opened the door, leaned out, and waved. The sedan pulled into a spot beside him. William MacCrivag got out. He wore his puffy black coat that made him look like a bald penguin. Philip Morrison followed. He wore a thick, tan, oilskin coat and matching hat.

"Thank you so much for coming. I know it was a long trip," Daniel said. He greeted the two men. Ellie waved from inside the van.

"Smart lass. It's freezing out," William MacCrivag said, waving into the window.

"You always think it's freezing. Tis a fine Scottish winter's day, it is," Philip Morrison said. He breathed in dramatically. Mr. MacCrivag huffed and stuffed his hands deep into his coat pockets.

"You look great, Mr. Morrison. A natural wilderness guide," Daniel said.

"Ta. Anything for Archie. Though I was surprised when you called. Reviving the business?" Philip Morrison said.

"Since you helped with Caird's Hebridean tours, you're just the man for the job. But we're only pretending to revive the business," Daniel corrected.

"Right, right."

"Did you bring the other thing I asked?"

Philip Morrison nodded. He patted the car's trunk. "Willie wouldn't let me keep 'em up front."

"It's bad enough smelling up my boot. Why'd we have to haul these things again?" William MacCrivag asked. He unlocked the trunk. Daniel saw a red cooler inside. Philip Morrison nodded. Daniel opened the lid. He winced at the smell. Mr. MacCrivag wasn't exaggerating. Dozens of black-shelled mussels lay inside, surrounded by ice.

"These are the bait," Daniel said.

"The best mussels in the Hebrides," Mr. Morrison said. "Scrubbed clean like you asked. But they're saltwater, not fresh."

Daniel picked one up, examined it, and returned it to the cooler. "Looks the same to me."

"That's why *I'm* the wilderness guide," Philip Morrison said. Daniel laughed and nodded.

"And they're not quite alive anymore," Mr. Morrison said.

"That's fine. Ellie insisted that if we went along with this plan, we use sterile, dead mussels. She didn't want to accidentally contaminate the local environment. Makes sense. We don't want to create another problem on top of the one we're trying to solve," Daniel said.

"Ah, now we know who's the brains of this operation," Mr. MacCrivag said.

"It's a joint collaboration," Daniel said.

"Sure it is, lad." Mr. MacCrivag gave Daniel a consoling pat on the back. "Now, let's get on with this before we're as frozen as those mussels." He handed Daniel the keys to his car. "Be careful with her. You're not driving, are you?"

"You've never even seen me drive," Daniel said. He knocked on the van's window. Ellie got out, and he tossed her the keys. Mr. MacCrivag hurried to take her place in the van.

Ellie pulled away from Tomnahurich Hill in Mr. MacCrivag's little green sedan. Daniel cranked up the heater, but even on high, it could not match that of the van they had just left. They crossed the River Ness and followed its southwesterly track across the Highlands. Before long, they could see the southern shore of Loch Ness. As they drove on, Daniel watched out the window. He hoped to see Urquhart Castle from the other shore, but the loch was too wide. Between the bare branches of the trees lining the road, he could make out the hilly northern shore, but no castle tower. Ellie slowed and turned into a side road marked by a small sign reading Inverfarigaig. They stopped at the nearby car park. Like Invermoriston on the northern shore where the freshwater mussel colony had been, Inverfarigaig sat at the mouth of a river feeding into the loch. The River Farigaig was smaller and lacked a tourist attracting waterfall. The relative seclusion of the place, though, made it perfect for their plan.

Daniel pulled the red cooler out of the trunk. He followed Ellie to a place on the river they had picked out the day before. The cooler's bulk made it difficult for him to see his footing. He slipped twice, though never fell. His rubber mud boots were stiff and did not fit as snuggly as his trainers, despite his donning two pairs of socks that morning. He sat the cooler down by the water's edge, where the bank was shallow, and the water made a small, calm eddy before continuing downstream.

"I'll be glad to get rid of these. I feel like their smell is permeating through all the layers of my clothes," Daniel said. He lifted the lid and pulled out one of the mussels. "Is there a particular way we should put them in?"

Ellie picked one out of the cooler. She stepped into the water a couple feet and placed the mussel in the sand. "On its side, kind of tilted up like this. They should look like they're ready to open to filter feed." Daniel placed his mussel next to hers in a similar position. Ellie placed another one. "Push 'em in a little so they won't float away. The water's calm here, but just to be safe."

"With any luck, they won't have to stay here too long," Daniel said. He placed two more and stood back to observe their progress. He chuckled.

"What?" Ellie asked.

"Nothing, just a silly thought."

190

"Tell me."

"This reminds me of the nativity scene at Church Street. Setting up an elaborate display for tourists. I was thinking of the weird aquatic extras Mr. Fisher would want to add. Some salmon, an octopus or two."

"Are you sure it was a good idea to leave him out of this plan? He was the only one of us that actually went on one of Archie Caird's tours. That could be helpful," Ellie said.

"Yeah, but I don't want him acting unusual. I don't know how good of an actor he is. Fisher has a habit of making everything about himself. I imagine if we let him in on our plan here, he'd want to play the part of tour guide himself," Daniel said.

"True. He'd especially hate being upstaged by the likes of William MacCrivag and Philip Morrison," Ellie laughed.

They continued arranging the artificial mussel colony until six mussels remained in the cooler. Daniel opened a pocket knife he had brought with him. He placed the blade at the lip of one of the mussel shells, wedged it in, and twisted. "Mr. Morrison made this look so easy," he said.

"Careful not to break it. It doesn't need to be opened all the way," Ellie said. She pulled a small bag out of her pocket. "Here, see if this will fit."

Daniel put down his knife and took the pearl from her hand. He held it up to the sun's light for a better look. He rolled it around between his fingers. "We did a good job on these. You can't tell where we filled in the hole unless you knew what to look for. I'd think it was real," he said.

"You couldn't tell these mussels from freshwater either," Ellie said.

"Is there really that much of a difference?"

"The pearls are a little big, but these are the smallest pet ID trackers the clinic has," Ellie said.

Daniel pried open the shell a little more and shoved the pearl inside. "I think the bigger size makes them more appealing to a would-be poacher."

"You're such a man," Ellie said, rolling her eyes.

Daniel inserted a tracking pearl in each of the remaining five mussels. He placed them with the others in the river but closer to the shore, where they could be easily picked up.

"Now we wait."

Chapter Thirty-One

Daniel Darrow and Ellie Gray had the rest of the day to fill together. Ellie had the day off from the veterinary clinic, and Daniel's work at the kirk had slowed down after the Christmas service. There wasn't much to do around Loch Ness other than explore the loch itself, but they didn't want to risk running into Mr. Morrison's tour. The parking area by the mouth of the River Farigaig only had room for a few vehicles. Fisher would surely notice Mr. MacCrivag's little green sedan there, so Ellie drove them back into Inverness. They spent the afternoon at the Eastgate Shopping Center, milling about the large indoor mall, looking out for after-Christmas sales. Around four in the afternoon, before sunset, they headed back to the carpark by Tomnahurich Hill, where they had met with Morrison and MacCrivag earlier that morning. The tour was set to return soon.

Ellie parked between two larger vehicles some distance from where their rented tour van was supposed to drop off their suspects, or clients. At four thirty on the dot, the white van rolled into the back of the carpark. "Mr. Morrison must be driving," Ellie remarked. Daniel squinted to see how many people unloaded. He held Archie Caird's original tour manifest checking off the individuals that appeared to match the list.

"It looks like everyone we invited showed up," he said.

"People love free things," Ellie said.

Daniel nodded. "We'll wait until they all leave."

After several minutes, they drove over to the van. Mr. MacCrivag stepped out from the passenger seat. He skipped hellos and instead circled his car, inspecting it for damage.

"Don't worry, Ellie drove the whole time," Daniel said.

"Don't mind Willie. I can't fathom why he's so protective of that old thing," Philip Morrison said. "Tour went fine. Showed 'em round the loch. Lunched down at Foyers. Even spotted a golden eagle. At least I kin it was a golden eagle. That's what I said it was, and no one seemed to question. It was quite far off."

"You showed them the mussels?" Daniel asked.

"Aye, of course. Cracked one open to see the pearl inside. They loved that, didn't they? You two did a fine job of planting them in the stream. Looked quite natural."

"Did anyone seem suspicious? Like they wanted to run off with them?" Ellie asked.

"No, not any more than you'd expect from tourists. Willie?" Mr. Morrison said. William MacCrivag shook his head.

"I'll tell you, I'm glad to be rid of that Mr. Fisher of yours, though. For a man who makes his living singing, he sure thinks he knows a lot about wildlife. If I didn't know better, I'd say he was a touch jealous he wasn't in charge of the tour himself," Mr. Morrison said.

Daniel and Ellie shared a knowing laugh. "We'd better head back out there if we're to beat any potential poachers. We brought dinner and a big thermos full of hot coffee to keep us going," Daniel said. They all piled into Mr. MacCrivag's sedan, William and Philip in front, Daniel and Ellie in back. "Are you sure you want to come along? It'll probably be pretty boring. Definitely cold. We don't even know if anyone will show tonight," he asked Ellie.

"If you think I'm going to sit this one out, after all the trouble it was getting those trackers into those pearls, you're crazy. Besides, I can't let you boys have all the fun," Ellie said.

Daniel shrugged. "I hope it won't be too much fun," he said, thinking of his last stakeout with Young Hugh Macpherson.

* * *

Mr. Morrison pulled into the small parking area at Inverfarigaig. "Is it fine to leave the car here?" he asked.

"I don't see why not. It's nearly dark, and the only person from the tour that might recognize it would be Fisher," Daniel said.

"Mind if we take the first watch? I enjoy a brisk winter's day, but night's another story," Mr. Morrison said.

"Finally, you're talking some sense," Mr. MacCrivag said. "Now where's that hot coffee you mentioned?" Despite the car's heater, William MacCrivag hadn't unbuttoned his large puffy coat since they'd left Inverness. Daniel poured them each a mug. He watched them walk slowly down the path that led to the stream.

"Do you think it's smart letting them go down there by themselves? After what happened to Archie Caird?" Ellie asked.

"There are two of them. And we'll see anyone first if they drive in here," Daniel said. He thought for a moment and pulled out his phone. *Remember to call us if you see anything,* he texted. "Just in case," he said. Ellie nodded.

"So now we just sit here and wait?"

"I told you it would be boring."

"It doesn't have to be," Ellie said. She scooched over close to him.

"Well, I guess it's not likely anyone will show up for a while," Daniel said. He pulled her in closer.

Ellie gave him a quick kiss, then a playful slap on the chest. "Ha! That was a test, and you failed!"

"What?"

"We're on a stakeout. We're supposed to be watching for a poacher and murderer. Men—no wonder you and Young Hugh never found anything on Carmen's ship."

"To be fair, he's not as pretty as you. Far less distracting," Daniel said. He took his arm from her waist.

"You don't have to do that. It's still cold in this car. We won't see anything if we freeze to death," Ellie said. She pulled his arm back. "Just stay focused on the mission."

Daniel laughed. "Sure thing."

Several hours later, Daniel woke to the sound of Ellie's voice. "You fell asleep," she said, rubbing his shoulder.

He sat up, confused. "I'm sorry, where? Did something happen?"

"Morrison and MacCrivag are back," she said. She nodded toward the path leading to the river. The light from a flashlight bobbed up and down with the gait of the man holding it, growing larger with each step. They did not appear rushed. No poacher yet.

Daniel and Ellie reluctantly gave up the relative warmth of the car to take their place on lookout beside the river. Daniel was taken aback by the freezing temperature outside. He knew it would be cold, but not this cold. No wonder the two older members of their stakeout crew had returned an hour before their shift was set to conclude. Luckily, the forest path was easy to navigate, even in the dark. It had a gentle slope, and the vegetation was more sparce than it would have been in summer. Still, Daniel was thankful when he heard the sound of the running water. Despite his thick gloves, the fingers that held his flashlight were numb by the time they reached the river.

They found the calm pool near the mouth of the river. The mussels lay undisturbed where they'd left them that morning. A few yards away, Daniel and Ellie hunkered down behind a large bush. It wasn't a great hiding place, and, in the daylight, they would have been easily spotted. But there was little other cover large enough to conceal two people while still providing them a good view of the pool. Daniel brushed aside a stamped-out cigarette stub before settling in. Mr. Morrison and Mr. MacCrivag must have found this same spot. Daniel hoped the light from the cigarette hadn't already scared away any poachers.

Ellie huddled close and pulled a thick blanket over them. Daniel turned out his light. Before long, their eyes adjusted to the dark. The sky was mostly cloudy, but every few minutes, the moon would peek through and reflect its cool light onto the pool. Daniel was surprised at how warm he was under the blanket with Ellie. It wasn't as nice as the inside of Mr. MacCrivag's car. His toes were tingling with cold. But if he and Ellie stayed close, they would at least not freeze to death.

Minutes or hours passed. It was hard to tell with nothing but the slow, intermittent movement of the moon across a cloudy sky to keep the time. Ellie nodded off a couple times. The woods remained quiet except for the sound of the stream and the occasional breeze rustling through the bare tree branches overhead. Daniel swallowed the last of the coffee from his thermos. It had lost its warmth long ago and was now good only for its caffeine. Now even that was gone. He had to pee, but he dared not venture out from under the warmth of the blanket.

Snap.

Daniel froze. His eyes scanned the area. Nothing. But he had heard something. Hadn't he? A footstep? Likely just a squirrel. *Snap. Crunch.* There it was again. Something, or someone, was definitely out there. Daniel's ears strained to detect the location of the sound. He slowly removed the blanket from his head so he could see better. To his left, he saw movement. Something was coming down the footpath toward them. It was far too large to be a squirrel or even a dog, not large enough for a bear. Did Scotland even have bears? Daniel couldn't risk turning on his flashlight and scaring it away. He would have to wait until it got closer.

Chapter Thirty-Two

Ellie felt a nudge. "Wha...?" She opened her eyes to see Daniel's face with his finger over his lips. He nodded left. She pulled down the blanket and shuddered at the sudden chill. The lower half of her glasses fogged over. She adjusted them and looked in the direction he indicated. She gasped and looked back at Daniel. *What is that?* she mouthed.

Daniel shrugged. They watched the figure approach. There was no doubt now that it was human. Whoever it was carried no light and walked clumsily down the path. Maybe the stranger's eyes hadn't yet adjusted to the dark. The stranger held something in one hand. A bag? Despite his or her ungraceful approach, the stranger appeared to know exactly where he or she was headed. The person walked directly to the pool where Daniel and Ellie had planted the mussels. The darkness concealed the figure's identity, but Daniel could see that it was a tall person. Too tall to be Carmen Oteiza. But then, Carmen had never seemed the type to get her own hands dirty. Could it be one of her henchmen, Allen, or the burly Luka? Had one of the guests from Mr. Morrison's tour told Carmen about the pearls?

The figure stooped at the river's bank. Daniel heard a faint splash as it waded into the pool. "Should we stop him?" Ellie whispered. Daniel retrieved his phone. He shielded the screen's light with one hand. He pulled up William MacCrivag's contact information and typed a quick text message. *Poacher's here. We'll drive him your way. Watch out.* He showed Ellie. She nodded. They removed their blanket, careful not to make a sound. Daniel made his hand into a fist with his first two fingers hanging down, like an upside-down rabbit. He walked them through the air in a semicircle and nodded toward the stooped figure in the pool. Then his hand opened and shook. Ellie looked at him with a raised eyebrow. She shook her head, confused. He made the motion again. "What?" She whispered.

"We'll sneak around and scare the poacher toward the carpark," Daniel whispered.

"What are you doing with your hand?"

"It's us walking over there," he whispered. He made the motion again. "Then we make a lot of noise and scare him," Daniel whispered, shaking his hand.

"It looks like scissors that exploded into jazz hands," Ellie whispered.

Daniel looked at his hand. "It's legs," he said, moving his two fingers back and forth.

The figure suddenly stopped searching the pool. Daniel put his hand over his mouth. The figure turned toward Daniel and Ellie. Had they been too loud? Or had the poacher simply finished collecting all the mussels? Daniel and Ellie remained still. If it was too dark for them to make out the poacher, it had to be too dark for the poacher to see them, right? The figure stood and took a step toward them.

Daniel looked at Ellie. He squeezed her hand. "Now!" he whispered. He jumped up and ran to the far side of the pool. He stumbled, fell to his knees, but caught himself with his outstretched hands before he could faceplant into the dirt. His foot had fallen asleep while they had been waiting, huddled under the blanket. Ellie pulled him up. His foot was a heavy, numb block. They had certainly made enough noise to spook the poacher. Daniel patted his pockets, searching for his flashlight. He must have dropped it when he'd fallen. "Light," he said.

Ellie turned hers on and shined the beam at the pool. But she was too late. The stranger was already on the shore and sprinting up the trail. All they could see was the poacher's back: rubber mud boots, dark slacks and coat, and a green woolen hat. The bag, now noticeably fuller, was slung over the poacher's back and rattled as they fled. Ellie pulled Daniel along in pursuit, but he was unable to keep up. His foot had regained some feeling, but every step felt like landing on a pin cushion.

When they reached the end of the trail, they heard a car door slam shut. Daniel saw Mr. MacCrivag's little green sedan. Headlights flashed on. Good, he had received the text. Then the lights pulled away, but the little green sedan remained in place. The lights must have been from the poacher's car, parked on the other side of MacCrivag's. Daniel and Ellie ran to the sedan. Daniel attempted to open the door, but it was locked. He banged on the window. He saw movement inside, and a light shined in his eyes, blinding him. The driver's side window rolled down an inch. "What's all this?" William MacCrivag muttered from inside.

"He's getting away!" Ellie shouted. She pointed to the tail lights speeding away, growing smaller by the second.

"Open the door," Daniel said. He heard a click and tried the handle again. He followed Ellie into the backseat. "Quick, go after him!"

Mr. MacCrivag started the car. Philip Morrison turned around from the front passenger seat. "You saw him? Who was it?" he asked.

"Too dark to tell. Why were the doors locked?" Daniel said.

"There's a murderer about," Mr. MacCrivag said. He pulled out of the carpark.

"You were supposed to be on watch. I sent you a text," Daniel said.

"Philly must've fallen asleep," Mr. MacCrivag said.

"I fell asleep? You were snoring away long before my eyes shut," Mr. Morrison said.

"He's getting away!" Ellie said.

"Which way?" Mr. Morrison said. They pulled onto the main road along the southern shore of Loch Ness. No other lights could be seen. The road was empty.

Philip Morrison slammed his fist against the dashboard. "We lost him!"

"He's likely headed back to Inverness. Maybe we can catch up?" Daniel suggested.

"You'll have to go faster than this," Mr. Morrison said.

"Not if you want to get back in one piece," Mr. MacCrivag said.

"Shoddy ol' car," Mr. Morrison said.

"Don't take your anger out on her. She's doing the best she can," Mr.

MacCrivag said.

"Did you not hear the other car? That lot wasn't very big," Daniel said.

"Couldn't hear anything over his snoring," Mr. Morrison said. Mr. MacCrivag grumbled, but remained focused on the road. "You said you didn't see who it was?"

Daniel shook his head.

"But it was a man? You said *he*. That should eliminate several of our suspects," Mr. Morrison said.

"Yeah, I think," Daniel said. He looked at Ellie. "I don't know. He seemed tall. Or she seemed tall. I don't know. It was dark."

"All we saw was the person's back," Ellie said.

She slammed into Daniel's side as Mr. MacCrivag took a sharp turn. The car shook and groaned. Mr. MacCrivag grumbled. He was coaxing all of the speed he could out of the old engine, but still, they saw no tail lights in front of them.

"Well, we can track whoever it is with those wee trinkets you put in the pearls, can't we?" Mr. Morrison asked.

Ellie shook her head. "They don't work like that. They're made for identifying lost pets. You have to have the pet, or pearl in our case, in hand to scan for the chip."

"You might as well slow down, Willie. We've lost him. Don't want to break down and spend the rest of the night stranded on the side of the road." Mr. Morrison shook his head. "What a waste. We're right back to where we started."

"Not quite," Daniel said. "Now we know for sure that someone from Archie Caird's last tour killed him. That also means that Young Hugh is innocent."

"Sure, *we* know that. But who's going to believe us? We have no proof," Ellie said.

"No, but what we do have is a list of addresses," Daniel said.

Chapter Thirty-Three

"Hi, my name is Daniel Darrow, with Caird Highlands Adventures. I was wondering if you might be willing to answer a few questions about your recent tour?"

The man at the door gave Daniel a suspicious eye. "Isn't this the sort of thing typically done through email or phone?"

"Yes, but as a small, local business, we pride ourselves in taking a more personal touch. It's what sets us apart from the big corporate touring companies. This won't take long, I promise," Daniel said. He held a clipboard with a series of questions that he, Ellie, and Young Hugh Macpherson had come up with the night before.

"Em, sure," the man relented, "if it's only a minute." He left his door open halfway, not willing to let this stranger inside his home, but equally not wanting to fully step outside into the cold.

"Great, thank you! Okay, first, How would you rate your overall experience, on a scale of one to five, one being greatly unsatisfied and five being very satisfied?" Daniel asked.

The man thought a moment. "Four."

Daniel marked his question sheet and moved on to the next. They'd included a few generic customer experience questions at the beginning to make the survey sound legitimate. These were meant to hide the real questions—the ones meant to ferret out any clandestine poachers or murderers. In between questions, Daniel tried to peek inside the house without being too obvious. He quickly glanced through the narrow opening for any clues that its occupant hadn't been home last night: muddy rubber boots, a green woolen hat, a sack of stolen mussels.

"In the future, what would be your preferred mode of transportation for getting to a day tour: public transportation, tour bus, or personal vehicle?"

"The van we took for the tour round Loch Ness was fine, so tour bus, I suppose," the man said.

"Not personal vehicle then?" Daniel asked.

"No, we don't own a car. When it was time to retire our last one, we decided to see how we'd fare without one. With the city buses and rideshares now, we do just fine. Save loads on mechanic's fees."

Daniel nodded. He marked on his form. *No car.* He skipped to the last generic question. "On a scale of one to five, what is the likelihood you would join another tour with *Caird Highlands Adventures* in the future?" Daniel didn't even pay attention to the response. No need. Their poacher hadn't driven away in an Uber. Wrap this survey up and move on to the next.

When he finally arrived back at his flat, Ellie and Young Hugh were already there, talking in the living room.

"We waited as long as we could. I think the kettle might still be warm," Ellie said, indicating the steaming cup of tea in her hands.

"That's okay. My last place was farther out than I thought," Daniel said. He took off his coat and sat down next to her.

"Did you find anything?" Young Hugh asked.

Daniel shook his head. "No. They all seemed like regular non-murdery folk to me."

"Mine too," Ellie said. She put the list of addresses she had surveyed on the table in front of them. Daniel added his and looked them both over.

"I don't get it. These are the only people that could have known about the mussels we planted. If none of them came back to get them, then who did we see last night?" Daniel asked.

Young Hugh looked over the lists, then sank back into his chair. "There is one other person that knew about the plan," he said. Daniel gave him a questioning look, then paused. Young Hugh nodded. "Me."

"But you wouldn't. You didn't. Right?"

"Of course, I didn't. I know the pearls are fakes. But what does it matter?

The whole city is already convinced I killed Mr. Caird. Even when we set a trap for someone else, it still comes back to me." Young Hugh put his head in his hands and sighed. He remained in that position for several minutes, sunken into himself, resigned.

Ellie gasped. She looked up from the list of names she had been studying. Daniel and Young Hugh turned toward her. "Hold on, boys. Don't give up just yet. I had a thought."

"What?" Daniel asked.

"It's going to sound mad," she said.

"What?" Young Hugh asked.

"There is one other person that would have known about the pearls."

"Mr. MacCrivag or Morrison? They were there with us, sound asleep in the car," Daniel said.

"No. Like Hugh, Willie and Philly knew the pearls were fake. But there's one other person that was present at both tours *and* didn't know our pearls were fake."

Daniel and Young Hugh stared at her.

"Mr. Fisher," Ellie said.

* * *

Daniel left his flat early the next morning. The temperature had to be close to freezing, given the way his breath billowed out of his nostrils like an angry bull. But he didn't feel angry. He felt confused, shocked. Only a slight breeze blew through Inverness that morning, largely following the course of the river. Without a strong north wind, the freezing temperature was tolerable, even invigorating. Daniel walked across a footbridge to one of the small islands in the center of the river. He fluffed his scarf to cover more of his neck. He was walking in the opposite direction from his intended destination, but he needed time to think. A few other pedestrians were out this morning as well. They passed one another with a smile or slight nod, each caught up in their own thoughts.

Daniel crossed another bridge to the other side of the river. He walked past

Whin Park, site of the once grand Winter Wonderland. Now all the rides and festive displays were gone. It was once again a simple city park with kids' play equipment and lawns suitable, in warmer weather, for family picnics. Daniel knew that the display at Church Street Kirk would soon follow. The small barn stuffed to overflowing with its mismatched menagerie of ceramic animals and wisemen. Daniel breathed in deeply, filling his lungs with the sharp winter air. He exhaled. Enough procrastinating. No amount of early morning walks could clear his mind of the task that lay before him. He took in one last look at the empty park and turned toward Church Street.

When he arrived, the light from Reverend Calder's study shined out from the space between the bottom of the door and the stone floor. If he had not heard her talk about her own house before, Daniel would swear she lived at the kirk. He knocked on the door.

"Fisher, is that you? Come in, come in."

"Sorry, it's just me," Daniel said, cracking open the door.

She motioned for him to enter. "Did I forget we were meeting?"

"No, I was actually looking for Fisher too. I guess you haven't seen him this morning?"

Reverend Calder shook her head. "He was supposed to return a pair of mud boots. Perhaps he'll stop by after his interview. I think it was an interview. He'd mentioned something about a job opportunity. I do hope it works out. He's been rather down since the school made his position redundant. And now, with the holidays over, he needs a pick-me-up as they say."

"He really does like Christmas, doesn't he," Daniel said.

"Mr. Fisher likes pageantry," Reverend Calder said. Daniel laughed and nodded in agreement. "Now that the choir practices are over and the decorations put away, I fear he might fall into a depression. We must keep an eye on him if he needs a bit of post-holiday cheer," she said.

Oh, I'll keep my eye on him, Daniel thought. "You said he was returning a pair of mud boots to you?"

"Aye, we're the same size, can you believe it? I prefer to think he has dainty feet rather than the alternative," Reverend Calder said with a laugh. She tapped the toes of her clogs together. "He said he needed them for a tour round Loch Ness. It was rather last minute. Something about Philip Morrison taking over Archie Caird's old business? You're friends with Mr. Morrison, right?"

Daniel nodded.

"Did you have anything to do with that?"

Daniel shrugged. "I may have planted the idea in his head."

"I think it's wonderful, Archie's name going on after him. I'm sure Edna will be pleased."

Daniel nodded again. "Well, if you see Fisher, can you tell him I'm looking for him?" He said goodbye to Reverend Calder and headed to his own small broom closet of an office.

He had calls to make and the kirk's Christmas donations and budget to reconcile, but he had trouble focusing on his work. He couldn't stop thinking about the day of the tour. He and Ellie had watched the guests arrive and depart from a distance. He had seen Fisher there, but what had he been wearing? Daniel remembered seeing a beige coat, but footwear? Had Fisher worn his borrowed mud boots that day – an innocent, practical choice for a walk along the loch? Or had he needed them for a return trip, late at night, when he thought no one else would be there?

How could Mr. Fisher have murdered Archie Caird, though? And what would he want with a bunch of endangered mussels? Was he selling the pearls to Carmen Oteiza? A little side hustle after he lost his position at the school? Did he even know Carmen? Was that the "job interview" Reverend Calder had mentioned? Gangly, potbellied, pageantry-loving Mr. Fisher?

Daniel shook his head. He had made false accusations before. The embarrassing consequences had nearly lost him the trust of the kirk and his job. He knew he would not survive a similar mistake. Nor should he. Who would feel comfortable confiding in a reverend who was constantly suspecting his own parishioners of murder? Daniel thought of Young Hugh. The allegation of murder hung heavy over his friend's head. It had lost Hugh his job, ruined his reputation, or more likely confirmed it, and would likely very soon cost him his freedom. Daniel sighed. If he was going to accuse Fisher, he needed solid proof—more than the mere coincidences of time and place and borrowed boots.

A knock sounded at the door. It opened a crack, and a blond, balding head peeked through. "Reverend Calder said you wanted to see me?"

"Fisher, yes, thank you. Come on in," Daniel said. He stood and moved the pile of books that occupied the only other chair in the cramped room. Mr. Fisher sat down. He stared at Daniel expectantly.

"Oh, sorry, I wanted to ask you…." Daniel paused. He couldn't ask right out if the choir director moonlighted as a pearl poacher. Daniel's mind raced for a plausible question. "I wanted to ask you, um, you went on a tour of Loch Ness the other day, right? How was it?"

"Fine, fine. Philip Morrison is no Archie Caird, but I don't know that anyone could replace Archie."

"Did you see anything interesting? Any wildlife?"

"Not much. It is winter. A rather inconvenient time for a wilderness hike. I tried to tell Morrison as much, but he didn't want to listen. Those Hebrideans are a stubborn lot. They have to be though, don't they, to survive up there," Fisher said. His pocket buzzed, and he pulled out his mobile phone.

"Do you need to take that?" Daniel asked.

"It's just a text," Fisher said. He looked at the phone's screen again. "Was there anything else you needed, Reverend? I have other things I need to do."

"Good news? Reverend Calder mentioned that you had a job interview this morning?" Daniel said, indicating Fisher's text message.

"No, that was Car—em, no one important. I'm still waiting to hear back about the job," Fisher said. He stood, attempting to make his exit.

"There was one other thing," Daniel said. "The Christmas eve service. I forgot to take any pictures. I was hoping you might have? For the kirk website. I need to update it," Daniel said hastily.

"I have a few. Sadly, I didn't catch those Gaelic singers Reverend Calder brought in," Fisher said. He shrugged and scrolled through the photos on his phone. "I still don't know why we needed them. I think our choir did a splendid job on our own."

"Y'all did sound very nice," Daniel said.

"Ah, here." Fisher showed the screen to Daniel. Daniel took it for a closer look, though Fisher seemed reluctant to let it go. "I can text them to you," Fisher said.

"I got a new number. Here, I'll just put it in your contacts," Daniel said. He held the phone closer to himself, farther from Fisher.

"That's not necessary. I can—"

"Not a problem. Almost done," Daniel said. He quickly closed the photos and searched for the messaging app. He knew it was dishonest, but he had to. He needed proof. And Fisher had nearly said her name. At least it had sounded like her name. Daniel had to be sure. He opened Fisher's messages and pulled up the last text. He was right. Carmen Oteiza had texted. So, Fisher was involved with her somehow.

The exchange was brief. It began with a number from Fisher, *N319*, to which Carmen had responded with a single word: *Tonight*. Daniel had expected some secretive message, like criminals or spies use in moves. *The package has been delivered.* Or, *The eagle has landed.* But a simple number? What did it mean? A code of some sort?

Daniel glanced up at Fisher. The man had clearly lost his patience and was reaching for his phone. Daniel tapped out of the message app just as Fisher took it back. "There you go. All up to date," Daniel said.

Fisher glared at him, then looked at his phone screen, returned innocently enough to its home screen. Fisher stuffed the phone back in his pocket and walked out the door.

"Thanks for the photos!" Daniel shouted after him.

Chapter Thirty-Four

Daniel Darrow sat behind his desk, staring at the open door through which Mr. Fisher had just made a quick exit. He heard a chirpy meow as Sir Walter Scott announced his presence. The kirk cat rubbed his cheek against the door trim and entered. "You just missed a most interesting conversation," Daniel said to the cat. The cat ignored him. Though from the animal's body language, Daniel could see this was more than Sir Walter's usual aloofness. The cat walked in slowly, measuring each step. Without warning, he crouched with his head flat to the ground. He gave his hind end a little wiggle, then pounced.

Sir Walter landed beneath the chair that Mr. Fisher had previously occupied. He rolled and held onto his prey with his front paws while kicking it viciously with his back feet. Daniel stood and reached for the chair to steady it from falling over. "What have you got there?" Daniel asked. It was a piece of green-colored fabric. Mr. Fisher must have dropped it in his haste to leave Daniel's office.

The cat hissed, grabbed the material in his mouth, and raced out the door. Daniel squeezed out from behind his desk and followed Sir Walter down the hall. Whatever the cat was carrying slowed him down. He waddled more than ran. Still, Daniel had to jog to keep up. Daniel followed him into the kirk sanctuary, past rows of pews, to the large wooden front doors. Finding the doors closed, Sir Walter abandoned his prize and fled down the length of the far wall. Daniel paused to catch his breath before stooping to retrieve the item.

He held up a green woolen hat. Something about it sparked a sense of familiarity. The material was well worn and frayed in places, likely in part from the abuse it had recently endured from Sir Walter. Daniel moved to a corner of the room shaded from the morning light that shone through the stained-glass windows. In the darkness, he was now sure of what he suspected. This was the same green hat he had seen two nights ago as its wearer fled from the pool at the edge of Loch Ness carrying a bag of stolen mussels.

Daniel rushed back to his office and grabbed his coat. On his way out, past Reverend Calder's office, he shouted his intention to make a house call to a shut-in parishioner. This was technically true since Young Hugh was forbidden from leaving their flat as a provision of his bail. When he reached Bellfield Park, he found his flatmate on the couch. Daniel moved in between Young Hugh and the TV. He pulled Fisher's green hat from his coat pocket and tossed it triumphantly on the table.

"What's this?" Young Hugh asked.

"Proof!"

Young Hugh picked up the hat. "Proof of what? Looks like something you nabbed from the bin."

"Ellie was right. Mr. Fisher is the only person who went on both tours, didn't know the pearls were fake, and doesn't have an alibi for the night they were stolen. This is his. It's the same one the thief wore—I know it," Daniel said. He sat down, out of breath from his hurry to get home and share this revelation.

Young Hugh placed the hat back on the table. "I don't know. This doesn't seem like much."

"What do you mean? This proves he was there! Fisher is the poacher. He killed Archie Caird. This proves you're innocent."

"This ratty old hat doesn't prove anything. How can you confirm it's even his? Loads of people have hats like this."

"DNA evidence? That's a thing, right?"

"Even if you can link it to him, it'd just be your word against his. He'd deny stealing the mussels. It was dark, hard to see. Could've been anyone."

"Ellie was there. She saw him too. She can corroborate," Daniel said.

"I'm sorry, mate, we need something more solid than a hat you found that looks sort of like another hat you saw on a dark night. Thanks for trying." Young Hugh sighed and leaned back.

"No, I'm not willing to give up yet. Especially when we're so close," Daniel insisted.

"Who would side with me over him? This is Mr. Fisher we're talking about. He was a school teacher. He directs a church choir. People trust him. *I* don't even believe he could hurt anyone, not really."

Daniel slumped into his own seat. "I certainly didn't expect him to be our top suspect."

"Then there's me. I'm a screwup. Everyone knows it. Always have been, always will be. That's all anyone expects from me."

Daniel shook his head and stood. He paced the length of the room. "Wait," he paused. "There is one more thing. N319."

"What?"

"N319," Daniel repeated. "It's a text message sent from Fisher to Carmen. I snuck a peak at his phone."

"Carmen Oteiza, my old boss?" Young Hugh asked. Daniel nodded. "Why would they be texting? How do they even know one another?"

"I was wondering that too on my way over. The nativity displays, maybe?"

"What does it mean?" Young Hugh asked.

Daniel shrugged. "I don't know, but we have to figure it out before tonight. That was her reply—one word: *Tonight*."

Daniel and Hugh were silent for several long minutes. "Stop pacing. It's distracting," Young Hugh said.

"Sorry, it helps me think," Daniel said. He froze beside the kitchen. He tapped his foot, unable to remain still.

"We need your girlfriend. She could get this."

"Ellie's busy at the clinic. I already tried calling before I got here. We're on our own for now," Daniel said.

"I'm doomed."

"Ha ha," Daniel sneered. "Let's look at the facts. Fisher has some kind of connection with Carmen. Carmen smuggles illegal animal parts. Fisher poached endangered mussels for the pearls...."

"That's an assumption, not a fact. You're assuming Fisher is the poacher," Young Hugh interrupted.

"The green hat," Daniel said. Hugh shook his head. "Okay, forget it. Let's look at the facts *and* assumptions. Assuming Fisher did poach the pearls, he would need someone to sell them to. That's the Carmen connection," Daniel said.

"And we saw how she smuggles them—in the display figures, which you have at the kirk," Young Hugh said.

"Yes, exactly!" Daniel was pacing again. He froze and opened his mouth, but didn't speak.

"What?" Young Hugh asked.

"Now we really do need Ellie," Daniel said. He retrieved his phone and started to dial.

"What?" Young Hugh asked again.

Daniel held up a finger. "Voicemail," he said. He waited a few seconds. "Hey, would you be up for playing another round of happy new parents after work today? Meet me at Church Street and bring a fresh doggie blanket. Love you!"

* * *

Daniel waited on the front steps of Church Street Kirk for Ellie. He answered a few work emails on his phone while keeping an eye on the nativity scene nearby. Once the sun began to set, the temperature felt like it dropped a degree a minute. Daniel hoped she hadn't gotten held up at the clinic. He put his phone away and stuffed his hands in his pockets for warmth. Ellie's car pulled to the curb. She stepped out with a small blanket folded in her arms.

"I'm here. Now, care to explain your cryptic message?" she asked.

"Good, you remembered the blanket," he said.

"I tried to find a pretty one for you." It was light pink with blue dog bones printed on it. She handed it to him. "What do you need this for?"

CHAPTER THIRTY-FOUR

"You know the Old High Church?" Daniel asked.

"Sure, I passed it on the way here."

Daniel nodded. "Just hold on a minute." He scanned the street in both directions. It was empty of pedestrians and had light vehicle traffic. He walked to the nativity display. Two camels and a sheep blocked his path. He squeezed through and stopped at the manger. He pulled the Joseph figure in close so that it half covered the manger. Then Mary. He knelt down, snatched up the baby Jesus into the blanket, and walked calmly but quickly to Ellie.

"Why did you take that?" Ellie asked once they were both inside.

Daniel pulled back the blanket and turned the figure upside down. "Look at its foot."

"I don't see…." Ellie leaned closer and squinted. "Wait. N319? A serial code?"

"It's definitely some kind of code. There were numbers on the foot of our original baby and the replacement—the one I was so sure had contraband in it and smashed in Carmen Oteiza's office. I didn't think anything of it at the time, but then I saw this exact number, N319, today in a text message to Carmen. It's more than just an inventory system. I think it's how she communicates with her people. How she knows which figures have stuff in them and which are empty."

As they walked up Church Street, Daniel told Ellie about his encounter with Fisher, the green hat, and the texts. "So, you think Fisher put our pearls in there for Carmen?" she asked.

Daniel lifted the figure to his ear and shook it. "I don't hear anything rattling around in there. They're probably wrapped up tight," he said.

"Never shake a baby!" Ellie said. Daniel looked at her, surprised. She rolled her eyes and shook her head. "Try this." She handed him a boxy, plastic device taking up nearly the entire space of her purse. "Microchip scanner," Ellie said.

"How does it work?"

"Just push the *on* button and hold it to the baby. If our pearls are in there, it should pick them up."

213

Daniel turned the device over twice before finding the *on* button. He pushed it and ran the scanner up and down across the ceramic figure. The screen blinked a series of blank lines.

"Give it a sec and hold it still," Ellie said. "Here, let me hold him."

Daniel tried the scanner again as Ellie held the infant figure. The screen blinked, and then a multidigit number filled the length of the screen. Daniel gasped. "It's there! I was right!"

"You sound surprised."

"I am, a little," Daniel said. He sighed.

"Don't get too excited now," Ellie said. She passed him the baby and looked at the scanner's screen before returning it to her purse.

"I am excited for Hugh. But this also means we're right about Mr. Fisher."

Ellie nodded. They continued on in silence.

"We're here, Old High Church," she said. "What's the plan?"

They paused in front of the building. It dwarfed Church Street Kirk. The street lamps and night lighting gave the ancient structure an eerie feel. The attached graveyard didn't help. Daniel led Ellie over to the nativity display at the front of the graveyard. He was relieved that, like Church Street Kirk's, it hadn't yet been removed. Unlike Church Street's this display was an uncrowded affair with only a few ceramic animals and the correct number of wisemen in attendance. Daniel loosened the blanket that was wrapped around the baby. He walked quickly to the manger, knelt, and switched out its occupants.

"Oi," someone shouted from the sidewalk. "Get out of the display."

Daniel stood and backed away from the manger. "Sorry, he wanted to get a closer look at the animals," Daniel said, wrapping the blanket over the new baby's head. He grabbed Ellie's hand and hurried her away from the church. Once they were a safe distance away, Daniel unwrapped the new figure and examined its foot.

"N315—a different number. Does this one feel lighter, or am I imagining it?" Daniel said.

"Are you switching them out to prevent Carmen from getting the pearls? You remember they're fake, right?" Ellie said.

"Just meet me back at the Old High tomorrow morning. Behind that row of shrubs near the cemetery wall. I have to make a few phone calls."

Chapter Thirty-Five

Daniel Darrow checked his phone for the time. He had more than usual this morning, enough to stop for a coffee before heading to the kirk. He wanted to arrive before Mr. Fisher, so he had left his flat extra early. Even though the choir director was not scheduled to come in today, Daniel imagined that he would and did not want to miss it. But he had one person to see first. He knocked on Reverend Calder's door. He knew she would be there. She always was. As expected, a cheery, "Yes? Who's that? Come it, come in," sounded from inside her office. He balanced two to-go coffee cups in one hand and opened the door with the other. He handed one cup to his boss.

"Ah, and what's this for?" she asked. "Low-fat milk?"

Daniel nodded. "I had a little extra time this morning."

"You do seem earlier than usual. Anything wrong?"

"After today, I think everything is going to be okay."

"Cryptic, aren't we? What is today?" Reverend Calder asked. She sipped her coffee, thankful for the hot, unexpected caffeine boost.

"Do you remember when you told me the story of the trial of Susanna?"

She thought for a moment. "Aye, she was falsely accused by two cheeky old men. You were concerned about Young Hugh Macpherson. Any progress there?"

"What if I accuse the right person, but I don't want to be right?"

"Do you mean Mr. Fisher? When you called me last night, I couldn't believe it. I've known the man for years. He has his vices, we all do, but poaching, murder?" She shook her head and took another sip of her coffee.

"I'd hate to lose either of you, but if you're right? Or if you're wrong and you bring this to the police? I'll just say that you'd better be very certain before making any accusations."

Daniel nodded. "I know. And I'm hoping I won't actually have to—accuse anyone, I mean. Speaking of Mr. Fisher, can you let me know if he comes in today?"

"He's already here. Didn't you see him when you arrived?"

"I came in the back through the garden. Where is he?"

"Last I saw, he was rummaging around the nativity display. Seems he's lost something in there. I'm not surprised. It's so stuffed full of figures and props. Just between you and me, it's become a bit of an eye sore."

"Excuse me, I have to, um, there's...." Daniel stood, unable to finish his sentence. He hurried out of the office, down the hall, through the empty sanctuary, and out the front doors. Daniel was counting on Fisher coming this morning to check on the baby Jesus figure. He wasn't counting on him being so early. When he reached the nativity display, he could not immediately see Fisher through the crowd of ceramic figures. He heard movement somewhere near the center.

"Mr. Fisher?" Daniel said as he approached. More sounds of shuffling through dirt and hay, but no response.

He heard mumbling: "It was here. I know it was. She must've made a mistake."

"Mr. Fisher, is that you?" Daniel asked, finding the man on his hands and knees by the manger.

Fisher sat up, surprised. "Reverend, I didn't see you there. I'm sorry, I must look a mess down here." He dusted off the knees of his slacks.

"Do you need any help? I thought I heard you say something should be here?"

"The infant, eh, never you mind, I'm sure you've got more important things to do," Fisher said.

"The infant Jesus? He's right here tucked away in his manger. Where else would he be?"

"No, it's nothing, just something's not right. Nothing to bother you,

Reverend."

"You might look under the mastic tree," Daniel said. Fisher gave him a questioning look. "Have you ever heard the story of the trial of Susanna?" Daniel asked. Fisher shook his head. "Never mind. Are you sure I can't help?" Daniel knew it was wrong, but he couldn't help himself. After all the pain Fisher had caused, he could deal with a little toying.

Fisher stood and put his hand on the infant figure, turning it over. "This is the same one? You haven't gone and broken another, have you?" he asked.

Daniel laughed. "Those things are surprisingly fragile. But, no, I didn't break it—at least not that one. Funny story though—"

"What did you do?" Fisher interrupted. He had a sudden intensity in his eyes. Daniel took a step back.

"The reverend over at the Old High Church called me yesterday asking if he could borrow our Jesus figure. Seems theirs was chipped, and they needed a replacement asap. I know you've got a bit of a rivalry going with their choir, but I thought this would be a nice start at ecclesial bridge building."

Fisher glanced at the figure. "This is theirs? It doesn't look chipped."

Daniel shrugged. It wasn't a great lie, but he hoped it would be enough.

"So, our baby Jesus is at Old High?" Fisher asked. Daniel nodded. "Right now?" Daniel nodded again. "I have to make a call. Excuse me," Fisher said. He began making his way out of the display.

"But weren't you looking for something?" Daniel asked. Fisher responded with a dismissive wave. "Mr. Fisher!"

"What?" Fisher asked, irritated.

"I know it's your day off, but before you leave, could I ask a small favor of you? I'm having trouble with the sermon for this Sunday and could really use a look at the hymns you were planning."

"Can it wait until tomorrow? I must be off."

"It really can't," Daniel said in his best pleading voice.

"I'll go fetch it," Fisher grumbled. He headed toward the front doors of the kirk.

"Thanks! You can leave it in my office," Daniel said. He headed in the opposite direction, toward the northern end of Church Street. On the way, he sent a text to Ellie: *Advance in plans. It's happening now. I'll let our friends know.*

When he arrived at the Old High Church, he found the meeting place he and Ellie had agreed on the previous night. She was not yet there. He settled in behind a row of shrubs near the edge of the cemetery to wait. He moved some branches aside to get a clearer view of the nearby Old High nativity display. "Oh, nearly forgot," he said to himself. He dashed out of the bushes, snatched the baby Jesus figure from its manger, and returned to his hiding place. Several minutes later, Daniel heard footsteps. He turned to see Ellie walking toward him, crouched low, stealthy. She knelt beside him.

"Have I missed anything?" she asked.

Daniel shook his head. "No, Fisher's not here yet. I sent him on an errand to buy us time. Though, he shouldn't be much longer." His phone buzzed. He read the text. "Our friends are set up over there." Daniel motioned with his eyes to a covered space on the other side of the nativity display.

"I guess the party can get started. Look who else has arrived," Ellie whispered.

Fisher approached the nativity display, followed by Carmen Oteiza and two men. One was of average size and height, not much taller than Carmen. The other was a hulk, surpassing even Fisher for height. Daniel recognized them immediately: Carmen's men, her lackies, Allen and Luka. None of the group appeared happy to be there, Mr. Fisher least of all.

"You better be right about this," Daniel heard Carmen say.

"It's here, I promise," Fisher said.

"That's what you said yesterday and had me up in the freezing cold of midnight on a wild goose chase," Allen said.

When they reached the manger, Fisher stood silent. He riffled through the straw bedding. He knelt, frantically inspecting the ground around the manger.

"Where? I, I don't understand," Fisher stammered.

"There is nothing here, Mr. Fisher," Carmen said.

"But he said it was here. It has to be," Fisher said.

"Do you think this is some kind of joke?" Carmen asked.

"No, I—" Fisher said.

"I am not laughing," Carmen interrupted.

"She's not laughing, mate," Luka chimed in.

Fisher stood and searched around the other figures. "It has to be here. I just need more time to find it," he said.

"I am a patient woman, Mr. Fisher. I have already given you more time than you deserve. Yet, still your debt remains unpaid. You should be careful before you meet the same fate as that wilderness man. What was his name? Card? Caird? I warn you, my patience is now quite thin," Carmen said. She gave a nod toward Luka. Luka stepped to Fisher, cupping his fist in his palm like a baseball glove.

From behind the row of shrubbery, hidden from view, Daniel and Ellie exchanged looks of shock. "Did she say Caird?" Daniel whispered. Ellie nodded and put her finger over his lips to silence him.

"What happened to Archie was an accident. I told you that. If he hadn't interfered," Fisher said. "He wasn't supposed to be there. I just meant to go back for the pearls. I didn't mean to kill him." Fisher looked from Carmen to Luka, pleading.

"But you did kill him, Mr. Fisher. And I took on a big risk framing our young friend. A shame too. I always liked Hugh. He at least paid his gambling debts on time," Carmen said.

"And Hugh was smart enough to know when to throw in his hand. He never racked up a tab like yours," Allen said, circling Fisher like a buzzard. He clearly enjoyed watching the older man squirm.

"Your time is up, Mr. Fisher. If you have no more pearls, we will have to think of some other way for you to pay. Luka," Carmen said. She nodded to the big man. Luka smiled, contorting his face in an unnatural, sinister way. He grabbed Fisher by the shoulder with one hand. With the other, he struck him hard in the stomach. Fisher cried out and buckled over.

Back behind the bushes, Daniel and Ellie watched with growing unease. "Are you sure our friends are here?" Ellie whispered.

Daniel nodded. He had wanted Fisher to pay. But this was not justice. He closed his eyes and took a deep breath. He stood. "Stop!"

CHAPTER THIRTY-FIVE

"Get down! What are you doing?" Ellie said. She pulled at his coat.

Daniel held up the infant Jesus figure. "Are you looking for this?"

Carmen and her crew turned, surprised. "Reverend?" Fisher gasped for breath.

"Boys," Carmen said. She motioned toward Daniel as if she were offering him up, fresh meat.

"With pleasure," Luka said. His large strides closed the gap between him and his prey in seconds.

Before Luka could get within arm's reach, Daniel tossed the figure to him and darted away from the bushes. He didn't want them to know Ellie was there too. Allen, who had anticipated the Reverend's escape attempt, reached for Daniel's arm. He caught hold of Daniel's coat sleeve. Allen's grip was insufficient to hold him, but it did succeed in spinning him sideways. Unbalanced, Daniel tripped. He scrambled to regain his footing, but Allen was quicker and pinned him to the ground.

"Halt! Hands up!"

Between Allen's arms, Daniel saw four police officers appear from their hiding place on the opposite side of the nativity display. Fisher, still reeling from Luka's punch, submitted to the officers without protest. Carmen attempted to run, but, fashionable as ever, her heel stuck into the soft ground. One of the officers grabbed her. Luka, baby Jesus in his arms, had a bewildered look on his face.

"Hands where we can see them."

Luka dropped the figure and raised his hands. The figure broke open, spilling a small black bag on the lawn beside it. Daniel was too preoccupied to notice the bag or worry about the cost of a third broken figure on his security deposit. Allen held him down. He struggled, but Allen's grip was tight. Allen was so caught up in the assault, he was unaware of the police's sudden appearance. One of the officers put a hand on Allen's shoulder. "Let go of him, mate."

Allen swung blindly and missed. Daniel took the opportunity to wriggle free. Startled by Allen's swing, the officer released his grip. Allen, now very aware of the police presence, jumped away and ran toward the row of bushes at the cemetery's exit. "Ellie!" Daniel shouted.

Just as Allen reached the row, Ellie stood and stretched out her arm. The purse, which she flung toward Allen, contacted him smack in the face. Allen's feet flew out from under him, and he hit the ground with a thud. The officer beside Daniel raced to put handcuffs on Allen before he could recover. Daniel ran to Ellie's side. "Are you okay?"

"I'm fine," Ellie said. She dropped her purse. It clanked against the soft ground. She reached down and opened it. "But I don't know how I'm going to explain this to my boss," she said, pulling out a microchip scanner broken in half, loosely held together by exposed dangling wires.

Chapter Thirty-Six

The cloudless, sunny afternoon made Daniel ache for spring. It was a rare January day in Inverness, almost warm enough to go without a winter coat. He could not have asked for better weather for the day's task and Daniel tried his best to keep everyone on task so that they could finish before the clouds and precipitation inevitably returned. He was helping William MacCrivag unbolt a rafter from a wall support beam when Reverend Calder and Philip Morrison returned from the kirk's storage room.

"I don't know how Mr. Fisher fit all these figures in there. We could hardly shut the door, and there's so much still out here," Reverend Calder said.

"I know he borrowed some of them, but only Fisher would know which ones belong to us and where the rest should be returned," Daniel said. "Mr. Morrison, I could use your height on this beam." Philip Morrison reached to steady the rafter as they lowered it to the ground. "You're not putting away the coded ones, right? The police might still want some of those for evidence," Daniel asked.

"They've been up and down every meter of this kirk. Whatever's left mustn't be too important," Reverend Calder said.

"Well, I wish they would've taken the whole lot. Save us the trouble," William MacCrivag said.

"You know we could just leave it up year-round. Folks do that all the time back home with their Christmas lights," Daniel said.

William Morrison and Reverend Calder exchanged worried glances, unsure if he was serious or joking. Reverend Calder assumed the latter.

"I'll never understand your American sense of humor," she said.

"Ha, next you would have us watching American football and eating cheese from a can," Mr. MacCrivag said. "Actually, that second part sounds quite good. He may have a point, Reverend."

Reverend Calder rolled her eyes. Daniel and Mr. MacCrivag started on another rafter. "It feels weird taking this all down without Fisher. I guess it would be weirder now with him, knowing what he did. But I…I don't know what I'm trying to say," Daniel said.

"I understand. I keep wanting to ask him about a choral arrangement or what hymn to pair with a scripture—he was always so good with that kind of thing. Had an encyclopedic knowledge of hymns, didn't he? It's hard to imagine our own Mr. Fisher, fussy, sweet Fisher, capable of such deceit and violence," Reverend Calder said.

"I've known the man for years. Always thought there was something off about him," Mr. MacCrivag said.

"No, you didn't," Philip Morrison said. "You thought the Macpherson lad did it."

"Hmf, we all thought Young Hugh did it," MacCrivag said. "But never mind that. Philly, tell us some good news, eh? How'd your talk with Edna go?"

"Edna Caird?" Reverend Calder asked.

"Aye, there's a few sticky points still, but I believe we can sort it all out. Looks like you'll be seeing a lot more of me soon."

Daniel and Reverend Calder gave him a questioning look.

"Philly enjoyed our wee faux-wilderness tour round Loch Ness so much, he wants to do it for real. You're looking at the new head of *Caird Highlands Adventures*," William MacCrivag said with pride.

Philip Morrison waved off this compliment dismissively. "I'm no head of anything. Edna still owns the business. I'll just be leading the tours. Seems like a good way to honor Archie. Keep his spirit alive."

"Plus, you like it," Mr. MacCrivag said.

"Aye, that I do," Mr. Morrison smiled and slapped his friend on the back.

"That's wonderful. I think Archie would be pleased," Reverend Calder said.

"I'm happy for you. Wilderness guide is a good fit," Daniel said.

"And I will be one of your first customers! I've been meaning to get out of my office more. Will you do a tour of the smuggling coves?" Reverend Calder asked. To Daniel and Mr. MacCrivag, she added, "Philip has been telling me the most extraordinary tales of his ancestors."

"Well, hopefully now all talk of smuggling can remain in the past," Daniel said. The others shook their heads in agreement. "If y'all've got this, I want to go check in on Ellie and Young Hugh," Daniel said. They were piling hay into the back of a rented truck.

"It didn't look like this much when it was set up," Ellie said.

"Looks like you're almost done," Daniel said. He leaned in to kiss her.

"Watch out. I'm sweating in this heat," she said.

"Heat? And people say I have a bad sense of humor," Daniel said. He kissed her despite her warning.

"I'm serious. It's practically balmy out. When's our lunch break? We do have fair labor laws in the country," Ellie said. She sat on a square bale of hay and wiped her brow dramatically.

"Hugh, you'd said your folks might bring by lunch?" Daniel asked.

"That's what they told me." Young Hugh retrieved his phone to check the time. "I'll text them a reminder." He typed on the screen. "Rev, I've got one last favor to ask of you."

"Sure," Daniel said.

"Mrs. Caird, she gave me her husband's watch. You know, the one the police found in my room. Well, she says she wants me to have it once it's no longer evidence. I still can't believe it was Mr. Fisher who planted it there. Crept into my room while I was asleep. How did I not notice?"

"I didn't either. I didn't think anything of it when he said he wanted to see stop by and see how you were holding up," Daniel said.

"Who'd have thought he could be so, I don't know, conniving?" Ellie said.

"People can do surprising things when they're desperate," Daniel said. "But Hugh, you mentioned a favor?"

"I can't take the watch. I know Mrs. Caird means well. Kind of an I'm sorry for thinking badly of me and jumping to conclusions about her husband. Evidently, it's a rather expensive watch. That's why Fisher stole it off Mr. Caird's body. He thought it might pay off his debt to Carmen. But with Mr. Caird dead, Carmen thought it would be of better use in framing me," Young Hugh said.

"She didn't want anyone casting a suspicious eye toward her or her business," Daniel said.

"Exactly. All I can think of when I see that watch is betrayal. How two people that I thought cared about me instead used me to try and save themselves. I don't want to offend Mrs. Caird, but I simply cannot accept that watch. You have to take it instead. Tell her you're holding on to it for me while I'm away."

Daniel nodded. "Of course. I can do that. So, you really are leaving then?"

"I've never been one to stay in one place for too long. And after being cooped up here, in that little flat. No offense, Rev, but a cup of tea and a dusty book before bed is not exactly the kind of nightlife I'm used to."

Daniel shrugged. "Beats being chased off a boat in the middle of the night. Do you know where you're headed?"

"I'm ready for a new adventure. Somewhere farther afield this time. South America or Australia, perhaps," Young Hugh said. He had a distant look in his eyes, as if he were already on a ship sailing far away.

"Don't look now, boys, but someone's ears must be burning," Ellie said. She nodded toward the sidewalk. Eliza MacGillivray, in her long black and white checked coat, rabbit in tow, walked toward them. Beside her was Edna Caird.

"If she mentions the watch," Young Hugh whispered.

"I'm holding on to it for you. Don't worry," Daniel whispered back. "Ms. MacGillivray, Mrs. Caird, what a nice surprise. Did you come to help with the demolition job?" he asked them.

"Oh, my, no," Ms. MacGillivray said. We were out for a walk, and I had a feeling you would be here just now."

"I mentioned it in the announcements Sunday," Daniel said.

"No, that's not it. I knew you would be here. I have a message for you."

"Oh, this should be good!" Ellie sat up straight and gave Daniel a wink.

"Come closer, love. This message is for the both of you," Eliza said.

"Both of us?" The smirk disappeared from Ellie's face. She took a timid step toward them.

Eliza MacGillivray handed her rabbit's leash to Edna. She unbuttoned her coat collar and fished out the gold chain necklace that held the smooth, donut-shaped stone. She grasped the stone between her finger and thumb and rubbed it gently. Her eyes glossed over.

"When the river Beauly is dried up three times,

and a scaly salmon is caught in the river,

that will be a time of great trial."

Eliza blinked slowly, and an alertness returned to her eyes. She returned the stone under her coat. Daniel and Ellie exchanged concerned glances then they looked to Young Hugh.

"Hey, I'm just glad it's not about me this time!" he said.

"That sounds quite dire, Eliza. I liked it better when you simply prophesied I'd go to veterinary school," Ellie said.

"Is it? I rather think not," Eliza MacGillivray said.

"There're no bloody pearls, but I'm going to have to side with Ellie on this one. Is this a Brahan Seer prophecy or an Eliza original?" Daniel asked.

"Aren't they the same?" Eliza said. "I don't know why you two are so concerned. I never interpret my messages, but I will this once because of how you've helped Edna and the young Macpherson lad. There is no greater trial, in my view, than the bonding of two souls. That is the way it was for me and my late husband, anyway. The greatest trial and the greatest joy of my life." Eliza put her hand to her heart and sighed. She knelt down for her rabbit and held it tight. The rabbit squirmed and kicked once, then settled down into her embrace.

"I never knew you were married?" Ellie said.

"Really? That's what you took from her explanation?" Daniel said.

"Calm down, Daniel, love. The Beauly's run dry at least a couple times since the Seer's time, and we're in a good place, you and I. No need to rush things," Ellie said. "Look, Eliza, you've made him blush!"

Daniel turned away. "I'm not blushing. It's just hot out here, like you said. Back me up, Hugh."

"Leave me out of this, mate. Oh, look, there's my parents just now." Young Hugh leaped away to greet his parents despite their car having just turned onto Church Street. When the silver Land Rover pulled to the curb, he helped them unload several containers of food. He brought an armload back to Daniel.

"That smells delicious. I'm starving," Ellie said.

"You might want to sit back down for this," Young Hugh said.

"Why? What is it?"

"Smoked Salmon."

Ellie's eyes grew as wide as half-pound coins.

"Look who's blushing now," Daniel said. He helped Young Hugh with the food and directed everyone back to the kirk hall for a meal and some much—deserved rest.

About the Author

Daniel K. Miller holds advanced degrees from the University of Edinburgh and Duke University. He is the author of *Fire on the Firth* as well as several short fiction and nonfiction pieces, one of which was named finalist for best short story in 2021 by the Texas Institute of Letters. He lives in Texas with his wife and a motley assortment of horses, cats, and wildlife. *Loch and Key* is his second novel. Visit him at www.danielkmillerauthor.com.

SOCIAL MEDIA HANDLES:
  @danielkmiller

AUTHOR WEBSITE:
  www.danielkmillerauthor.com

Also by Daniel K. Miller

Fire on the Firth

Lightning Source UK Ltd.
Milton Keynes UK
UKHW012013120123
415233UK00004B/255